S0-BIH-881

THE
CLARK
INHERITANCE

THE
CLARK
INHERITANCE

Sophia Yarnall

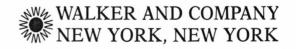

WALKER AND COMPANY
NEW YORK, NEW YORK

*To my children and theirs,
in tribute to our forebears*

Library of Congress Cataloging in Publication Data

Yarnall, Sophia.
  The Clark inheritance.

  I. Title.
PS3575.A73C59 1981   813'.54   80-54812
ISBN 0-8027-0679-7   AACR2

First published in the United States of America in 1981 by the Walker Publishing Company, Inc.

Published simultaneously in Canada by John Wiley & Sons Canada, Limited, Rexdale Ontario.

ISBN: 0-8027-0679-7

Library of Congress Catalog Card Number: 80-54812

Book Design by Marjorie E. Reed

Printed in the United States of America

10 9 8 7 6 5 4 3 2 1

PREFACE

IN THE LATE 1700s homesteaders moving one hundred miles or so north from Philadelphia discovered that the fertile, rolling fields of the Pennsylvania Dutch farmland ended abruptly in rugged, timber-covered mountains. Inhabited by bear, wildcats, and wild boar, the untamed beauty of the mountains held less attraction for future settlers than the occasional outcroppings of black and gray mineral along the mountainsides. Suspecting it was some form of fossil fuel, they dug it up and tried to burn it but with no success.

After many attempts, a group of workmen in a Philadelphia wire factory, in a final gesture of frustration, slammed the door on a furnace where they had piled the mineral, opened a draft and left in disgust. Several hours later one of the men returned to find a marvelous fire burning. They had stumbled on a solution that immediately made anthracite coal an important factor in producing household heat.

This story concerns itself with one family's ownership and development of anthracite coal mines during the last half of the nineteenth century; their struggle to survey the land and police it against squatters; their efforts to find mine sites near enough to rivers and streams for proper drainage; their hiring of hundreds and thousands of workmen, miners, engineers, and mule drivers; their purchase and manufacture of equipment—pumps, boilers, engines, coal cars, mules, and mule carts; their logging of timbers to shore up the mine chambers; their construction of houses for miners, technical employees, and their families; and finally the investment of hundreds of thousands of dollars before the first ton of coal was shipped.

It is the story of a family mystique so powerful that men of substance were inexorably drawn to leave their comfortable lives in Philadelphia for a remote and highly speculative future. It is the

5

story of doubts and anxieties before these men could confirm their hopes that they owned deposits of coal that could be developed. It is the story of their stormy relations with labor and their efforts to keep their company alive in competition with the burgeoning railroads, which themselves were acquiring mine sites. It is also the story of the men's wives and children, their loneliness and isolation—and their share in the venture.

Names of places and people have been changed. Some episodes have been added and some transposed, but it is basically the story of the author's grandparents and their brothers and sisters

THE CLARK FAMILY

*The Children and Grandchildren of
Judge Samuel Edward Clark (1791–1879)
and Anna Brewster (1800–1876)*

Brewster Clark–Amanda Tucker
(1833–1885)   (1847–1933)

    Caroline   Pamela
    Sandra   Ernest

    Jemima Clark
    (1835–1898)

Frederick Brewster Clark–Eliza Morris
(1838–1906)   (1841–1924)

    Daniel (1866)
    Anna (1870)
    Freck (*Anna's son*)

Dexter Brewster Clark–Jessie Tucker
(1839–1895)   (1841–1926)

James Brewster Clark–Marjorie Tillinghast
(1841–1904)   (1843–1922)

    James, Jr.
    Frederick Clark II
    Alfred

Philip Brewster Clark–Emmy Sheldon
(1843–1873)   (1845–1925)

    Philip, Jr.

Susie Morris Frazier (*Eliza Clark's half-sister*)
Sumter Frazier, *her husband*
Griswold Frazier, *their son*
Mr. and Mrs. Josiah Tucker (*parents of Amanda and Jessie Clark*)

PROLOGUE

Clarkston, Pa. 1871

'GET IN, ELIZA, and let Maria sit next to you with the baby. Danny and I'll sit facing you.''

It was only a mile to the house, Eliza told herself, and she prayed it wouldn't be too much for Danny after the three-hour train ride from Philadelphia.

Frederick Clark sounded more confident than he felt. He had postponed bringing his wife and children to the mines in Clarkston until five-year-old Danny had learned to use his crutches and Anna was weaned. He lifted his crippled son from the station steps outside Clarkston Junction, placed him carefully in the victoria, and climbed in himself. "I think you'll see a lot of changes in the past months," he said to his wife.

It was late May and the mountain laurel was in bloom, the air smelled fresh and cool, and the gashes cut in the green hillsides by the mine openings and railroad tracks were less noticeable than they had been in the winter.

A group of men working on the ditches looked up as the carriage passed, lurching from side to side in the muddy ruts.

"Pretty much of a swell for round here," one of them observed at large.

Eliza's cashmere shawl covered the shoulders of her plum-colored velveteen dress, and a jaunty little straw bonnet confirmed the impression that she was more appropriately dressed for Philadelphia than for Clarkston.

"Will the horses go very fast, Pappa?" the boy asked.

"Not too fast," his father answered. "The road is very rocky and it's all uphill to our house. Everyone's safely in, Janos," he

9

called to the Hungarian coachman. Janos had been recruited from the mines six months before in anticipation of the arrival of Fred's family.

"We'll drive past the colliery, Danny. That's where the breakers are and the tracks the locis use to bring the coal from the mines. This is where the coal gets sorted and put into freight cars."

"What are locis, Pappa?"

"There's one right now—that little engine pulling the narrow cars. They have specially narrow tracks so they can go down in the mines."

Eliza sat in her corner of the carriage, trying with all her might to put down her rising sense of fear and desolation. She must not let Fred guess her panic. Her visits up to now had been few and far between, but she had known ever since they had been married that she and Fred would eventually have to live here.

"What a lot you've done since the fall, darling," she said aloud. "And I'm dying to see our house now that it's finished."

"It's just like all the others," Fred said, laughing. "Big and roomy and comfortable. But you'll make it really ours, Hodie darling, when you start fixing it up inside." Hodie was Fred's private name for his wife in moments of special tenderness.

As Janos turned the corner past the colliery and started up Clark Hill, Eliza recognized a familiar landmark. On the right was Judge Clark's three-story wooden mansion, painted brown, with a long wooden porch across the front, its five gables accented by windows framed in heavy shutters. Beyond the mansion stood Dexter Clark's shops, his office, and his mining and engineering library.

"There's Dexter just coming out of his shops," Fred said, waving to his brother. "I hope you and Jessie can come over later," he called—and to Danny, "Your Uncle Dexter's shops are full of all kinds of fascinating machinery. I bet you'll spend a lot of time working there with him."

"What can I make there, Pappa?"

"Perhaps one of these days you'll help him build an engine to run in the mines." Fred was half serious.

On the left as they drove up the hill came, in regular succession, Philip's, Dexter's, Fred's, and Brewster's houses. Each of these was protected from the road by clumps of spruce, pine, and fir trees, and each was surrounded by lawn and gardens recently cleared from the forest.

"Oh Fred, how lovely!" Eliza exclaimed as she caught sight of the new white board fence surrounding their place.

Janos got down from the box to open the double gate and led the horses up to the front door.

"I love it here, Pappa," Danny said with a ravishing smile. "And I bet I can climb on that gate and swing on it."

"Good boy. I bet you can, too." Fred glanced at his wife. If they could match Danny's courage, perhaps life here would not be all bad—and perhaps his father, the Judge, would overcome his indignation that fate had struck down his oldest grandson with a mysterious and debilitating disease.

Eliza managed a smile. "First thing to do is get settled," she said gamely. "Then you can swing on the gate, Danny."

Janos handed the reins over to the gardener, who met them at the front door. He lifted the little boy out of the carriage and took his crutches while Danny laboriously crawled up the front steps.

"That's the fella," Janos said as the child fell exhausted on the porch.

Fred left Eliza and the children at the house and walked across the road to his office next to Dexter's. Despite Danny's enthusiasm for his new home, Fred could not shake an insistent sense of foreboding. Little can the boy guess, he thought, how dismal it's going to be for his mother, away from her friends and the music she loves and the balls and parties where she has such a wonderful time. Why, he asked himself, had he knuckled under to his father's bland assumption that what was best for the mines was best for his sons. Fred straightened up and walked toward Dexter, who met him at the office door.

"You look splendid, Fred." He put his hands on his brother's shoulders and held him at arm's length. Slighter than Dexter and two inches taller, Fred's figure was spare and muscular. His service in the Union Cavalry and in the Philadelphia City Troop gave his legs the slightly bent look of a good horseman "Have you been riding a lot?"

"No, but since the beginning of spring I've had my shell on the Schuylkill every decent day. I'm going to miss it terribly—the exercise and the friends."

"You're too stylish for Clarkston, Fred." Dexter released his grip on his brother's shoulders and stepped back to look him over.

"For God's sake, Dexter, I didn't stop to change my clothes," Fred protested.

"I know that. I wasn't thinking of your clothes. I must say you got all the looks in our family, and that goes for your beautiful brown eyes as well as your fashionable hair and moustache."

"Oh, shut up," Fred said affectionately.

As Dexter ushered him through the office door, he held his elbow tight. "You've no idea how wonderful it is to have you here for good, Fred—and Eliza and the children."

Fred shrugged. "I hope it will work out," he said. "God knows I want it to. But I've been dreading this day ever since Father sent me to get trained in the accounting office in Philadelphia. He said, 'You'll make a splendid pair, you and Dexter. He has the genius for engineering and mining and you've got a head for figures. Between the two of you, the mines at Clarkston will surely flourish.'"

Fred looked at his brother. Better not say what was in his mind—that Dexter had no children, a profession that fascinated him, and a wife whose temperament was more that of a social worker than socialite. For the hundredth time Fred wondered why his father and his grandfather had set such store by developing this lonely wilderness. What had possessed his grandfather to leave the comforts of colonial Philadelphia and travel miles on horseback to encourage homesteading that would result in thousands of acres still uninhabitable when he died? What had possessed his father, a successful judge with a growing family, to leave the security of the federal bench and spend his mature life fighting timber thieves and poachers, searching for money to pay taxes, and living for weeks on end in prospectors' huts or primitive inns?

"It's wonderful for Jessie and me to have you here," Dexter said again, breaking the awkward silence.

"Well, Eliza and I will do the best we can," Fred said, forcing a smile, "but I'll admit I'm frightened for her and the children. The agony and anxiety of Danny's illness never leaves either of us. I confess, Dexter, I've never understood why Father wanted to follow up on Grandfather's crazy ideas that the Clarks would one day be landed gentry in a godforsaken place like this. It's as though Father were obsessed."

Dexter's face was serene. "The coal, Fred. Don't you understand? The coal. Grandfather suspected it. Father was sure of it. And I'm to prove it."

"Yes, I understand," Fred sighed

CHAPTER 1

Clarkston 1874

AT NINE IN THE MORNING on a blustery day in March of 1874 the colliery whistle blew three piercing blasts, the signal of disaster. Jessie Clark's horse reared, nearly unseating her. She hoped that the animal wouldn't sense the terror that had seized her the minute the whistle sounded. Jessie was riding on a muddy, rutted road, an eighth of a mile from the colliery. After she managed to quiet her horse, she turned her in the direction of the mine, touched her shoulder with the crop, and galloped headlong to the colliery.

Once through the gates, she could see twenty or thirty men and a few women gathered around the mouth of the mine. Schlenker, the superintendent, with Dexter, Jessie's husband, by his side was bellowing orders. Except for Schlenker's shouted commands, the colliery was filled with eerie silence. Everything had stopped; the machine shops, the locis, the breaker; workers were assembling swiftly and silently.

Jessie dismounted and looked on in silence as Dexter ran over to her.

"Clarkston Number One, Jessie. Schlenker thinks it's only one man, and I pray he's right." Dexter turned back to stare at the mine opening. "There," he pointed toward the shaft, "The foreman is coming back up now." Dexter started toward him.

Jessie handed her horse's reins to a mule driver standing nearby, adjusted the skirt of her fashionable riding habit, and hurried after her husband. In spite of his broad shoulders and air of authority, there was something about him that touched her—touched and intimidated her. The crowd around the mine automatically stepped aside to make room for her.

"One man trapped, sir," the foreman said. "I'm afraid maybe he's badly hurt. He's pretty near completely buried. The roof must have fallen in on him, and as far as I can figure, he had been working at least a hundred yards from the shaft, so it's hard to get to him."

"I want a fresh crew of six men to stand ready to go down every fifteen minutes," Dexter ordered.

In seconds the foreman had descended once more with his crew. When he came up again, he reported to Schlenker, "I think Stephen's back may be broken. His laborer wasn't caught, so the two miners working the next room started immediately trying to dig him out with their hands. But they couldn't get very far and all they've been able to free are a few of his fingers."

"Who is it?" Jessie whispered. She bit her lower lip to help control her trembling.

The foreman looked at her hesitantly. "It's Stephen Malloy, ma'am."

The blood left Jessie's face. Dexter put an arm around her as the foreman gathered another crew and went back down the shaft.

Jessie began searching the crowd, looking for Katie Malloy. "I can't find Katie anywhere," she said. "I suppose she doesn't know yet."

"No, I guess not. I'm terribly sorry, Jessie. God knows this is hard enough to bear no matter who the miner is, but when it's Katie's husband—" Dexter shrugged helplessly. Katie had worked as Jessie's maid from the time of her arrival in this country until her marriage, and Jessie had a deep affection for her. "Well, I'd as soon she didn't know until we get some kind of definite word."

The next time the foreman came back, he reported that he thought Malloy was alive, but so far they had only been able to free one of his wrists. "I hope we'll soon be able to reach his arms and shoulders," he said, "but right now he can only move his head a little."

"That's bad. Means his back may be broken." An older miner, standing in the crowd, edged forward.

After the rescue squad went down for the fifth time, Dexter

turned to Schlenker. "How in God's name did it happen, Schlenker? Malloy is one of our best miners."

"Greed," Schlenker replied coldly. "I'm sure he used one charge instead of two or three and brought that roof down on himself."

Jessie turned away, unable to stand Schlenker's smug expression. She loathed him as much as the men did.

During an interminable two hours, rescue crews came and went; Malloy's wife, Katie, arrived. Black-haired, blue-eyed, she still had the pink cheeks of her Irish childhood. Finally Malloy was brought to the surface.

The doctor from Hazleton, waiting since the first alarm, gave Stephen a dose of laudanum, helped wrap him in blankets and load him onto a mule cart. Katie, Jessie close behind, ran to the stretcher to hold her husband's hand, but mercifully the laudanum had begun to take effect and Stephen lapsed into unconsciousness. The doctor climbed into his buckboard and hurried ahead as the mule cart started with Katie walking at its side.

Watching the pitiful cortege begin its journey, Jessie moaned. She knew it was not the right moment but she couldn't stop herself. "Oh, Dex, if only you had built the hospital in Clarkston. Those awful seven miles to Hazleton will probably kill him."

"Jessie, for God's sake, why bring that up again now? Dammit, you know the reasons as well as I and I'm sick enough about this as it is. Please get out of here and go home." Dexter turned away.

Silenced, Jessie took her mare's bridle from the mule driver and left.

Seven and one-half hours after the accident Stephen Malloy reached the Hazleton hospital. Over rough and rocky roads, the trip had taken three hours. Stephen was more dead than alive. Although his back was not broken, he had suffered a fractured pelvis and probably a splintered leg. His grave condition was greatly aggravated by the grueling journey.

"I'm sorry about this morning, Jessie," Dexter said. They had finished dinner and were in the living room. "I shouldn't have lost my temper."

"That's all right, Dex," Jessie said quickly, "I was wrong—it wasn't the time to bring up the hospital."

"No. It was a good time. Today's accident convinced me. After you left, I told Schlenker to go ahead with the plans for it."

"Oh Dex," Jessie got up and ran to him. She bent down and kissed his cheek.

He took her hand and held it, then got up and put his arms around her, drawing her to him.

"Jessie, could we—could we go upstairs?" He breathed the words against her hair.

Jessie stiffened. "Dexter," she said, pulling away, "after today, I'm exhausted. I'm too tired now to do anything except go straight to sleep."

Dexter's arms dropped to his sides. "Good night, Dex, and thank you for the hospital." Jessie leaned forward and kissed him once more and left the room, walking rapidly toward the stairs.

Dexter felt a wave of frustration and self-pity. Fred, he was sure, was never so rebuffed by his wife, Eliza.

CHAPTER 2

Philadelphia and Cape May
May 1868
Clarkston
1885

Jessie Tucker Clark had had the shock of her life on her wedding night. She was not prepared for the realities of marriage and the only warning of what was to come was the peculiar conversation she had had with her mother the afternoon before her wedding.

Mrs. Josiah Tucker, whom no one ever failed to take seriously, turned abruptly to Jessie after Mr. Tucker said grace at the noon meal. "Jessie, I want to talk to you privately after lunch."

To Jessie's astonishment, Mrs. Tucker led her up the curving staircase, down the long hall, past two Sheraton highboys. When they reached her bedroom in the east wing, Mrs. Tucker motioned Jessie to sit by the dressing table. Then she bolted the door and settled herself nervously on the edge of the chaise longue. "Jessie—ah—you are about to be married." She was stammering.

There didn't seem to be much to answer to this, so Jessie, although she was beginning to feel uneasy, remained silent.

"You see, my dear, there are certain things in marriage that will come to you as a surprise. Things that—ah—you may not quite know . . ." Evidently Mrs. Tucker was finding it hard to go on. She was making Jessie very nervous now. She even seemed to be breathing hard when she began again. "These may be, well, quite painful. But, of course, you will have to bear them. I am afraid there is no other course than to submit."

Jessie could not help echoing, "Submit?"

19

"Don't interrupt, my child." Since the art of reprimand came naturally to Mrs. Tucker, the interruption had restored her poise. "Yes," she said. "Submit. You will know what I am speaking—"

Submit. To what?

"—of later. Meanwhile remember that in time you may be able to avoid this unpleasantness altogether, particularly if your husband—"

Unpleasantness. What on earth was going to happen to her?

"—is considerate, and I am sure Mr. Clark is that. Certainly once there are children, there is no need—"

Children. But after you're married, children arrive via an act of God.

"—to continue the physical side of—"

Physical. Of course she would help Dexter every way she could, but her mother was putting it strangely.

"—marriage, although at first a wife has a duty to allow her husband to impose—"

Duty. She understood now. The marriage ceremony said, "love, honor, and obey."

"—his presence on that of his wife's. However, while she is not bound to enjoy it, she must not show her displeasure."

Presence. Enjoy. Displeasure. She was at sea again.

"So, my dear Jessie, I hope this little talk has been helpful and that you will enjoy the blessings of a long and productive marriage."

Jessie said, "But Mamma, I'm not sure I—"

Her mother stood up. "You will," she said.

"Not a cloud in the sky," Mrs. Tucker noted with satisfaction. It was the twenty-third of May 1868, the country was in the grip of the Reconstruction era, Andy Johnson was in the White House, but Philadelphia's elite could afford to ignore both. It was also Jessie's wedding day, and Mrs. Tucker had personally inveigled the Lord into giving her a smiling, sunshine-filled day so that her daughter's reception could be held in the Tucker garden. Lilac purple and white, peonies pink and red surrounded a cleverly conceived vegetable garden, divided by borders peppered with alyssum and mertensia. In the background was a row of flowering dogwood, its waxlike petals in sharp contrast to the evergreens behind. All was at its peak, in silent tribute to Mrs. Tucker's superior planning.

"Jessie," said her mother as she watched the maid help her daughter out of her wedding dress, "it was a perfect wedding."

It had been, but it seemed to Jessie this was the tenth time her mother had congratulated herself. It was nearly time to go and Jessie's thoughts were hovering around the night ahead.

"Mamma, I think I'm almost ready. Do I look all right?"

"Um, yes," Mrs. Tucker said absently. She was clinging to what was left of her day. Even Mr. Tucker, although he generally had the good sense to remain invisible, had emerged temporarily to compliment her on her arrangements.

Jessie, standing in front of a long mirror, examined her appearance critically. A pearl gray silk dress from Worth with a tightly fitted bodice topped a flaring skirt supported by several bouffant crinoline petticoats. She placed her new leghorn hat on her head, tilting it forward fashionably. "I think it's time, Mamma," she said.

Her mother's obscure warnings kept creeping back into her mind all during the honeymoon trip to Cape May. Dexter, solicitous and ebullient at the same time, had an air of eagerness about him that made him look as though he might become dangerously unrestrained. He had kept his eyes fixed on hers. Conversation that once had flowed unreservedly was now halting and meager. The drive to the wharf in Philadelphia, the ferry to Camden, the train trip to Cape May seemed endless. By the time they arrived at the Breakers Hotel, where they were to spend a week, Jessie was wracked with nervousness. A bellboy took them to their suite and deposited their luggage. The steamer trunks would come up later.

"I think," Dexter said, gripping Jessie's elbow firmly, "we'll go straight to the dining room. We haven't time to change for dinner."

"Whatever you think, Dexter." Out of fright Jessie was developing a submissiveness totally foreign to her nature.

The sight of the long, white, high-ceilinged room had an immediate effect on Jessie's anxieties. For the moment she was back in familiar territory. Dexter ignored the headwaiter and seated Jessie himself. Lightly touching her shoulder, he asked, "Will you be comfortable here? Is this all right, Jessie?"

"Oh yes," said Jessie, staring fixedly at the silver vase with three pink carnations in the center of the table.

Moselle arrived with the Little Neck clams. Waving his glass and his fork simultaneously, Dexter attacked his plate with relish.

Jessie toyed with her fork.

"Dex," she said brightly. The waiter took away the plates and placed a tureen of soup on the table. "You remember those choruses the Welsh miners have? The Eisteddfod? Do you think we could have anything like that in Clarkston?"

"Um," Dexter mumbled. He looked at her again with the same frightening intensity. "Probably. Some time later."

"It would be wonderful to develop a choir," she persisted. "Your brothers' wives could help. Two of them are very musical."

"Yes. Certainly, Jessie." He smiled at her. The soup plates went out to the kitchen as a noisette of lamb appeared. The head-waiter showed a bottle of claret to Dexter, who nodded his approval and instantly turned his attention back to Jessie. "You look lovely, Jessie," he said shyly.

"Thank you, Dexter." Jessie's voice was almost a whisper. She began again. "Dex, you—remember you asked me to be your partner and I know I can't help you much with the technical side of mining, but perhaps I could do something about the other . . ."

His proposal had indeed seemed an offer of partnership. They had come back from a cross-country ride. As Jessie slipped gracefully from the saddle onto the mounting block, he said, "You ride beautifully, Jessie. You must have been born to the saddle and you've got the best hands I've ever seen." He gazed appraisingly at her.

Jessie felt a thrill of excitement. Each of the five Clark brothers was considered a catch by all her friends in Philadelphia. Eliza Morris, that gay, sophisticated debutante, had already snared Frederick, but this was Dexter, the ablest of them all.

Abruptly he reached for her hand. "Jessie—I want you as my partner. I don't know anyone else who has—well, you're the only girl I know who has enough courage to spend her life as the wife of a Pennsylvania coal miner. Will you marry me and come to Clarkston to live?"

Jessie laughed. "Are you offering me a position in your mine Mr. Clark, or are you proposing marriage?"

"Both," said Dexter.

What had happened to the ambitious practical man, her former friend and companion, who had made that straightforward proposition? Jessie was unnerved tonight by a peculiar urgency in Dexter's eyes. He kept them trained on hers as he raised his glass of claret and said, "To you, my darling." The waiter returned and exchanged dinner for dessert plates.

Jessie plowed on. "Dex, I am so looking forward to our life in Clarkston. Have you come any closer to solving the problems of the miners' houses?"

"No, not really."

She couldn't believe it. He sounded indifferent, and the way the men lived was something he had agonized over.

"Jessie, oh, I've longed so to be alone with you," he said haltingly. His rapid leaps from exuberance to diffidence were as disconcerting as his intensity.

As the waiter traded the dessert plates for finger bowls, Jessie decided to try changing the subject. "You know, Mamma never stopped saying what a beautiful wedding it was."

"Oh, it was, Jessie," he said enthusiastically. Then, dropping his voice, "And Jessie, we're finally married. Tonight begins our married life."

The finger bowls retreated to make place for a tray with coffee. The familiar sight of the after-dinner coffee service produced panic. "This is a marvelous hotel, Dex," Jessie said. "It's—it's . . ." She couldn't seem to go on.

Later they were in their suite preparing for the night. Dexter pulled the heavy green velour curtains to one side. They had been drawn across the entrance to the bedroom and across the French doors that looked out on the sea.

"Come look at the view, Jessie," he said, "it's magnificent." He put an arm around her and looked down at her. Her back was tense and stiff. He released her and said gently, "Jessie dear, call me when you're ready."

She nodded mutely, went into the bedroom, from there into the dressing room. Her underclothes and nightdresses had been placed in the tall highboy in the corner. Jessie removed her dress and jacket. Her hands shook as she unfastened the twenty or more hooks that held each of her crinoline underskirts in place. She poured warm water from a pitcher into the washbasin, washed her hands and face, and slipped into a lawn nightdress. Finally she took her ruffled peignoir from the wardrobe and walked slowly into the bedroom.

She was trembling as she knelt by the side of the bed. She did not know what she should ask God for or what, if anything, He could do to help her. All she was able to murmur was, "Please God, please help me through whatever is coming." She blinked rapidly to hold back tears as she said, "Amen," and slid between the sheets. In a thin voice she called out, "All right, Dexter."

Dexter came into the room and crossed to the bed. He stood there for a few seconds. Finally, he said, "You look very small lying there, Jessie. I won't be long. Would you like me to turn out the lamps while I undress?"

"Yes." Jessie began to relax a little. Now that the gaslight had been turned off, moonlight flooded the room and she could see Dexter's shadow through the dressing-room door. He was a tidy man but awkward and noisy. He hung up his jacket, took off his shoes, placed them beside hers, pulled off his socks and piled them along with his underwear on a chair. Next he fumbled around inside his valise long enough to make Jessie want to help him, extracted a nightshirt, put it on and went to the washbowl. Jessie watched all this with quiet fascination as though she was another person, quite unconnected with herself. Then he poured water into the bowl and, with a jolt, Jessie realized how intimately she was sharing this man's life.

The scene she had just witnessed made him even more of a stranger. He was walking toward her. She shivered. She could not think what it would be like to sleep next to a man. He was in her bed now and she was wide-eyed with apprehension. He put his arms around her, crushing her to him. As he sensed the rigidity of her response, he began to stroke her back with his free arm.

"Jessie, Jessie, relax. I've waited so long . . ." His next words were lost as his mouth was on hers. She could feel the pounding of his heart when he placed his body on top of hers, still holding her in an unbreakable grip. With no warning at all, a terrible weakness betrayed her; she was terrified, suffocated, and helpless. For a brief moment she was paralyzed, unable to escape from the horror in which she was caught until suddenly she felt pain. The shock made strength return to her and with a tremendous surge, she managed to free her body from his. Submit, her mother had said. It was impossible, grotesque, but all she could do for the moment was to beg for time. As he reached for her again, she cried out, "Please please, wait—I can't—"

The next morning they were stiffly self-conscious with each other. After midday Sunday dinner, they went down to the bay to look for the famous "Cape May diamonds," the brilliant quartz pebbles varying in size from those as small as lentil seeds to some as large as bricks.

On the way back, Dexter took her arm to guide her through the narrow streets. With each step, Jessie's skirt brushed against his ankle. It was a minor annoyance until with no warning Dexter stopped walking.

"Jessie, your skirt—I think I could do something with it."

"What?" Jessie was defensive. Hoops were out of style but much easier to walk in than the longer skirts in current vogue. "It's more comfortable to walk in than the new dresses," she said lamely.

He laughed. "Oh, I don't care how old or new it is. It's the hoop. I think we could use it for surveying."

Jessie listened attentively. This was the way it used to be.

"Remember we surveyed the Oneida property last week and had a terrible time with it? The terrain is so rough that the chains and stiff wires we were using were impossible to manage."

"And the hoop in my skirt is—"

"Exactly. Strong and pliable. Do you think, I mean, would you mind if we cut the material and pulled the hoop out?"

"Of course not, Dex." Jessie's voice had a lilt. "Let's hurry back."

Together, like children, they removed the tempered steel band from the skirt. Using a tape measure from Jessie's sewing kit, Dexter took down the specifications. "I'd better ask them for five hundred feet, Jessie." He would write the specifications to Heller and Brightly in Philadelphia. "This tape measure of yours leaves something to be desired, but I make it approximately a fifteenth of an inch thick and an eighth of an inch wide."

"Let me look, Dex." Jessie checked his measurements. "That seems right to me."

"It'll do," he said. "You didn't bring along a scale, too, did you?"

"No." Jessie was delighted. "But don't you think I've already done enough?"

"Not quite. Here, hold this thing and see what you think it weighs."

"Between two and three ounces," she said serenely.

"Good girl. I made it two-and-a-half ounces, too. We'll leave it at that."

Jessie felt almost gay as they went downstairs for supper. "There's a great deal I still have to find out about you, Dexter. I've often wondered, for instance, how you and Brewster managed to escape the war."

"That's something I'm not very proud of, Jess, especially when Fred, Philip, and James had such fine records. If you must know, Father bought substitutes for both Brewster and me."

"How strange!" Jessie looked puzzled. "Your father always seemed to glory in the fact that three of his boys served in the Union Army."

"That's true. But having them in the army didn't interfere with his own plans at all. As I look back, it seems to me he was pretty highhanded with us."

"How do you mean?"

"He was torn between his duty to his country and the responsibility laid upon him by my grandfather to develop the mines."

"I see. And he thought you the best qualified for the mines so he sent you to the École des Mines in Paris and on to Germany for training?"

"That's right," Dexter accepted his superiority in the field matter-of-factly, "and Brewster also went to Germany to study law, which Father thought would be needed. But that was a bad investment because Brewster has neither the health nor the inclination to spend much time in Clarkston."

"I see! . . . Dexter, did you have to go to Europe for a technical education?"

"I did," Dexter answered. "There's not a university in this country where I could have gotten the mining and mechanical skills I was taught abroad."

"That's awful. Maybe someday"—Jessie's face lit up; her

feelings seemed to seesaw between anxiety and assurance—
"maybe someday we could help to get engineering courses introduced here."

"What a wonderful idea! There's still a backbreaking job to
be done in Clarkston. But with you to help me there's no limit
to what we can accomplish." He lifted his glass and the look in
his eyes temporarily brought back last night's sense of panic.
Then he leaned across and took her hand in his very gently.

"It—I'm sure it will be better tonight."

Jessie could only hope her misery didn't show. Privately, she
had begun to realize she must do as her mother said.

That night in an agony of pain she was able to satisfy him.
In the morning, she tried valiantly not to rebuff his gestures of
affection. All that week she felt bewildered and frightened for
the future.

Years had not dimmed the memory of the horror she had
endured during the first days of her marriage. Over the years her
husband had made fewer and fewer demands on her, and Jessie
believed it when she told herself that their busy life together in
Clarkston, the town they had literally built themselves, used up all
Dexter's energies.

"For what we are about to receive, we thank Thee," Dexter
mumbled. Having satisfied the Lord, he reached for a slice of
bread, spread it thickly with butter, and added a solid layer of
marmalade. Jessie looked at him disapprovingly; it couldn't be
good for him to eat as much as he did, but if she tried to stop him
she would be fighting a deeply ingrained Clark habit.

"I told Schlenker I'd drive over to Buck Mountain with him
this morning," Dexter said. "I want to see for myself that everything's all right now. Do you have your sewing class this morning?"

"Yes. Emmy and I are going."

"How about taking Eliza, too?"

Jessie frowned. Eliza and Emmy were both her sisters-in-law
and Jessie's devotion to Emmy, Philip Clark's widow, was as great
as her dislike of Eliza, Fred's sophisticated wife. She wished
Dexter would stop trying to arrange a truce between them.

"Even you admit she's an expert seamstress and a good teacher, Jessie."

"Yes, I do, but what's the use? The minute she gets a group of girls started, she rushes off to Philadelphia or Atlantic City or Florida or anyplace she wants." Jessie spread her hands. "If it isn't Danny's health, it's that Fred has to be in town and she feels she has to tag along with him. But she doesn't mind leaving Fred here without her or the children either when she takes it into her head to get out of Clarkston. There's always some excuse."

"I know, Jess, but think of how she must feel about Danny. Can't you be a little more tolerant?"

"No, I can't," Jessie snapped. "Eliza is a frivolous woman."

Dexter patted her on the shoulder. He said, as if talking to a child, "My brother loves his wife, very, very much. I love my brother and there is no one to take his place in the business. You know that, and that I depend on him as I depend on you to help me with my job. I have enough worries without adding to them by knowing you can't get on with Eliza." He kissed her on the forehead and walked out.

Driven nearly to tears by a sore conscience on one hand and sympathy for herself on the other, Jessie went to her desk and wrote Eliza a polite note asking her to join Emmy and herself at the sewing class that morning.

CHAPTER 3

Clarkston 1886

On a Thursday in January, twelve years after the mine accident, as soon as he had finished breakfast, Heinrich Schlenker, the superindendent at Clark Brothers, kissed his wife and each of his six daughters with military precision, walked to the front door, picked up his felt hat, and let himself out.

At this hour Clarkston's main and side streets were empty. Mountains of slag as black as coal surrounded the houses. On Main Street the houses occupied by the upper-echelon Clark Brothers' employees were ugly, wooden, middle-class houses equipped with heavy board shutters. None of these things troubled Schlenker; his concerns were limited to his job, his daughters, and his wife and in that order.

He reached Black Creek Hall and glanced at it with distaste. It was a typical Clark indulgence that was to provide both education and recreation for the employees. In Schlenker's eyes it was a waste of time. It reminded him that he would have to report more cases of dockage to Dexter Clark. His employer's peculiar insistence on knowing everything about employee grievances was a major irritant. No other mine owners paid the slightest attention to their laborers; they expected their superintendents to take full charge, and if strikes threatened, they hired Pinkerton detectives as well as Coal and Iron Police to protect their property.

Schlenker started up Clark Hill. He was on his way to Dexter Clark's house rather than his office because Dexter had been confined to his home for a week with the grippe. Schlenker hoped he wouldn't run into that bossy Jessie Clark, who he knew despised

29

him. Mary, the parlor maid, let him in and he went straight to the octagonal book-lined study.

Almost immediately he heard his employer coming down the stairs.

"Ah, yes, Schlenker," Dexter said absentmindedly. "Good morning."

He sat down behind his flat-topped oak desk, motioning to Schlenker to sit opposite. He was frowning as he unlocked the right-hand drawer. He pushed aside the company code book lying on top, took out a sheaf of papers, and relocked the drawer. Waving the papers at Schlenker, he asked, "You know what these are?"

Schlenker nodded.

Dexter looked at the papers with distaste. They were Pinkerton reports. "As you know," he said, "I was very reluctant to use Pinkerton to spy on our own men."

Schlenker restrained a sigh. Dexter's naiveté often made life difficult. He was unrealistic about the facts. In the mid-1880s all over the country labor was in a ferment. Persuading Dexter, however, that his men, the men in his mines, whom, he believed, he treated so well, were ungrateful was like trying to tell a man his children were murderers. Dexter's brother Frederick and Schlenker had finally pushed Dexter into hiring Pinkerton men, like all the other operators. Schlenker had little love for either of the Clarks, but he recognized that Frederick at least had common sense, which was more than he could say for Dexter, with his head full of dreams of breakers and jigs and other mining equipment. At first Dexter stubbornly insisted that the detectives confine their spying to outsiders. Eventually Fred and Schlenker made him see that this was ridiculous and a waste of money. But using the detectives had never ceased to appall him.

Dexter ran a hand through his hair. The gesture told Schlenker that his employer was more upset than usual.

"Have you had any rumors of a new strike lately, Schlenker?"

"No, sir."

"Have you seen any signs of unusual unrest among the men?"

Schlenker had not. He admitted to himself that he had sensed discontent and rebellion in the air, but there was no point in telling Dexter that.

"*Nein*," Schlenker said, lapsing into his native language as he did whenever he was put off balance. "Just the usual. The men don't like dockage and Huxley and Browning had to dock for slate last week."

"Are there new men working the Number Three and Seven mines?"

"Yes," Schlenker answered. "Hungarians. In both cases the Irish foremen blame them. But as you have said, dockage is the only way we can make them produce clean coal."

Dexter turned away for a moment to look out at the landscape, still barren despite his wife's heroic efforts to soften it with planting. Only a few hundred yards away, the black dust of Clarkston Number Two, a working anthracite mine, covered the ground where trees had been leveled, the earth's surface ripped away and the mouth of a shaft opened. Dexter's shops, the place where he was happiest, were up the hill and across the road, a two-minute walk from the house. He looked at them longingly and wished that he was hard at work on an engineering experiment instead of talking to his superintendent about the problems of the men. The recent influx of immigrants from middle Europe had raised racial and religious conflicts that seemed bound to end in violence.

He turned back to his superintendent. Allowing a trace of a smile to cross his face at the thought of Schlenker's discomfort, he said, "Remember that Irish miner you called down for letting a load of coal go by with too much slate who had the nerve to tell you, 'What God hath joined together let no man put asunder'?"

Schlenker nodded glumly.

"Seriously, I wish to God I could design something mechanical to do the job, something that would do for slag and coal the same thing the traveling grate we've built does for sorting sizes in the breaker."

Schlenker concentrated on the week's tally of coal mined and shipped while his employer let his thoughts drift. Dexter would never forget his first breaker. Anthracite coal mining demanded the services of a breaker, an awkward, rambling structure named literally for its vital function of breaking large pieces of coal into smaller units. The excitement Dexter felt the first time Clarkston Breaker Number One was tried out could still stir him. He had devoted a year's effort to making structural innovations. He knew a moment of terror as he watched the first car filled with coal

emerge from the mine and, hooked to the pulley operated by a
stationary engine, start uphill. He trembled then, sharply aware
that the angle at which he had built the trestle to the top of the
tipple might be too steep for the weight of the car and the strength
of the pulley. The peak had to be eighty feet from the ground to give
the coal, being sized inside the breaker, the force of gravity to flow
unimpeded all the way to the ground. What worried Dexter most
was the perilous trip the car, carrying coal from the mine and
known for some inscrutable reason as a gunboat, would first have
to make to the top of the breaker. As it reached the summit the
gunboat paused briefly. A workman waiting astride the trestle
pulled a handle on the side of the car, opening the bottom. The coal
slewed out in a thundering mass, separating itself into various
troughs according to size, passing through iron rollers and screens
designed to crush and sort the lumpy black stream. Dexter felt like
shouting.

Now the same urgency that had bedeviled him when he was
building the breaker began to seize him again. He had not invented
the breaker, but he had built an extraordinarily competent one and
he was sure he must be able to invent a method other than manual
for separating the slag from the coal before it went into the
breaker.

Reluctantly he glanced down at the file of papers on his desk.
Why was his skill with machines so much greater than his com-
petence in handling men? Leafing through the Pinkerton mem-
oranda, he said, "These indicate that some of the men have organized and may be inciting others to strike."

Schlenker pushed aside the colliery tallies. "There's been
some trouble at Buck Mountain, Mr. Clark, but you know already
about that and it's quieted down."

"I know. Anyway, keep your eyes open. I'll be back in my office
tomorrow and glad to be there. I wouldn't have stayed home if Mrs.
Clark hadn't insisted. She's always so afraid I'll catch pneumonia.
She fusses over me as though I were a growing boy." His smile was
rather prim. "We can go over these tallies in the morning."

It was a dismissal. Relieved, Schlenker stood up, said good-
bye and left.

Dexter looked at the superintendent's retreating back curiously and then returned to the Pinkerton file. He had only had time

to glance through the reports, but now he must read them thoroughly, no matter what it cost. His eye fell on one especially unpalatable sentence. A detective reporting a discussion among a group of miners and laborers in a bar in Freetown overheard a carpenter, employed in Hazleton, saying that "some of Clark's men, especially at Clarkston, were suckers and they would do whatever Clark told them; that Mr. Clark had as much influence or more than all the other owners combined; that he had had a special train to bring him from Philadelphia to Clarkston." He had used it last year, when he wanted to get back to Clarkston immediately after his sister died. The carpenter quoted the Clark employee as saying, 'I wish to God it was himself that died.'"

Dexter wondered if Schlenker was concealing anything from him.

Weekday mornings Jessie Clark memorized sonnets, saving longer poems for Saturdays and Sundays. The last lines of William Wordsworth's "On the Extinction of the Venetian Republic"— "Men are we, and must grieve when even the shade/Of that which once was great, is passed away"—were running through her head as she turned to look out the window. The soothing effect of the poet's language was immediately erased by the sight of Heinrich Schlenker striding down the front walk.

Putting him from her mind, she began planning her day. She would go immediately for her usual visit to the miners' hospital, come home for lunch, and then go and see how Katie was getting along.

By three o'clock, Jessie was bundled up in an ulster of dark blue broadcloth and ready for her afternoon call. She stood on the top step of the buckboard while Eroh, the Lithuanian coachman, holding two corners of a heavy buffalo robe, put it and his arms around her from the front and skillfully pushed her into a sitting position.

"Mercy, Eroh," Jessie said, "I feel like an Egyptian mummy. Go straight to Katie Malloy's. If there's time afterward, I'll stop at Black Creek Hall."

"Yes, ma'am," Eroh answered, climbing into the front seat. He gathered up the reins and gave Betty's flank a gentle flick. When they reached the bottom of the hill, Jessie glanced to the left at the seething activity in the colliery. The locis were darting back and forth along the tracks like eager water beetles, picking up dump carts full of refuse at the breaker and depositing them on one of the banks of culm and slate across the colliery. Mule teams, coal cars, stable boys, breaker boys, and miners made a changing but orderly pattern as roads and railroad tracks crossed and recrossed one another. In the center of a bare and dusty area two tall thin smokestacks spouted plumes of white steam. These came from the boiler, whose function was to force thousands of gallons of water per minute through the breaker.

Half a mile farther on was a row of young chestnut trees Jessie had ordered planted five years before. She looked at them and at the tidy yards in front of each frame house with satisfaction.

Eroh turned right into Fourth Street and stopped in front of a gray clapboard house. He helped Jessie stand up, unwind the buffalo robe and step down on the ground. Then he reached into the buckboard and handed Jessie a basket with jars of calf's foot jelly, tomatoes, beans, and peaches.

"I won't be long, Eroh," she said and walked a step toward the gate. Then she added, "You could turn the buckboard round while I'm inside."

Eroh muttered under his breath that she might at least credit him with that much sense.

Glancing out her front window, Katie spotted Jessie stepping down from the carriage. She also noticed Eroh's exasperated expression as he turned the horse around. She smiled a little, remembering that, unlike some, when she first started to work for Mrs. Clark, she had never resented her mistress nor been intimidated by her.

Katie O'Toole was seventeen when she was first brought to Jessie Clark by Heinrich Schlenker. The superintendent was on one of his periodic trips to Ellis Island to recruit labor for the mines. He had interviewed Katie at the suggestion of Father O'Flanagan, who before leaving Ireland had been a friend of the O'Tooles's parish priest. The interview convinced Schlenker that

Katie could be trained as the chambermaid Mrs. Clark needed. His decision was based partly on the fact that Father O'Flanagan said she had been a scullery maid in an Irish castle. Schlenker, ignorant of the customs of the Irish gentry, could not have known that Katie never left the castle's dark kitchen and that her "experience" consisted solely of learning to scrub.

Schlenker persuaded Father O'Flanagan that Katie would be in good hands and took her direct from Ellis Island across the Hudson River and by train to Bethlehem, Pennsylvania. There they changed for Clarkston Junction, where Eroh met them in the buckboard—one hundred and thirty miles and four-and-a-half long hours from New York.

By the time they reached the back door of the Clark house, Katie was paralyzed with exhaustion. She had not yet recovered from the terrible crossing, the confusion at Ellis Island, and the newness of her sourroundings. Mary, the parlor maid, greeted them. "Come and sit down," she said and pushed Katie into a chair. "You must be tired from the trip and all. Mrs. Clark's expecting you. She'll be down directly."

Stop! Katie wanted to scream. Too much was happening too fast. From the moment she had decided to go to America, she seemed to be swept along by outside forces over which she had no control. She felt dead inside. The desolation that had engulfed her at leaving her family became unbearable the moment her father put her on the ship. From then on terror piled on terror. The crowds on board, shoving, pushing, some battling bravely for what they hoped would be survival; her own loneliness until she found Stephen Malloy, a fellow traveler as miserable as she; the hunger, the retching with seasickness during the first bad storm; the death from typhus of two old men and their instant burial at sea to prevent contagion; the longing for and anxiety about arrival; and finally Ellis Island, with its hardened officials, the runners, the procurors who had come to size up candidates for the world's oldest profession; and at last Father O'Flanagan's kind Irish face.

Then, with no time to get used to the change, here she was in Clarkston, Pennsylvania, in what appeared to be a large house, being introduced to a new mistress before she had even taken in her surroundings. Dazed, she got to her feet and looked at Jessie Clark coming through the kitchen door.

"Ah, yes, Katie. Katie O'Toole, isn't it?" Jessie said, smiling at her. "Mr. Schlenker has just been telling me about you. You must be tired from your trip. Please sit down."

Katie managed a "thank you, mum" and sat.

"You know," Jessie said, "I've been all over Europe but never visited Ireland. It's a very beautiful country, isn't it?"

"Yes, mum," Katie murmured.

"Tell me, Katie, you worked for Lady Ross, I believe. At Birr Castle?"

Katie nodded.

"I wonder what the castle was like," Jessie said musingly. People said of Jessie that she could pry conversation out of a stone. "What did you do there, my dear?"

"I worked below stairs," Katie said.

"Oh. I guess that means the kitchen?"

"Aye. I scrubbed pots, the stoves, well everything, mum." She hesitated before adding apologetically, "I didn't do upstairs, ye know."

"How about your family, Katie? Are there many of you? You were very brave to leave them."

Katie swallowed and raised her head to look directly at Jessie. "I had to, mum. Ye see there's not all that much—well, there be nine of us and me youngest sister, she be going on fourteen, same age as me when I started at the castle, and I got her me old job at the castle and she'll be bringing home the wage and I can send some over from here and that way, why, with every one of us working, there'll maybe be enough to eat."

"We'll try our best to make you happy here, Katie," Jessie said. "I can tell you're a worker and I'm sure you'll have no trouble. But first, you must have some rest. Then Mary will show you your duties and later on I'll be able to devote some time to your training myself."

Jessie stood up and smiled again. Katie rose quickly. Jessie's face seemed kind. She thought she saw compassion in the deep-set, beautifully shaped blue eyes, and there was gentleness in the smile. As she studied Jessie, Katie felt a surge of hope; life here might not be the misery she had been used to.

That first impression had never changed for Katie. Jessie Clark was exacting, demanding, and a relentless teacher, but she asked as much of herself as she did of others and Katie never forgot how much she owed her. Jessie passionately believed in self-improvement, and she had brought first grade readers home from the local school for Katie, had corrected her grammar, and had devoted half an hour a day to giving her English lessons.

As Katie watched Jessie coming up the walk and again noticed Eroh's defiant expression, she was reminded of the time Mary, whom Jessie had just finished reprimanding, had turned to her after Jessie left and hissed, "That woman. What in God's name does her husband see in her?"

Katie had given Mary an astonished look and said, "But—she'd do anything in the world for him."

"Come in now out of the cold, Mrs. Clark," Katie said. "I've a good fire going in the kitchen and the children are asleep upstairs." She took the basket from Jessie and motioned her toward the front door.

"How are they, Katie?"

Katie stopped to conquer a short coughing spasm. When she could, she said, "We'd put the sign in the window last night so the doctor came early this morning. He says Ellen's pretty bad with fever but Moira's on the mend. Tommy and Stevie's bound to get it sooner or later."

As she talked, Katie led the way into the kitchen. Jessie stiffened slightly. She would never get used to the homes of the miners. Neat, clean, careworn, and shabby. The pattern never varied. Two rooms on the ground floor, kitchen and parlor. The parlor was furnished with a large bed for miner and wife and often a cradle. The kitchen, dominated by the coal-burning stove, had a tiny window, open shelves for foodstuffs, a wooden table covered with shabby oilcloth, four or five straight chairs and a tin tub resting in a corner.

Katie made a gesture toward the table. "Please sit down, Mrs. Clark. Wouldn't you like a cup of tea?" She picked up the kettle and started for the door. "It'll only take a minute."

Jessie held up her hand. The pump was outside on the street. "Oh, no thanks, Katie," she said. "Really, I haven't the time. I just wanted to see how the children were and I want to talk to you—

about your cough." She paused to look at Katie's thin, flushed face. The eyes were too bright. "It isn't any better, is it?"

"Oh, it's all right. Truly, not as bad as it was." She was deathly afraid of what was coming.

"No, Katie. As soon as the children get over the measles, you've got to go to White Haven for a few weeks."

Katie looked at her desperately. White Haven was a sanatorium for TB where lung specialists, after testing their victims, pronounced their verdict. "And what if they do find something?" she asked. "What am I to do with Stephen and the children if they keep me? With Tommy at the breaker and Moira not old enough to manage Ellen and Stevie?"

"We'll think of a way, Katie," Jessie said soothingly. "But meanwhile you must get as much rest as you can. See that the girls help you now. They're not too young to start learning to cook and wash. The trouble is you spoil them."

Upstairs, Ellen started to cry. "My head hurts, Mommie."

Katie looked harassed. Her cough was always worse when she was tired. She'd been up and down the stairs twenty times. She wished her visitor would stop lecturing her and leave so she could go see what was wrong with Ellen and then flop down and rest.

Jessie stood up. "Go to Ellen," she said. "She needs you and I mustn't keep Eroh and Betty out there in the cold any longer. Why don't you take Ellen a dish of the jelly I brought? It might taste good to her."

Katie's thanks were mumbled as she helped Jessie on with her coat. Jessie's visit, although full of good intentions, had succeeded only in increasing Katie's fears.

Outside the winter dusk had intensified Clarkston's natural melancholy. In the buckboard, reenveloped in the buffalo robe, Jessie was struggling with an unusual feeling of gloom. Katie had been such a bright, gay young thing when she had worked for her and afterward as a bride.

"Oh, Mrs. Clark," Katie had said to her, shaking with excitement, "Stephen and me, I mean I, we've waited four years and now we've picked the date, the date to be married, next April the twentieth of the month, oh, Mrs. Clark," overcome with shyness and lapsing into her native way of speech, "Oh, Mrs. Clark, would ye come to the wedding?"

Of course Jessie would and after Katie had literally danced away delirious in the belief she was about to begin her life in the great American dream, Jessie began to wonder if she should warn her. Not that the dream might differ from reality but that even the kindest of men could be transformed into a terrifying spectacle by lust.

CHAPTER 4

Philadelphia 1886

THE MOMENT SHE GOT ONTO THE TRAIN, Eliza Clark's spirits improved. The weather was typical of December; cold, gray with lowering clouds that held a threat of snow, a day that emphasized the bleakness of the town. The solitary parlor car, with the promise of escape, looked welcoming and comfortable.

Eliza handed the porter her sealskin dolman and took a seat in the middle of the car, pushing the bustle of her russet skirt slightly to one side. Her tailor-made habit jacket of cream color had tight sleeves set high on the shoulders, giving a "kick up" effect. Her olive green hat was decorated with birds and feathers and two olive green ribbons that tied under her chin. Her customary erect carriage was enhanced by the tightness of her stays.

She was going to Philadelphia with her sixteen-year-old daughter, Anna. Fred would join them later in the week, in time to go to the Assembly. Eliza had been brought up on the Assembly, that exclusive, snobbish annual ball to which her father had taken her as a debutante and for which her marriage had entitled her to act as patroness as "the Bride of the Year." Philadelphians certainly take their Assemblies seriously, Eliza thought, always reminding their wives and daughters that attendance was hereditary through the male line and that General Washington was an honored guest when he was in Philadelphia in 1790. In spite of the formality and ceremony, Eliza always looked forward to it every year as a wonderful, gay party, where she could waltz her heart out. In the not-too-distant future she and Fred would be taking Anna to the Assembly.

Eliza glanced across at her daughter with affection. Radiantly healthy, with bright pink cheeks and a willowy figure, Anna looked like a shy eager fawn. She was perched on the edge of her green plush seat; a beaver hat sat on the back of her head. She had on a striped wool dress with a bodice fitting tight over her slight bosom and tiny waist. It was the first time she had been allowed to wear anything more sophisticated than a pinafore, and it seemed to Eliza that the dress gave her self-confidence. Eliza hoped that perhaps this time things would go smoothly for her.

"Anna," Eliza said tentatively, "I thought we might ask the Barstow girls to luncheon before Wednesday's matinee." She had ordered five tickets for *Rip Van Winkle*, the Washington Irving classic that Dion Boucicault had dramatized for Joseph Jefferson.

"All right, Mamma," Anna said docilely. Then added, "But you know what it will be like. They'll just talk to each other and they're always giggling."

The last time they had been in Philadelphia, Eliza had given a small afternoon tea for Anna. Among the carefully chosen young ladies had been the three Barstow sisters. Like most girls their age, the guests quickly separated into little groups, none of which included her daughter. The result was that when the last girl left, Anna fled from the living room, crying, "I hate those stupid girls."

Slowly the train pulled out of the Junction. Eliza frowned at the scene she was leaving; a towering hill of black refuse was piled close to the wooden train shed; the area around it was crisscrossed with miles of track, leading to the gaping mine pits; the only trees visible were on top of the surrounding mountains, ominously dark against the turbulent sky. No wonder, Eliza thought angrily, Anna couldn't adjust to a normal social life. These surroundings were enough to make a melancholy recluse out of the most cheerful temperament. If the environment was bleak, so were the available companions. Anna never saw anyone but her governess, the Clark cousins, and the Shipley girls, whose insignificant father was a distant relation of Fred's. Anna's contemporary, Barbara, was the prettiest of the three sisters but a superficial little flirt with whom Anna never seemed entirely comfortable.

Returning to the problem at hand, Eliza said, "Don't worry, darling, luncheon will be easy and we'll go to the theater afterward. It's important for you to know these girls because you'll be coming out in Philadelphia in two years."

Anna looked unconvinced.

Eliza laughed. "Come on now, you'll have a wonderful time, lots of parties, lots of beaux. Remember I've told you what fun I had when I was a girl."

That was certainly stretching the truth. Eliza's own childhood was so miserable that she kept it largely a secret. Her mother died when she was born, and before long she was old enough to understand that her grandmother was always urging her father to marry again.

When she was seven, her father took her to a leading eye specialist, who pronounced her blind in one eye. From that time on, she began to compensate consciously for the vision she lacked by standing very straight and turning her head frequently and sharply to the left.

On the day she became eight, her father brought her stepmother home. She smiled at Eliza nervously and said, "Why, here's my little Eliza. You come over here and give your new mother a big kiss."

"I hate kissing," Eliza said, trying to wriggle out of a smothering embrace.

From that day on, Eliza eluded her stepmother whenever possible. Seven stepbrothers and stepsisters arrived with oppressive regularity. Of them all, only Susie, the eldest, laid any claim to Eliza's affections, although there was nine years difference in their ages. Only Susie prevented Eliza from wanting to escape permanently from her crowded home. Unlike Anna, she found her pleasure and interests outside it, with her contemporaries.

Eliza saw with relief that the train was pulling out of Hazleton. The track twisted and turned down the mountain to a deep gorge, then a narrow valley. The mountains dropped behind them like a sinister curtain, while in front the landscape widened into a series of rolling Pennsylvania Dutch farms. Eliza always felt at this particular spot that she was escaping from prison.

In three hours they were in Philadelphia. The first thing Anna saw when she got off the train was her Aunt Jemima's new carriage. She wasn't prepared for its elegance. "Oh, Mamma, it's beautiful," she said.

"What, dear?" asked her mother, keeping her eye on their porter.

"The carriage," Anna said impatiently. "How much did it cost?"

"Nineteen hundred dollars. Oh, hello, Patrick," Eliza said abstractedly to the coachman. "I'm glad to see you. Over here, please, porter. Anna, you must never, never ask what things cost."

It was worth it, Anna thought. Dark green with red stripes on the running gear and the inside in matching dark green silk satin with Patrick, on the box, in a dark green woolen overcoat and fawn-colored top hat. She climbed in and sat back contentedly beside her mother.

Aunt Jemima's house, once lived in by the Judge and Mrs. Clark and all their children, had always seemed forbidding to Anna. She climbed the marble steps leading to the heavy walnut door with misgiving. Built in the 1840s at 1512 Spruce Street, it was a typical Philadelphia row house, identical with its neighbors on Walnut, Locust, and Pine streets.

As she crossed the threshold, Anna was struck by the stiff, formal surroundings. A vestibule paved in black and white marble led to an inner door of frosted glass. Halfway down the hall a steep staircase mounted abruptly from the gloom, and immediately on the left a pair of double doors opened into the front drawing room.

"It's so stuffy, Mamma," Anna said. "I feel smothered."

"Those were your grandparents' best brocatel and lace curtains. Your aunt just loves them. They're designed especially to keep out the light." Eliza's tone was sarcastic.

The globes of a gaslit chandelier were reflected in the tall mirror over the mantle, but the flames barely penetrated the far corners of the room.

Eliza looked at her daughter and laughed. "Isn't it awful," she whispered, dismissing with a sweep of her hand the rosewood chairs and overstuffed sofas scattered over a figured Brussels carpet. "You'd better learn what they are, though, because your Aunt Jemima and your father and uncles all think everything in this house is beautiful."

"It's all so gloomy," Anna said. "That room," she said, pointing to another set of double doors draped in green velvet with black silk fringe and opening on the second parlor. "Is it exactly like this one?"

Eliza shook her head. "Not quite, darling. You haven't had a chance to see the formidable collection of rubber plants. They seem to thrive—even in the dark."

"Well, they give me the horrors," Anna said and turned on her heel.

Their first night in Philadelphia Eliza took Anna to the opera. Gertrude Robinson went with them. She was the widow of Henry Robinson, a special partner in Clark Brothers. Henry had died eight years before of a heart attack, leaving Gertrude alone and with an inadequate pension. When the Clarks tried to make Gertrude's life financially more secure, they were surprised to have her refuse all their offers. Instead, with Dexter's help, she got herself a position in the Philadelphia Public Library. Eliza had invited her this evening because she found Gertrude more interesting than many of her contemporaries. She also knew she loved music.

Eliza and Gertrude, with Anna trailing them, hurried up the steps of the Academy of Music. The six octagonal Venetian lamps on the façade framed the brilliance of the arriving audience. Anna was dazzled by the ladies' velvet cloaks in reds, purples, blues, and greens, but the men, in their black silk hats, dress suits, and opera cloaks, seemed to her the most romantic creatures she had ever seen.

Eliza picked up her train. "We'd better get to our seats. I love the overture and don't want to miss any of it."

From the Parquet Circle, where they were sitting, there was a good view of the crescent of boxes four rows in front. Mr. and Mrs. Tucker, Jessie's parents, sat in one not far from Anna and the two women. Gertrude cringed as she saw Eliza's scornful nod in their direction. She wished the Tuckers were elsewhere.

The orchestra was assembling in the pit under the apron of the stage. As the lights dimmed, Gertrude glanced toward the Tuckers, Mrs. Tucker a redoubtable seventy, looking energetic and severe, Mr. Tucker mild and shrunken. Gertrude wondered for the thousandth time about the enigma of Jessie. Although Dexter spoke about her freely, he had never really explained their marriage. Their relationship seemed paradoxical, if nothing else; they were close to each other in many ways, poles apart in others.

She supposed the same thing could be said of her own relationship with Dexter. Except for Eliza, she was always uneasy in the presence of his family, although she was sure that none of them had any inkling that she was more to him than an acquaintance.

If Eliza guessed, Gertrude knew her secret was in safe hands. Eliza was so happy in her own marriage she had no need to feed off the love affairs of others. And what a heavenly evening this was! Gertrude sat back and allowed the lovely arias of Gounod to envelop her. She hated to come back to reality at the end of the last act.

Eliza insisted that Patrick should drive Gertrude home after he had dropped Anna and herself at 1512 Spruce. All the way out Walnut Street and after she had let herself into her house and climbed into bed, Gertrude was under the romantic spell of the evening. The music went round and round in her head, making her restless and lonely. She could not sleep but gave in to the painful indulgence of reminiscence.

Gertrude's affair with Dexter had started seven years before. Once he found her the library job, he began stopping in to see her in the late afternoons when he was in Philadelphia. One balmy spring evening they were sitting in her living room, drinking after-dinner coffee. Dexter got up and walked over to the window. "May I open it?" he asked. "It's such a lovely night."

"Of course," she answered and stood beside him to look out at her lilac bushes just come into full bloom.

"It reminds me of my student days in Paris." Dexter inhaled deeply. "The same marvelous smells used to drift through the windows of the École des Mines from the Luxembourg Gardens. Not very conducive to study."

"I can imagine," she said, and although her shoulder barely touched his arm, a sudden speedup of her pulse warned her there was more that intrigued her about this man than his mining career. Better be careful. Everything about him—marriage, temperament, position—put him beyond intimacy. But there was still a lot she would like to learn about him.

"That's enough fresh air," she said abruptly. "I wish you'd explain to me about Clarkston, Dexter. Your family's feeling for it seems like that of the devout toward a religious retreat."

Dexter smiled and settled down in his chair. "I never thought of it like that," he said, "but as soon as the war was over, Father wasted no time bringing his five sons together. We met in Clarkston in a rooming house. Father had the incorporation papers ready and before we knew it, we were partners in the firm of Clark Brothers."

"It must have been terribly remote and lonely in those days."

"It was. There were a couple of turnpikes connecting the Delaware, Susquehanna, and Schuylkill rivers, but they were full of rocks and tree stumps and barely passable for a carriage. The best way to travel was on horseback."

"I bet you loved it," she said.

"I did. But I remember worrying about Fred. Even in those early days, it was obvious our three other brothers weren't going to be much help in the mines and that Fred and I were saddled with the responsibility. And Fred's heart wasn't in it the way mine was. And I remember worrying about Jessie. I was courting her then and wondered how she'd take to starting married life in a boarding house in a wilderness, waiting for our own house to be built."

He stopped for a moment and Gertrude looked at him curiously. He had smiled, and there was something about the smile she couldn't quite define.

"I needn't have worried. Jessie took to it immediately. Jessie *is* Clarkston."

Why shouldn't Jessie fit into Clarkston, she thought? She was apparently queen of the little kingdom. Gertrude found herself irritated at Dexter's smugness about his wife and moved in her chair to cover up her annoyance. "One of the things I would find hard to live with," she said, "would be the responsibility for the accidents that seem to be an inevitable part of your business."

"Obviously we take every possible precaution," Dexter said, "and we're constantly improving our safety record. But no matter what we do, accidents in mines result ninety percent of the time from the ignorance and carelessness of the miners."

"Hard to believe," she murmured.

"Incredible," he said, entirely missing her point. "For instance, take firedamp, the miners' term for gas, a danger every miner is scared of. Yet I remember a very competent Irishman who one day, instead of putting his safety lamp on the front of his hat, absentmindedly put his naked lamp there. Safety lamp in hand, he went in to test the gas. When he was in the middle of making his examination, the flame on his hat blew him up.

"Dexter, that's—"

"Horrible, yes. It's also typical." He paused for a moment. "It's true miners are exposed to many hazards: bad ventilation and impure air, black lung, as they call it, and occasional caveins, but they are rare, and—thank God—have never happened to us. I'm happy to say our men are mostly content, as they should be. We treat them well. We're trying to educate them and they are better off than any other miners I know."

He was maddeningly complacent and Gertrude wondered how he could be so obtuse. Was he unaware of the formation of a strong new union, the American Federation of Labor? "You don't expect strikes or anything like that?" she asked.

"Good heavens, no. There hasn't been a strike in two years, and I've made it clear to the men that I won't negotiate."

"I see," she said coolly. She wondered how he would feel about her father, who had taught her to respect all individuals, laborers included. "But suppose they strike anyway?"

He shrugged. "We'd close down."

"But you'd lose money."

"We'd lose money if we gave in to demands for higher wages and shorter hours, and I have no intention of committing suicide. I don't commit suicide. I don't arbitrate, I don't argue. I simply do not speak to them."

"But suppose the men get violent? I mean, for instance, like the Mollie Maguires?"

"What do they have to do with anything? They're dead."

"They may be dead," she said through tight lips, "but Dexter, you must see why they acted as they did."

"Why do you bring them up now?" Dexter was flushed and angry. "I don't know how they got into this in the first place. They were a dreadful bunch, terrorists. Thank God we got them hanged!"

The Mollies, a violent and lawless group, had sprung up in the late 1860s. Like the members of an antilandlord organization in Ireland who dressed as women on their raids, the American Mollies created havoc in the coal mines of Pennsylvania for eight long years. They burned breakers, murdered mine superintendents, and paralyzed the region. When they were finally caught, all of them were hanged. Gertrude supposed they deserved their fate, but she wondered why Dexter couldn't grasp that the wholesale hanging had engendered a deep resentment among the Irish working class. Why was she so attracted to him?

"Don't you think," she said carefully, "that a lot of the Irish in the cities as well as in the mines are bitter about the Mollies?"

He shrugged. "They were murderers. Everyone knows that. They deserved to be hanged. It's a matter of law and order."

"Whose law and order? Yours?"

"What? What do you mean by that? Don't you believe in punishing murderers?"

She had made a mistake. "I shouldn't have taken the Mollies as an example. . . . Of course, they deserved what they got. But I still believe there will be a lot of resentment. You see, I believe in the right to strike."

He was appalled. "My God, that's anarchy. You can't mean it."

"But I do. Can't you see why the men have a right to bargain for a better wage?"

"No, I can't. The first strike we had almost made me sick. I've got more sense now. We pay these men well. They have no right to strike or belong to a union. The unions are all a bunch of communists out to ruin the country."

She shook her head. "Times will change, Dexter, and I—" She was ashamed of being so inarticulate.

"They're not going to change as long as I'm around," he interrupted. He was standing, his back rigid. "The trouble with reformers is that their thinking is fuzzy. I'm beginning to believe even you have managed to collect a lot of impractical theories. I realize you're intelligent, Gertrude—but you don't know the workers. You have absolutely no idea how limited they are. Believe me, they're their own worst enemy."

At least he had granted her a brain, if a fuzzy one, but his own was certainly full of misconceptions. She had recovered her poise and was beginning to enjoy herself. "Perhaps I've been misinformed," she said. "But haven't I read of cases where mine owners have neglected to put in proper safeguards? I don't mean Clark Brothers, of course," she added hastily.

"We're accused of all sorts of things, Gertrude," he said coldly. "However, while there may be mine owners who are careless, it's the goddamned stupidity of the miners that causes most of the accidents."

He walked away from her and turned to look her straight in the eye. "I don't suppose you've ever been near the scene of an accident?"

She shook her head.

"Well, I've seen enough," he said grimly, "to last me a lifetime. And so has Jessie. You don't know what it's like"—his voice was accusing—"the sight of the miners' wives and children huddled around the entrance to a mine."

"I'm sorry. I didn't mean to get you upset," she said. But it was hardly her fault that she didn't live within sight and sound of his precious mines.

"No, no, of course you didn't and I'm sorry if I seem that way." He evidently realized he had been unfair. Sounding tentative, he said, "The accident that sticks in my mind is the one that resulted in building our own hospital. Malloy, a man we were fond of, was in it and we didn't know whether he'd ever walk again." He looked uncertain. "He was one of our best miners, but that damnable accident was strictly due to his own carelessness—and greed. Evidently Malloy found a rich vein in his room, and he wanted to save a few cents worth of powder and make one blast do for several, so the charge he set brought the roof down on top of him and he had to be dug out by hand, which took time."

"How ghastly!" Gertrude said.

"I guess it was four or more hours. Malloy looked terrible when he came up and was in bad shape when he arrived at the Hazleton hospital. Jessie convinced me that the trip to Hazleton was more dangerous than the accident, so I gave orders the day Malloy was hurt to start the company hospital."

His remote expression puzzled Gertrude. There was something very odd about what he said. It was as though he had to justify himself or Jessie—or both.

"They—I guess the accidents must be terrible," Gertrude said lamely. "I'm glad you have the hospital."

"Yes," he mumbled. Then abruptly, "I've got to go." He

seemed in a great hurry. At the front door he barely said good-bye, then he vanished into the night.

She wondered if she would ever see him again. She had been a fool to irritate him and make him uncomfortable. His wretched old mines and his pigheadedness about labor were not worth a fight. With all his faults, he was a man of overwhelming vitality and magnetism, his bombast tempered by a disarming humility. They were both too young, she told herself angrily, to enjoy a platonic relationship—and it was impossible to imagine this could be anything else.

Two days later, to her astonishment, he was back. She opened her front door to find him standing there looking oddly awkward and self-conscious. He was clutching a bunch of red roses in one hand and what must have been a bottle of wine in the other. He looked unsettled and said stiffly, "I hope I'm not intruding. I wanted to bring you something to—to thank you for the other evening." He thrust the roses at her and remained rooted to the spot.

"Dexter!" She didn't care if he knew she was delighted. "Please, oh, do come in." Frantically she tried to remember what was in the larder. She would have to find an excuse to change her dress. "I'm so very glad to see you," she said as she led the way to the parlor.

"I don't mean to bother you," he said clumsily. "It—it was an unexpected trip." He looked at her anxiously.

She stifled an impulse to laugh. He was as bumbling as a seventeen-year-old. "Oh, no—you're not—bothering me, that is." His awkwardness was catching, it seemed. "I do hope you'll stay for supper."

"Oh, no, I couldn't do that. I shouldn't impose myself . . ."

"But you're not. Please, please do stay," she said quickly, marveling at the transparent strategies of the male. Did he think she hadn't noticed the bottle?

"Here." He handed it to her.

"Oh, you shouldn't have brought . . . brought me so much," she said, extracting the bottle of burgundy from its sack. "Marvelous, we'll have a feast. Will you forgive me for a moment while I just take this to Bridget and put the roses in water. . . . They're lovely. Thank you." She darted out of the room and, once in the kitchen, said breathlessly to Bridget, "Mr. Clark is here. He'll stay to dinner and—"

"Again?" said Bridget.

"I know we haven't much on hand, but perhaps— We have sardines—we can have them on toast for a first course, unless there's still some chicken soup and, well, leftover lamb— shepherd's pie, and fresh peas, perhaps?"

Bridget nodded glumly.

"You do those beautifully, Bridget. Better than any cook I know. I'm sure he'll appreciate it."

Unconvinced, Bridget muttered, "Yes, ma'am."

"Thank you ever so much, Bridget. I'm sure everything will be absolutely perfect." She rushed to the pantry, seized a tall vase, filled it with water, plunged the roses in it, and went back to the parlor, where she found Dexter looking out the window.

"See," she said, holding out the roses. "They're beautiful. Perfect for this corner." She put them down on a small whatnot stand. "Will you excuse me for just another moment? I want to change."

"A moment? In my experience, that kind of operation is more apt to take an hour—or two." He was evidently feeling more self-confident.

"I won't be long, I promise." She left him and made another trip to the kitchen on the way upstairs. This time they would use the silver candlesticks and her best wine glasses.

She changed into a low-cut emerald dinner dress that brought out the depths of her eyes. It was one she considered mildly daring.

The candlelight in the dining room made her hair glint. Seated opposite Dexter, she felt exhilarated, relaxed, and happy all at the same time.

He raised his glass to her. "To you, my dear—my rebel." She blushed slightly and he laughed. "I thought about some of the things you said the other night. Where on earth did you ever get such ideas?"

"My father," she answered promptly. "He was—is pretty ad- vanced in his thinking, I guess. Well, for instance, he started out by being a good friend of the Motts."

"That's not so very radical," Dexter said, with benign toler- ance. "I was an abolitionist myself."

"Um. Well, you asked me where I got my ideas. Father told me that Lucretia Mott had taught him the mind has no sex, and that's the way he intended to bring me up and did." She ignored his frown.

"He teaches in the School of Philosophy at the University of Pennsylvania, and because he felt he ought to be able to give his students something more than a textbook approach, he began looking around. He visited all sorts of factories and talked to the workers." She stopped and looked at him. "He didn't like what he found. Child labor, fourteen-hour days, and if the workers strike, federal troops are brought in to break it up. The laborer doesn't have any way to defend himself, unions are scorned, locked out, anybody belonging to one is put on a blacklist—"

"And should be," Dexter said pleasantly.

Her smile was brilliant. "I know—that's the general sentiment. But my father says that someday labor will get itself organized and there will be a much fairer distribution of wealth." She had struck at the heart of Dexter's creed.

"I won't tell you what an unbalanced idea that is," he said with perfect good humor. "Sheer socialistic nonsense. We are a capitalistic republic, my dear, and there is no way in the world that socialism will ever get anywhere here."

Gertrude raised her glass. "Would you like to put a small wager on that?"

He shook his head. "I've made it a rule never to take money from a lady."

After dinner he settled himself happily in a chair by the fireplace.

"You know, I love my work," he said. "In fact, Jessie says I drive myself, but, well, recently I'm beginning to find it's a relief to be away; I guess I work all the time when I'm in Clarkston—but here, well, I seem to be able to relax—particularly when I'm with you." He looked directly at her, and there was something in the deep, brown eyes she had never seen before.

"I'm glad," she murmured.

"I want to say something to you and—I—don't know how."

"You—you can say anything you want to me." Her voice was almost a whisper.

"I—well, you see Jessie is wonderful, but there is one thing that doesn't work for us. I've been living like a monk for years and . . ." He paused to examine her expression, evidently safe, and then went on. "Ever since I was a student in Paris, I've loathed the idea of buying a woman, so when my wife would have none of me, I tried to forget the fascinations of your sex." From his chair he made her a funny little formal bow and then looked at her gravely. "It's no longer so easy since I've found you."

She hesitated. A false move would destroy his confidence. Her fingers closed on the arms of her chair. "I think," she said slowly and almost under her breath, "you must have guessed how I feel."

He stood up, came over, and pulled her to her feet. He put his arms around her, his mouth on hers, and kissed her gently. When she responded, he opened his eyes with a look of wild incredulity. Then his mouth, his hands, his whole body reached for her.

When they woke in her bed several hours later, his face had an air of serenity that was new to her. He took her in his arms and kissed her gratefully.

That had been the beginning. It was a relationship that would never be free of conflict; her joy in being with him was overshadowed by her loneliness when he was absent.

The day after the opera the Barstow girls arrived for luncheon. Eliza and Anna were waiting for them in the front parlor. All three Barstows were squeezed into their corsets, and each wore a slightly pinched expression. Virginia was the oldest, Beatrice the youngest, and Priscilla was Anna's age. They made their proper curtsies to Eliza, who then led them into the dining room.

Unlike Anna, the Barstow girls were not affected by the formidable array of Clark and Brewster portraits on the walls. The minute they were seated, Virginia spoke up. "I understand," she said, addressing herself to the table at large, "that *Rip Van Winkle* is a bit tedious. I mean"—she paused to giggle—"there's very little romance in it."

"You mean you're not excited about seeing Mr. Jefferson?" Anna was genuinely surprised. "Why, he's the greatest living American actor."

"Naturally I've heard of him," Virginia said quickly.

"We haven't much time to go to the theater," Priscilla said.

"Because we have one 'At Home' a week and four days calling with Mamma."

"How boring!" Anna said, without thinking. Then she turned pink and continued in a rush. "In Clarkston we all go to Aunt Emmy's most afternoons and evenings in the winter. My cousin Philip has a bowling alley with a stage at one end where we put on lots of plays and charades."

Eliza sat in silent wonder. What had happened to her shy, demure daughter?

"You mean you don't go calling in Clarkston?" Virginia said and sniffed.

"Do you mean you dress up and really act a part?" Priscilla asked.

"Certainly," Anna answered. "And every time we come to Philadelphia, we go to the theater." She looked directly at Virginia. "Don't you get tired of calling with your mother?"

"Mamma says it's very important to learn how to behave in a drawing room." Virginia refused to be bullied.

"But don't you ever do things outdoors?" Anna was bewildered. "Like sledding or skating on the river? If we lived in Philadelphia, I'd skate on the river every day it was frozen."

"Mamma says there are too many undesirable young people on the river," said Beatrice. The youngest Barstow was an anemic replica of her sisters. "And besides," she added, "we might get chilblains."

"Oh," Anna said, shrugging. "Well, in Clarkston we coast down the mountain, right past our house. Then in summer we go on picnics, do archery, and play tennis. On bad days or in the evenings we do plays and charades." She stopped and took a deep breath. "I would hate to go calling all the time and just sit with my hands in my lap."

Eliza gasped before Beatrice asked, "Do the boys act with you?"

"Of course, during the holidays—and I have lots of cousins. Only winters they're away at school. But the aunts always help us. They teach us our lines."

"Do you have an audience?" Beatrice seemed fascinated.

"Yes, all the family comes about once a month. And Aunt Emmy's maids bring lemonade and stay to see the performance."

Eliza decided she had better step in. The conversation had undertones of peril. "Perhaps Anna and I appreciate the theater more than you do," she said, "because in Clarkston it's all homemade and we get hungry to see professionals."

Lunch finished on a muted, pleasant note and afterward Anna was aware that the elegance of her Aunt Jemima's carriage was not lost on three pairs of worldly Barstow eyes. If their guests found Joseph Jefferson's performance boring, Anna and Eliza were enthralled.

The Philadelphia Assembly fell on the following evening. Eliza, at Fred's insistence, had bought a madly extravagant Worth ball gown of powder blue velvet. She looked at herself critically in the mirror. I'm not much of a beauty, she thought, with that slightly drooping lid over my blind eye, but I have more style than the other Clark wives. She allowed herself a moment of satisfaction as she studied her erect carriage and the way her long neck and bare white shoulders emerged from the blue velvet bodice. She picked up her train, walked to the door, turned, came back to the mirror, and curtsied. Satisfied, she gathered up her long white kid gloves, a dark blue velvet cape and her evening bag.

It was snowing lightly when Eliza and Fred arrived at the Academy of Music. The stairways on either side of the big foyer on Broad Street were shrouded in potted palms and giant poinsettia plants. In the foyer Fred looked at his wife. "You're beautiful tonight, Hodie." He smiled possessively.

"And you're the handsomest man in town," she answered. "You look ten years younger than when you trudge back and forth from the office in Clarkston."

"Never mind. I don't like it any better than you do. Let's forget it for one glorious night."

Eliza swept ahead of Fred into the ballroom. The patronesses, with their fixed smiles and tightly laced figures, were carefully arranged in a semicircle. Eliza's five curtsies, one for each patroness, came off smoothly. Fred finished his bows, opened his arms, and waltzed her the length of the room. Eliza's card was full; she danced the polka and the waltz with equal ease. Supper was served in the lobby at twelve. The musicians returned at one, and at three the guests finally disbanded to the strains of "Good Night, Ladies."

The snow had stopped and the night was clear and still. Eliza and Fred walked the two blocks to 1512 Spruce, basking in the afterglow of a beautiful party.

"You were made for Assemblies, Hodie." Fred pressed her arm as he said it. "I'm sorry, my darling, that Clarkston isn't—well, I know how you feel."

They reached the house and as they came into the vestibule, Eliza said, "Can we sit in the drawing room for a moment? I'm tired but wide awake, and I want to talk to you."

"Only if I can take these things off." Fred shook off his dancing pumps and turned up the gas chandelier.

Eliza settled down on the sofa. "It's about Danny. I don't know why, but somehow an evening like this makes his illness seem particularly bitter. Oh, I don't mean that I mind terribly that he can't go to dances. It's—the fact that he can't have any kind of normal life. I may as well be blunt, Fred. No girl will ever look at him."

His reply was swift and hard. "There are some things we don't discuss, Eliza." He stood up.

Eliza reached for him. "Fred, oh, darling, don't shut me out like that. Please."

Fred's face was a mask. "Eliza, it's pointless for you to concern yourself with things you don't know anything about. Danny will work out his own salvation."

Obviously, he would not face the fact that Danny was hunch-backed and crippled and that women would probably be forever out of his reach. Danny was twenty and showed every sign of being attracted to girls.

"I suppose you're right, Fred," she said wearily. There was nothing more to say. She stood up. "And now I'm very, very tired."

The lovely party mood was broken. In two days they would be back in Clarkston.

CHAPTER 5

Clarkston
November 19, 1887

Snow had been falling all day and by afternoon two and one-half inches had accumulated, a sleigh rider's dream. When he came out into the open from the breaker, Tommy Malloy shouted with pleasure. At fourteen, Tommy was small, thin, and wiry. He was made, his mother often thought, of skin, bones, and energy. On his way home he hopped, skipped, jumped, turned a somersault now and then, and ultimately arrived, grinning, his white teeth brilliant in a face covered with coal dust.

Katie, watching at the window, came to the door to greet him. She started to laugh as she saw his face, streaked with black and white where the snow had erased some of the day's accumulated coal dust.

"It snowed, it snowed, it snowed," Tommy yelled, gathering up a handful and flinging it in the air.

"I can see that," said Katie. "And you should see your face. You look like a patchwork quilt."

You go get washed up and hurry up about it. I'll want you to fetch some carrots and turnips from the shed after. Moira picked four buckets of coal from the slag for me this morning and she's resting now."

"Stew again?"

"Now, never mind. It's the last time. Tomorrow we'll have salt pork and cabbage." It was the fourth night for the stew and by now the meat in it was scarcely discernible.

Tommy skipped off in the direction of the pump. Katie

watched him, a shadow of anxiety clouding her face. Even if she wanted to, it would be impossible to dampen Tommy's spirits, but she wished she could instill in him a normal respect for danger; each day he left for the mines she prayed he would come home whole.

Tommy was the brightest, the most lovable of her children. If only she could get him out of the mines and back to school. Jessie was her only hope, but Katie shrank from approaching her, even though she realized it would make Jessie happy.

Jessie had already done too much. A week ago Katie had returned home from the White Haven Sanatorium. It was her second trip in two years. The first time the doctors reluctantly allowed her to go home after six months. They told her her tuberculosis could be kept under control provided she had sufficient rest and sunshine and that she "fattened up." By late summer Katie suffered a relapse and was returned to White Haven for sixteen weeks. She had learned her lesson and this time she was taking care of herself.

Stephen came in carrying two pails of water. He put them down and gave Katie a wan smile. She knew instantly something was wrong and was tempted to ask him then but decided to wait.

Tommy followed his father into the kitchen. Distractedly, Katie noticed that he was emptyhanded. "Tommy, the turnips and the carrots . . ."

"I forgot—in a minute."

Now, son, do as your mother asks, or there'll be no supper."

"Yessir," said Tommy cheerfully and made a running broad jump toward the door.

After supper, Katie waited until she was sure Tommy was out of earshot. "Stephen, what is it? What's the matter?"

Stephen touched her hand. "I hate like anything to worry you so soon after coming back from the hospital, Katie."

"Stephen, if there's to be trouble, it's a good thing I am back," she said practically. She got up and methodically began to cut into quarters the loaf of bread she had made that morning for Stephen's and Tommy's lunchpails. Their fare rarely varied: bread, Cheddar cheese, and black coffee.

"I think the men are going to strike," Stephen said. "At both Hanley and Clarkston. They're already agitating at Oneida and it'll spread to us here soon, sure as we're sitting here."

"Striking's no good, Stephen, and you know it. What is it this time? Or is it John making trouble again?"

"Katie, Katie, it isn't just John, though I know you'd like to think so. I—"

"I know very well how he feels about the Clarks and I know he's a troublemaker."

"And so do I feel the same way about the Clarks," Stephen said with heat. Then he added, "Somewhat, that is. Look, Katie." He pulled at a strip of frayed oilcloth. "I know how much Mrs. Clark means to you. But damn it, all she does is keep us tied to them by her charity, with the old man never paying me enough to care for my own family."

Katie wrapped the bread and cheese in a clean, damp cloth. "You can't deny they've been good to us, Stephen."

"No matter how I figure it, I can't make my pay come to more than $49.81 a month. When we're working well and I have a good laborer, we come out at $4.35 the day between us. Out of the $4.35 I have to give him $1.80. That leaves me $2.55, and out of that I have to buy powder, oil, and I just had to buy a new blasting barrel and squib."

"Maybe you buy too much, Stephen." But Katie knew in her heart her husband would never make enough for more than a bare living for the children and herself.

"I can't save on those things—so the most it ever comes to is $49.81." Stephen was silent thinking about his conversation with John Murray.

"You're a damned fool," John had said to him when Stephen asked him what would be the good of a strike. "You're making a lousy two dollars a day, and that's only if you don't get docked or laid off—or get killed, like you nearly did."

"It was my own fault," Stephen said. "I was hurrying it up so I put too much powder in one blast, and anyway the Clarks paid me all the time I was laid up."

"Now isn't that noble of the holy Clarks! They make you pay for your own powder, they pay you a lousy rate for the coal you bring out, so you naturally try to economize and you nearly lose your life, and, by God, the Clarks come all over grand and pay for your sojourn in the hospital." He spat viciously into the blackened earth where they stood. "An' on top of it all, you've a sick wife who's that way from working too hard trying to keep a starving family together, and your oldest son—me own godson—is a breaker boy, breathing coal dust every day, sure to die of black lung at an early age because the lousy forty cents a day he earns helps keep the rest of you from starving altogether." He looked at Stephen with contempt. "Will you never learn that unless you stand up fer your rights, it's never going to get better? And more than that, Stephen, any man who stands against us is going to get hurt." He started to walk away, stopped, and called back over his shoulder, "Even yerself—even though you be my friend."

Although John was Stephen's best friend, Stephen stood in his shadow. The Murrays had emigrated to America in 1856, eleven years before Stephen. John had not quite been ten then and his father, who had worked in a slaughterhouse in Cork, was lucky enough to find employment in New York City as a butcher. John was one of those who had been swept up in the bloody draft riot, the summer of 1863, a riot caused as much by tenement living conditions as by the draft. John, then seventeen, had been influenced by his uncle, a laborer in a New York iron foundry. The uncle with five hundred fellow workers marched on the draft offices at Third Avenue and Forty-sixth Street. They attacked the building with everything they could pick up and throw; they destroyed all papers, records, and books they could put their hands on. It was John's first taste of blood; for the rest of his life he remained an agitator, a passionate hater of privilege. Stephen feared and respected his superior knowledge of his adopted country.

The figure $49.81 was acting as a battering ram in Katie's head. It seemed increasingly impossible to get along without Tommy's forty cents a day. Perhaps she could get around asking Jessie directly for help by offering to do some sewing for her.

"I suppose," she said finally to Stephen, "we could move into a double house. It would mean a reduction in rent from $5.50 to $4.50 a month."

Stephen shook his head. "It wouldn't be worth it, Kate. I save that much out of the garden alone and a double house wouldn't give us the space of a big one—like we have now."

This was true but there were times when she felt working the garden at the end of a day in the mine extracted a murderous toll from him. But if they faced a strike of any duration, the garden and the cow would be crucial to survival. "Whatever we do, Stephen, please promise you won't get involved in a strike," Katie said. "John's no good for you, Stephen, he's a hothead and full of ideas about his rights and what's owed him. If he was married, he wouldn't dare cause so much trouble. He's probably even saved money what with paying only a dollar a month for that shack he lives in and no children to feed. What else has he been telling you?"

Stephen hesitated. He had better not tell her about John's threat; it would only make her angrier. "He—he says Father Kelly is as bad as the Clarks," Stephen said. "He says the priest works hand in hand with the owners to keep us down. And he says some of the men sent a message to old man Clark ten days ago demanding either higher wages or arbitration, and there's not been a word out of him since."

"That's a lie about Father Kelly, I'm sure of it," Katie said furiously. "It's just like something John Murray would make up. I—I'm beginning to hate him, Stephen. He'll get all of you all riled up, there'll be a strike, everybody will suffer, and in the end nothing will be any better. I wish you wouldn't—oh, what's the use?"

Stephen nodded uncertainly. He was terrified that a strike would come—and soon. If it did, he would have no choice. None of them ever did, even though they knew their wives and children might go hungry. Lucky man, John Murray. He had neither.

With the deliberation that accompanies a familiar ritual Frederick Clark took his silver cigar cutter from his pocket, snipped off the rounded end neatly, and placed the cigar in his mouth. His lips protruded slightly as he savored the combined taste and smell of the Corona Corona. He struck a match, partially closing his eyes as he drew in his first puff. Dexter watched him with mingled envy and disapproval. Jessie had indoctrinated him with the idea that both alcohol and tobacco were injurious if not sinful, and he only thought about smoking when he was with Fred and about drinking wine when he was with Gertrude. He pushed both thoughts away and said. "I found a copy of the *Freiburg Jahrbuch* two weeks ago with an article on a new jig that made me furious at my stupidity."

"Why?"

"You know how long I've been trying to develop a jig. And how much money we've spent. Over ten thousand dollars and in the end we still have to depend on the breaker boys to separate the slag from the coal by hand. This article describes a coal breaker operating in Saxony very much like ours except for the jig. Theirs is much simpler, it's bound to save coal, and as far as I can see, there are hardly any parts to get out of order."

His chair made a scraping noise as he turned it slightly to look out the murky window at his machine shop opposite. Impatiently, he swung his head and his attention back to Fred, seated facing him. Both men's offices gave Jessie the shudders. Cramped, with maps of the region, schedules and rates, time sheets, and calendars plastered haphazardly over the grimy walls, they suggested the brothers' myriad preoccupations. Each office was furnished with a huge desk, two chairs, and an uncomfortable bench. In addition to the clutter on the walls, three wooden pegs placed next to each door were draped in winter with overcoats, on one of which perched Fred's derby. Behind each desk was one small window offering a view of the colliery.

Fred guessed his brother was feeling guilty about money and time wasted and was also piqued to discover that a German invention had surpassed his own. He smiled encouragingly at him. "How much would the German jig cost?"

"Probably half of what it cost to build the cheapest jig we're using now. And I'm sure it will work."

"Fine," Fred said lightly. "But stop blaming yourself. We won't go broke for ten thousand dollars."

"I suppose not. But the months I wasted make me furious. My education is as good as any German engineer I know, and God knows I've got the best technical library in the world."

Fred ground his cigar into an ashtray and immediately picked up and lit another. Dexter was an exceedingly complicated man—driven, arrogant, often opinionated, and overwhelmingly ambitious when it came to technical problems.

"I'm certain you'll master the jig—especially if it saves coal, even though we've got enough here to last for generations."

"You sound like the South Americans who kill their cattle, take the hides, and leave the meat to rot on the ground. They figure it's easier to make money that way and that the cattle will last forever."

"They probably will, Dex," Fred said easily.

"I hate waste—it's wicked. Waste of animals, of coal, of money, of manpower, of talent—it's downright evil."

"Don't take it so hard, Dex. I don't, but then I'm not built like you."

"Be grateful, Fred, I know that I've got a mind that often produces a piece of useful machinery, along with a disposition that gives me a lot of trouble. You never have periods of black despair or whole nights when you can't sleep, do you?"

Fred inhaled his cigar and let the smoke out slowly. The unpredictability of Dexter's moods could be frightening, and burdensome, Fred thought gloomily. "No, Dex," he said aloud, "but I guess it's the price you pay for being brilliant. Now look, will you put that ingenious mind of yours on a problem I've been wrestling with?"

"The railroads?"

"Of course. They've just raised the rate ten cents a ton from Sheppton, Oneida, Hanley, and Stockton to Tidewater—in fact, from all the collieries. They're telling me the same old story. The idle cars lying at the collieries for a day or two cost them so much that—and I can repeat exactly what they said—'We're forced to do this, Mr. Clark, as much as we dislike it.' Damn them. They're trying to squeeze us out of business."

"Well, they won't." Dexter sounded irritable.

"Even so, and even if they change the way they fix their rates, I'm positive that we can't ever feel secure until we have our own railroad. As long as we have to depend on companies who own their mines as well as their railroads, we'll be at their mercy. Of course, they're going to charge us through the nose when they can get away with it and on top of that haul their own coal for practically nothing."

"I don't disagree. The expense—have the surveyors given you a better estimate of how many miles of track we need?"

"Yes. About sixty to hook up each of our collieries to one of the three big roads—the Reading, the Jersey Central, or the Lehigh Valley."

"And that means—in rough figures—somewhere between four and five million."

"I know, that's staggering, Dex, but I think we can do it. You and I are limited in the amount we can contribute because we've got so much tied up already, but if the rest of the family helps, I think we can get the New York banks to go along."

"New York? Are you planning to get much there?"

"Some. But I'll spread my favors around. A few old friends in the Troop are pretty comfortable now."

Fred glanced at Dexter. He knew it made his brother faintly uncomfortable whenever he referred to the Philadelphia City Troop, and he knew Dexter would never understand his pride in it. They were brothers, but socially they were poles apart.

"Danny's already finished the drawings for a heavy-duty engine that should haul at least twenty full cars," Fred said, veering away from the subject.

"I know," Dexter said, "and that's quite an achievement." Dexter was filled with admiration for Danny. Without any formal education he was a competent engineer. "Furthermore, we ought to be able to build most of the equipment in our own shops. That'll save us money, and it's the one place where I have very little trouble with the men, thank God. Largely due to Danny, I think."

It was true that Danny had a magic touch with the men. Fred wondered briefly if he was pushing the railroad as much for Danny's sake as for the company's. As soon as Danny had been told that the railroad might become a reality, his attitude had visibly changed. He had begun making a desperate effort to build himself up physically and had, in part, succeeded. He had recently insisted on coming to the table for lunch and dinner and forced himself to eat, if not with relish, with determination. He had started daily exercises prescribed by the doctor for his legs.

"Danny told me he wants to call it the Delaware, Susquehanna, and Schuylkill."

"I like that," Dexter answered. "These rivers have cradled our coal properties for centuries. It'll be called the D. S. and S. for short, and I like the sound of that, too."

Fred had allowed the ash on his second cigar to grow two inches long in the conviction that the longer you kept it, the cooler the smoke. With a flick of the wrist grown skillful through practice, he dropped the ash into the glass tray on his desk and leaned back satisfied. "That's settled, then," he said. "Now that we've solved all our problems, let's go outside and take a look at my new wagon. For a hundred and ten dollars, it should have a pretty fair motion."

Both men stood up and began putting on their coats. There was a knock at the door, and Dexter's secretary, Emerson Untermeyer, burst in, looking visibly disturbed.

"Word has just come from the Oneida colliery," Untermeyer said. "The miners are threatening not to come back tomorrow. They're demanding a pay raise of fifty cents a day. They asked for that or arbitration ten days ago and"—Untermeyer hesitated— "they say they have a right to a reply, that they're not going to wait any longer."

Dexter flung out an arm. "Calm down, Emerson. We're not going to be intimidated by a bunch of troublemakers in Oneida. I know they've stirred up the men in Clarkston and Hanley, but they'll quiet down when they learn they can't have what they want."

Fred knew what was in his brother's mind. "Dex, Schlenker told me the men in Clarkston and Hanley have sworn to follow whatever the men in Oneida do. Are you completely sure you want to tell them we won't arbitrate?"

"*I am not going to tell them we won't.*" Dexter pronounced each word with care. "I shall simply not have any direct communication with them." He buttoned his overcoat and to Fred's surprise, he spoke softly. "You know, Fred, I've always said that the operators and the men are like a man and his wife. They may quarrel and fuss, but they have to live together. Besides," he added, and Fred nearly laughed out loud at the tone of sweet reason that had now crept into his voice, "we can't pay the men any more without having to borrow to keep the mines going, so I'm not going to pay them any more." With that he headed for the door.

Fred shrugged and followed Dexter out, nodding good-bye to Untermeyer, who was still standing by the desk with his mouth open.

"Fred, wake up." Eliza shook her husband. Fred opened his eyes to see the ceiling of their bedroom pink with reflected light. In a single motion he sat up, was out of the bed and at the window.

"Oh, my God, Hodie, it's Number Two breaker. Quick, my trousers, shoes, coat."

Frantically, Eliza scrambled out of bed, found his trousers and tossed them to him. She didn't bother lighting the gas wall bracket; their bedroom was rapidly becoming as bright as day. Fred pulled his pants on over his nightshirt. Eliza threw him his shoes and ran after him down the stairs, helped him into a top-coat from the hall closet. He ran out the front door leaving it open and Eliza standing there, staring out at the crimson sky.

Fred had gone almost a hundred yards in the direction of the colliery when he nearly collided with Dexter.

"I'll go to the breaker, Fred," Dexter shouted. "I want to get the pumps going. See if you can get help from Freetown. Get them to drive both engines down."

Danny reached for the crutches that stood beside his bed and swung his feet onto the floor. He placed the crutches in position, hobbled to the window, and looked out. The sight made him damn the fact that he was unable to go farther. His old nurse, Maria, appeared in the doorway.

"Don't you dare try to get dressed, Danny. You know you can't go out."

"For God's sake, Maria, stop fussing." With a curse he leaned against the window frame, watching the changing sky. He listened intently. His parents' room was down the hall, three doors away from his. He heard a thud, the sound of a shoe dropping, and pictured his father struggling into his clothes.

As Eliza helped Fred dress, a corner of her mind worried about Danny. She saw Fred out the door, watched anxiously as he ran down the driveway toward the billowing flames, then turned back into the house, closing the front door behind her. She went up the stairs and straight to Danny's room.

"Breaker Number Two," Danny said, as she came in.

"I'll go down and make you both some coffee," Maria said and left.

Eliza hurried to the window. "Oh, where are those fire engines?"

"They'll damned well never get to the colliery in time to save the breaker," Danny said. "It takes fifteen minutes for someone to get to Freetown to alert them. I haven't even heard the colliery whistle yet, have you?"

"No. But your father's on his way. "They'll send a runner immediately if they haven't already."

"Even so. Fifteen minutes for a runner. It's all uphill. Ten minutes to harness the horses. Half an hour to get the steam in the engine going. If they know what they're doing, they'll start the boiler immediately. Eight minutes to get here. It's more than forty minutes or the best part of an hour, no matter how fast they go." He paused to search the skyline. "I'm not sure they'll be able to contain the fire."

"They have to," Eliza said grimly. "Oh, Danny, this will break Dexter's heart."

"No doubt. All that Georgia pine."

Eliza frowned. "You don't sound exactly sympathetic."

"I am and I'm not. It's no secret that Uncle Dexter makes the men see red. There are damned few who don't hate him. I don't blame them most of the time. My God—he's stubborn—and autocratic."

"I suppose he is, Danny, but in his own way he does his best for the men."

"That's right. His own way. Giving the poor the privilege of education, as Aunt Jessie says. And let's not forget 'we run the best company store in the area.' But the men still refer to it as a 'Pluck Me'. In the men's eyes, it's still a place where they get cheated. Besides, the Clarks run it. That's the trouble, the Clarks run everything. And in spite of all their overwhelming generosity, some of those men we do so much for don't have enough to eat."

Eliza was frightened by his anger. She had no answer to what he said and very little knowledge of the miners. Most of the time she avoided thinking about Clarkston and its inhabitants altogether. Obviously Danny knew more about the town and the miners and the people who worked there than all the other Clarks put together. Equally obviously Jessie's frantic efforts to do good hadn't really had as much effect as she had thought. There was some satisfaction in knowing that; Jessie always made her feel guilty.

"Then, all those things that Jessie does—I mean the sewing classes, the hospital, and everything else doesn't count for much?"

"No," Danny shifted his balance and turned to look directly at his mother. She had a lovely figure, he thought irrelevantly, and even in her warm velour wrapper, with her hair twisted in a simple coil on the top of her head, she was very pretty. No wonder Pappa was so crazy about her. He smiled at the difference between her and Jessie. He took a deep breath. "On the contrary. What my aunt does goes a long way toward helping. A lot of the men realize that she was responsible for starting the hospital, and a lot of them know that she cares. She's not called the Angel of the Anthracite for nothing, you know."

"But—" Eliza found herself suddenly irritated. Whatever Jessie's kindness to the miners and their families, her holier-than-thou attitude was exasperating. And now here was Danny singing her praises.

"I'm sorry," Danny said. "I suppose I shouldn't have said anything to you. But I don't like violence and"—he waved toward the window—"I'm pretty sure this fire was set and a man has to be damned angry to do a thing like that. But then have you ever wondered what it's like to work on an empty stomach? Look, maybe it isn't Uncle Dexter's fault. But the fact is, he treats the men like animals who can't think for themselves. He's still living by the standards Grandfather set. But eventually the operators are going to be forced to listen. Good God, have you ever had a look at our books? We make one hell of a lot of money, and those men who are responsible for making it for us get a pittance. If I said anything like that to Uncle Dexter, or to my father for that matter, they'd call me a bloody Socialist. I'm not. But the point is really that it would be a lot better if the owners gave in a little before they're forced to at gunpoint and before there are a lot more fires like this one."

The colliery whistle was shrieking. Four long blasts and two short. The whole area around the breaker was a sea of red, a greedy inferno that threatened to devour everything in its path.

Even after the whistle was quiet, the voices of the men calling directions were punctuated by the crackling explosions of the fire and by the clatter of the locis and coal cars being moved to the farthest corners of the colliery. Mother and son peered silently out the window, watching the geyser of flames and swarming black clouds of smoke cover the horizon. Then, in the distance, they heard the bells of the fire engine and within less than a minute, the sound of horses' hooves pounding down the mountain road. The

Freetown fire engine and tender were racing toward the breaker, a yapping coach dog running alongside.

Danny let out a cheer and was quiet. "I'd give a lot to be there," he said. "Damn it, why can't I be like other fellows? Is it some kind of curse on the Clarks that makes me such a mess?"

"I only wish we knew, Dan." Eliza hoped he couldn't see her cheeks quiver. "Someday we'll find out and you'll be cured. As it is, you're getting stronger all the time."

Danny turned away and Eliza suppressed a desire to put her arms around him.

Tommy and his father, wakened by the alarm, arrived at the colliery simultaneously with the engines. They stood to one side as the engines stopped dead in front of the gates. Over by the breaker tongues of flame were shooting several hundred feet into the sky.

"My God!" Stephen was out of breath. They had run up Main Street to the colliery as fast as they could. "What a terrible sight!"

John Murray came up behind them. "Quite a sight, eh, Steve?" He put an arm around Tommy. "You be careful now, Tom. That's a helluva fire, that is, and there's no use in the least anyone trying to put it out. They'll only get hurt for their pains."

"Stay clear away of it, Tom," Murray continued, reading Tommy's thoughts. "This is no place for boys like yerself."

Tommy waited until Murray's attention was distracted and then quietly insinuated himself into the crowd of men pushing through the gates. Minutes later, when his father turned to speak to him, he had disappeared.

Tommy worked his way over to where Heinrich Schlenker stood. Although the burning breaker was five hundred yards away, the heat was already unbearable. The Freetown fire engine looked like a toy pitting itself against a giant prehistoric creature bent on annihilating everything around it. As Tommy stood there, the walls of the breaker collapsed, setting off a series of explosions and sending sparks and debris flying for hundreds of yards in all directions. Flames swirled wildly around the structure from top to bottom and then from bottom to top. There seemed to be no orderly pattern to the fire's progress, to the inexorable, voracious flames consuming everything in their path.

Schlenker was barking orders to the men through a megaphone. He had given up trying to save the breaker. He instructed the arriving firemen to let it burn and go immediately to the shops; they might have a chance to keep the fire from spreading. He told them to concentrate their hoses on the roofs and walls of the buildings there. As soon as Tommy heard this, he started back to the gates. His godfather and Schlenker were right. There was nothing to be done near the breaker. The sight of the flames, the falling debris, and the intense heat were terrifying.

The fire engine and tender had turned around outside the gates. Ned Barker, the fire chief, realized when they came within sight of the colliery that neither his horses nor his men could get near the breaker. Trained not to fight the impossible, he agreed with Schlenker's instructions and started up the hill to the shops.

Tommy ran out of the gates and turned to the right up the hill, following the engine and tender. The horses, still steaming from their gallop from Freetown, snorted loudly as they were reined in opposite the machine shops. Both drivers jumped down, unbuckled the harness from their horses, and led them to an open field well out of range of the fire. As soon as they tethered the animals, they ran back to the shops to help the other firemen unreel the hose and hook the ladders together. The wind was carrying huge sparks across the colliery. They were falling at random on the boiler house, the shops, and on Dexter's library, the only fireproof building in the lot. The shops and boiler house comprised one building, twice as deep as it was long. The passage between it and the library was a narrow alley, no more than two feet wide, making access to the back of the structure extremely difficult. Ladders were placed against the front of the building. In a few minutes men were on the roof, playing their hoses and smothering the fires immediately in front of them.

One of the men called down to the chief, "We can't reach the back. We don't dare pull up any more hose without rollers. The edge of the roof will cut it."

Barker shouted in answer, "Try lifting the hose higher."

The men yanked it toward them, pointing it up to give it more play. It didn't work. They called down again, "Can you give us more pressure?"

"No," Barker yelled, "we're up to the limit. Hold on a minute and keep trying." He turned to his assistant, and together they started walking over to the alley, Tommy trailing them.

As they squeezed themselves into the passage, the assistant looked up and said. "They're still not reaching. We've got to get a ladder and man in here."

"A man—you mean a midget. Goddamn it," Barker stamped his foot. "There's barely room to stand the ladder, much less a man with a hose."

"Do you want to bring the other hose around to the back?"

"We'll have to, but that'll mean cutting down on the pressure on the front of the buildings. Even so we'd better do it. Damn it, I've told them often enough we need two engines."

Tommy plucked at the fire chief's sleeve. "Maybe I could get up, sir?"

Both men looked down at Tommy without saying anything. Finally the assistant said, "You Stephen Malloy's boy?"

Tommy nodded. He was holding his breath.

The chief said, "We can't take the risk. He's too small."

"He's not big, but he's a breaker boy, Ned, and a strong one." The assistant patted Tommy's shoulder. "How old are you, son?"

"Fourteen."

"And you're used to climbing, aren't you?"

"Yes."

Barker looked up at the sky. "Not too much danger from sparks back here if he keeps close to the edge. All right. Let's try it and pray he doesn't get hurt. What's your name, son?"

"Thomas Malloy."

Together they walked to the front of the building. The chief started bellowing orders. Two men put another ladder together while a third dragged a hose to the space between the buildings. Barker and Tommy followed them back to the narrow alley. The chief took off his hat, and, padding it on the inside with his handkerchief, put it on Tommy's head and pulled it down over his ears.

"It fits fine," Tommy said.

"Turn it around if you need to protect your face," Barker said.

The ladder was set in place, positioned about two-thirds down the length of the alley. Barker placed Tommy on the bottom rung and put the hose in his hand. "Now be very careful, son. Mother of Christ, I'll never forgive myself if anything happens to you." He started shouting. "You men back there, give this hose all the support you can. Don't for the love of God make it heavy on the lad."

Tommy, his right hand gripping the hose and his right elbow holding it against his ribs, started climbing. Rung after rung. At first, due to the support from the men below, the hose weighed practically nothing, but as he kept going up, it grew heavier and heavier. Three-quarters of the way to the top, he stopped to get his breath. After a moment, with a superhuman effort, he tugged at the hose, crawled up the remaining rungs and, reaching the roof, fell forward onto it. Once there, he scrambled to his knees and sat down panting. His legs and arms were trembling.

The fire chief called up, "Are you all right, lad?"

"Y-yes," Tommy's answer floated down. It could barely be heard by the men below.

"Are you sure?" Barker shouted back.

"Yes." This time the answer was strong.

"All right, then. Hold on tight. We'll give you some water."

Tommy grasped the hose with both hands just in back of the nozzle, felt it stiffen and begin writhing. It took all the strength he possessed to subdue it. After a minute he had it under control and was able to direct it to the part of the roof where the men in front could not reach. By bracing his back against a metal smokestack he was able to play the hose back and forth and send streams of water over most of the unprotected areas. When he first came onto the roof, the sparks had been landing fifteen feet away and he was able to keep them under control, but after ten minutes there was a subtle change in the wind and they came ominously close to him.

On the ground the fire chief held up a finger. "Holy Mother of God, the wind's changing. We've got to get that boy out of there. Tommy—Tommy, boy," he started yelling. "Stop. Stop. Drop the hose. Get down as quick as you can."

As the chief spoke, a burning strip of wood landed a foot away from Tommy. Accustomed now to the feel of the hose but weary and less careful about his movements, Tommy got up from his knees, stretched his aching muscles, and swung the hose toward the burning strip. The water splashed back underneath his feet; he lost his balance, his hat flew off, and he slipped on the wet surface. Desperately, Tommy hung onto the hose; too late he realized it would not save him. He threw it to one side, flung himself flat, both hands clawing frantically for something to cling to. Unfortunately the discarded hose, driven by the force of the water surging through it, began to behave like an animate creature. Viciously, it switched itself around, spewing its water directly at Tommy. He began to slide down, head first over the edge. Reaching frantically for a hold where there was none, he felt himself diving down with nothing beneath him, and instinctively he put out his arms to break his fall.

In the dream Tommy had been falling, down, down, down into a pool, a bottomless cavern that seemed to be filled with a kind of water, a strange mixture of air and foam. It was comfortable enough until one terrible moment when he was suffocating, being held down, unable to move or draw breath. Then he heard voices felt the cool pressure of a hand on his brow and opening his eyes, began dimly to perceive the neatly clipped Van Dyke beard of Dr. Grunig. The beard floated in the air for a moment, a disembodied thing, and Tommy closed his eyes again as he became conscious of his hands, his wrists, instruments of torture. He wanted to scream.

"Ja. Now he begins to come out of it." Dr. Grunig, the town doctor, spoke. He, Stephen and John Murray were in Dexter Clark's library with Tommy. "You will be all right, Tommy," the doctor said gently.

Stephen and Murray jumped. It was the first time they had ever heard concern creep into the doctor's voice. He dispensed advice and pills in exactly the manner of a German general issuing military orders.

"Two wrists broken," the doctor said, straightening up. "That is all. It is a miracle."

Daybreak had just begun. Tommy's father and John Murray were hovering opposite the doctor beside the couch where Tommy lay.

Murray was the first to speak. "Are you in pain, lad?"

The pain continued to ebb and flow. Tommy tried to answer but could only rub his head back and forth on the pillow.

"He will be like this," the doctor said to Stephen, "for some hours. I don't want to give him more morphine, so stay with him here. Mr. Clark said to use the library."

The doctor nodded curtly at Murray and picked up his bag.

"I'm sorry," Murray said, tightly.

Stephen turned away to avoid Murray's eyes.

"Look," Murray began, stopped, and took a step toward Stephen. He started again, "Stephen, listen to me. You can't think I meant to burn the breaker."

Stephen spun around. Katie's warning had come back to him full force. "What else did you mean? You said you'd get the Clarks no matter what it cost."

"Oh, for God's sake!"

Stephen looked at him and then down at the boy on the couch.

"Damn it, Stephen, you don't think I'm stupid enough to cut my own throat, do you?"

Stephen shrugged.

"Think about it, you dumb clod," Murray said angrily. "With that breaker gone it means over six hundred men are automatically out of work. Damn it to hell. How can I call a strike now with that many out already?"

Stephen's concern for his son had wiped out his fear of Murray. "Then explain to me exactly why that breaker went up. I heard the police tell Mr. Clark it couldn't have been an accident. What does that mean, Murray? You should know—you're our leader."

"Stephen, if I tell you, you've got to swear you won't tell a soul. Not even Katie."

Stephen nodded and kept his eyes on Murray.

"It was—well, it was supposed to be just a little scare for the Clarks to ponder on. You know the shed the breaker foreman uses? That was all that was supposed to go. But someone—and if I ever find out who it was, believe me, he'll pay for it—got carried away He set a fire in the breaker instead of the shed, and it wasn't discovered until it got beyond control. Then the wind came up and it was too late."

"And now," Stephen said slowly, "there'll be no strike, just men out of work—and no chance of getting better pay."

"Don't say that, Stephen," Murray said sharply. "The Clarks have lost a lot—it isn't what was meant to happen, but by God, it's a beginning. They'll have to know we mean business."

"I'm not sure," said Stephen, "that we're going about telling them the right way."

At dawn the breaker, built with such care and considered the finest in the region, was gone, completely destroyed. The brothers stood at the edge of the colliery watching the firemen trying to contain the fringes of the dying fire with axes and hoses.

"It's about a hundred-and-fifty-thousand-dollar loss, Dex," Fred said. "And the insurance company won't take care of the extra loss in production."

Dexter shook his head. "We were getting a thousand tons a day out of it with six hundred and fifty men employed. That ought to put quite a crimp in any strike they're planning. Pity those fools didn't think about the six hundred and fifty men they were putting out of work without going through the motions of a strike. Do you know what they've done? Handed me a ready-made scab force. Damn them to hell."

Fred had never seen his brother so enraged. He himself could hardly contain his anger; anyone who had watched the night's terrifying inferno had to be consumed with fury. He put a hand tentatively on Dexter's arm and wished he could find something to say.

Dexter shook himself free. "They'll never tell me I can't employ men who want to work no matter what names they are called."

Fred tried again. "At least they kept the fire from spreading to the boilers and the shops. I haven't had a chance to ask you— what do the police say?"

"I can't get any clue about who is guilty," Dexter answered. "While you were talking to the firemen from Freetown, I put the two night watchmen and six Coal and Iron Police through a third degree. They swear there was no sign of fire anywhere around the breaker when they made their rounds." He kicked at a stone on the ground. "I don't believe it. Lot of good it's done us hiring the extra police and Pinkerton men."

"There can't be much doubt now," Fred said. "With the Buck Mountain breaker burnt down just two days ago, also for no visible reason. This kind of destruction is frightening."

"They won't frighten me," Dexter started walking away.

Fred followed him helplessly. His brother, always stubborn, was now completely beyond reason. "Dex, they're not showing any sign of backing down."

"They will." Dexter tried to steady his voice. "Even if they do call the strike, they'll come back crawling. What's more, I'll build a new breaker that no fire can destroy. I'll build it of iron."

Fred stepped over a loci track twisted and tangled by the heat. "No reason you can't, I guess. In fact that's probably a very good idea. I'm sure it—"

Dexter didn't let him finish. "You're damned right it is. I'll do everything I can to make those sons of bitches straighten out. When I think of all we've done for them over the years and all we've gone through—" He stopped speaking and turned to stare for a long moment at the smoldering ruins of Clarkston Number 2.

Fred walked doggedly toward the colliery gate, his head down, his heart leaden. "What's the use?" he groaned under his breath. "This goddamned place, the goddamned miners, all Dexter's work for nothing and months of uphill struggle before we can get back to normal. Eliza's right. This is a hell of a life."

CHAPTER 6

Clarkston and Philadelphia
September 1890

IT HAD BEEN THREE MONTHS, one week and two days since that afternoon in June. It was useless for Barbara to deny the fact that she was pregnant.

There was no one to go to. She didn't know any midwives or even where to find one in Clarkston, and if she went to stern Dr. Grunig, he would only tell her family, and in any case he had about as much compassion as a counting machine. Her father would be worse. Griswold, even if she could get to him, would be both helpless and hopeless. Her sisters would be furious with her for disgracing them. That left her mother, whose rage would be monumental, but there was a chance that she also might be practical enough to think of a way out. The rehearsal of her limited choices was like a litany; it was the thousandth time she had gone over them. She had come to the end of the line. She would have to make herself tell her mother today, after breakfast.

She was supposed to teach a sewing class this morning, but she wasn't going to take a chance of running into her sister on her return. After breakfast she waited upstairs until she heard her father go to his office at Clark Brothers and she knew her sister Lucy had already left for the Miners' Hospital. Everyone was out of the way. Barbara, shoulders back, went downstairs and into the living room, where Mrs. Shipley was busy crocheting an antimacassar.

As she came into the room, her mother said, "Barbara? What are you doing here? Aren't you going to be late?"

"I'm not going, Mamma. I have something to tell you."

"But why aren't you—what do you want to tell me?"

"I think I'm going to have a baby."

Mrs. Shipley remained perfectly still, her crocheting in place on her lap, her right hand holding the crochet hook poised in midair, her mouth open.

Barbara, watching her closely, couldn't tell if she was unable to grasp what she had just been told or was taking it for granted. Her mother had never had much faith in her. Often enough Mrs. Shipley had prophesied that of all her daughters, Barbara was the one who would come to a bad end.

"By whom?" Mrs. Shipley might have been inquiring about the weather.

"I—I," Barbara stammered.

"Tell me who it is." The tone was stretched with patience.

"Griswold Frazier," Barbara said coldly. It would be useless to try to elicit sympathy. The figure in the chair was a graven image.

Then abruptly, as if electrified, the image came to life. In a single precipitate motion, Mrs. Shipley stood up and flung her antimacassar, crochet hook and all, in her daughter's face.

"Mamma, don't," Barbara screamed.

"Be quiet." An army would have jumped to obey. "You—you whore." Her mother started across the room. Barbara watched her warily.

Mrs. Shipley turned to face her. "When did it happen?"

"In—in June. At that picnic."

"June!" She nearly shouted. "June! That's over three months—" Sagging, she walked back to her chair, sank down in it, and began to moan.

Barbara could almost sympathize.

"Was he the first, Barbara?" This time the voice was deceptively sweet.

"Mother!" Outrage was beginning to replace fear.

"One single thoughtless act on an afternoon in June and you—you—"

Barbara could have finished the sentence. "Ruined everything" was probably what her mother wanted to say. Mrs. Shipley had managed to marry her father, but it couldn't have been for love. She could have had only one motive for spending a lifetime with the beaten little man, with no voice of his own, subservient to his wife and to all the Clarks who surrounded him.

Caldwell Shipley, who came from Philadelphia, was not above boasting of the Clarks' reputation as powerful mine operators and his relationship to them. It was this relationship that won him his ambitious wife, who persuaded him six months after their marriage to move to Clarkston. Soon installed as a lesser official in the company, Caldwell Shipley had not noticeably advanced twenty-two years later. His wife, abler and more ambitious, had, however, succeeded in getting one daughter married and another engaged to the two sons of James Clark, younger brother of Fred and Dexter. This was a considerable achievement, for though James was not connected directly with the mines, he shared in their profits and was also financially independent through a rich wife from New York. His two sons, graduates of Yale, represented everything Mrs. Shipley had dreamt of for sons-in-law.

Barbara knew her mother would never forgive her if the scandal of her pregnancy upset her remaining sister's forthcoming marriage. She was silent, watching her mother covertly. It would be best to let the worst of Mrs. Shipley's rage subside before she said anything. Finally she heard her mother sniff and saw her reach for a handkerchief.

It might be time to speak. "I—oh, Mamma, I wish I was dead."

The statement failed to move her mother. "Have you told anyone else?" she asked.

"No, I—"

"Don't." Mrs. Shipley bit off the word. "When was that picnic? Around the first?"

"The second. On Saturday."

"Have you told him?"

"No. He— Remember he went abroad for the summer? The picnic—the party was for him."

"I hope he's having a good trip," Mrs. Shipley said, looking at her daughter. "You are sure he was the first?"

"Mamma." It was time to begin to defend herself. "I've never been with anybody before, ever."

"Naturally. And what caused you, as you put it, 'to be with' Griswold? Don't tell me it was love."

It would be better, Barbara felt, to say nothing to that. She looked down at the floor.

Her mother stood up. Barbara glanced at her quickly, then away. Mrs. Shipley said, "Spare me the dramatics, you slut. And don't lie to me. All right, it was Griswold Frazier and he's not even around to admit it. I always thought he was a slick young man, with his oily black hair and his affected accent. What about his family?"

"They live in Philadelphia."

Mrs. Shipley raised her eyebrows. "I know that. Griswold Frazier is Eliza Clark's stepnephew."

"What does—?" Barbara stopped. Her mother was leading up to something.

"Griswold's mother is Eliza Clark's stepsister. It seems to me they ought to know what their son perpetrated."

Barbara turned pale. "Who ought to know? The Fraziers or the Clarks?"

Mrs. Shipley ignored her question. "Who else was on that picnic?"

"Everybody. You know, James and Margaret here from Philadelphia, Alfred, Fred Jr., Philip Jr., young Brewster, Caroline, Sandra, and Pamela, all the Clarks—and, of course, Lucy."

Silence. Then, "But Danny stayed home?"

"Of course. He couldn't possibly have come. We walked all the way to Pulpit Rock, slipping and sliding over that rough path. dropping pots and pans, loaves of bread and bacon. Luckily Lucy hung on to the eggs, although Alfred chased her most of the way." Barbara almost smiled.

Mrs. Shipley strode to the window. "If only, if only it could have been *her* son."

"What?"

"Danny, naturally."

"Danny?" Barbara asked. "That cripple." She made a contemptuous gesture.

"Never mind," Mrs. Shipley said impatiently. "The Clarks got us into this and they're going to get us out."

Barbara noted her mother's choice of pronoun. Evidently they would accomplish what was necessary as a team. However, it was difficult to follow her mother's twisted thinking. "Yes, Mamma," she murmured.

"She's soft, you know," Mrs. Shipley said to the window. "And easy to fool. Supposing 'that cripple' had proved his manhood. She'd be proud of him maybe. Maybe not."

Barbara began to see. "But Mamma, I barely know him. And he wasn't on the picnic. I've never even been alone with him."

Mrs. Shipley nodded and walked back to her chair. "Oh, merciful heaven, why, why, why?" She rubbed her eyes. "If this ever gets out . . ."

Barbara said timidly, "Mamma, if we—well—if I could get rid of it, why would anybody have to know?"

"Do you have any idea how much that would cost? *If* it were possible to arrange it."

"No, Mamma." They didn't seem to be getting anywhere.

"Have you any other suggestions?"

The question was put sarcastically enough to ignore, but something her mother had said made Barbara start to think. "Mrs. Clark. Do you think she might give us the money? You know. Quietly?"

"You'd tell her?"

"Me?" Barbara cringed.

"Who else, for pity's sake?"

"Well, I guess—I thought, I mean, you know her and you might be able to—" Barbara looked at her mother's face and stopped.

It was transformed with energy. She got to her feet again and began walking up and down. She started to speak, emphasizing her words with brisk, jabbing gestures. "No. You. You have to go to her. That's what we'll do. You go to Mrs. Clark. We'll leave the Fraziers out of this for now. Anyway, Griswold is Mrs. Clark's nephew. Tell her you're terrified. You can't tell me or your father. Tell her your father would kill you. Tell her we'd all be ruined, us, your sister, we'd have to leave town, we'd be disgraced for the rest of our lives, get on your knees, beg her to help you. Blame it on Griswold, tell her he made you do it, tell her you didn't really know what you were doing. She'll believe it. She'll help you—she's got to." Mrs. Shipley looked out the window. "Too bad about Danny," she said under her breath. "It would have been a sure thing that way." Then with new force. "You go to her tomorrow. If we wait, it will be too late— It's late enough now and you were a fool to wait— As much of a fool as you were to get into this, but it's done now. You have to go to her tomorrow. Don't tell anyone else. Your father mustn't know. He might indeed kill you, but he doesn't know how to manage anything anyway. Tell Eliza Clark you need money. Lots of it. No, don't. Don't take any chances and make her suspicious. Just throw yourself on her mercy, and be sure you blame the boy. Make her believe you can't come to us. That's very important. And be very sure you don't tell anyone else."

Mrs. Shipley returned to her chair and motioned to her daughter to leave the room and her in peace. Barbara nodded mutely and bent down to pick up the crochet hook and antimacassar. Quietly, she placed them on her mother's lap and walked out of the now silent room.

It was Eliza Clark's habit to spend two hours at the piano after lunch; for her it was the loneliest time of the day, the hour when the pall of being in Clarkston descended in earnest. Music became Eliza's only refuge.

She was startled at Nellie's announcement that Miss Barbara Shipley had arrived to see her. No one ever intruded at this time. Although she saw little of the Shipley girls, she remembered Barbara was the prettiest, the most alluring of the three sisters, with her curly yellow hair and slim figure. She couldn't imagine why she was here.

"Show her in, Nellie," Eliza said.

The girl looked dejected and ill, and Eliza, glancing at her, felt a tiny start of fear. She rose, held out her hand, "How are you, my dear?"

Barbara's hand was clammy to the touch, her words of greeting mumbled.

"Why, Barbara, I'm delighted to see you. I always love seeing young people, and this is, well, it's always an especially lonely hour for me." What an idiotic thing to say to a young girl, Eliza thought. But something in Barbara's face had made her babble on.

It was a moment before Barbara replied. Then to Eliza's discomfort, she said, "I have no one else to go to."

Eliza, in a flash of intuition, sensed what was wrong and

instantly rejected the suspicion. Whatever it was, why would the girl come to her? "You're in trouble, Barbara?"

The girl nodded and looked at Eliza piteously.

"Tell me about it. It's always easier if you tell someone."

"Oh, Mrs. Clark, I'm so ashamed. But I didn't know what I was doing. Honestly." Barbara began to cry.

Eliza went to her and put an arm around her. "There, there," she said helplessly. The tears were flowing freely now and Barbara's crying had turned to sobs. It seemed to Eliza an eternity until the girl quieted down. When she did, Eliza said, "Tell me what it is, Barbara. What can I do to help?"

"I'm going to have a b-b-baby."

"Oh, dear Lord!" Eliza said it under her breath. Then, aloud, "Have—have you told your mother?" She was afraid she knew the answer. Mrs. Shipley's pose of devoted motherhood was as brittle as a plaster saint's and would disintegrate with the first blow to her pride. Her outrage would be terrible, her righteous anger blistering. She couldn't blame Barbara if she had not wanted to face her mother.

"No, no . . ." The sobs began again. Patiently Eliza waited. When she could speak, Barbara said, "I can't. She woul— My father would kill me. The disgrace—it would ruin me for life."

"But who is the boy?"

"Griswold."

Eliza felt as if she had received a physical blow. Griswold Frazier, her nephew, aged seventeen, an irresponsible, thoroughly spoiled, precocious brat, the apple of his mother's, her stepsister's eye. Prophetically enough, she had often tried to warn Susie that unless he was better disciplined, Griswold was headed for trouble. "How did it happen?" Eliza asked.

"It was at the picnic, last June. We had lunch. Afterward Griswold asked me to take a walk with him, he held my hand, we went down to the ravine, below Pulpit Rock. It's so pretty down there where all the laurel grows, he—he told me he loved me, he wanted to be really close to me, and there—there, we, well he made me lie down, he took off some of his clothes and some of mine, he, ohhhhh . . ." Barbara collapsed once more into tears. When she recovered, she said, "I tried to tell him no and make him stop, but he's so strong he—"

Eliza stood up. "Oh, that ghastly boy," she said angrily. "Have you heard from him since?"

"No, don't you remember? He went to Europe."

Eliza groaned. Of course she remembered. How like him to have his little fling and then go wandering off halfway across the world. She was beginning to long for the peace of her lonely afternoons; this one was turning into a nightmare. Her stepsister, Griswold's mother, who was nearly forty, was seven months pregnant and having trouble keeping the baby. She must not be upset now. Although Eliza was desperately sorry for the girl weeping softly in her chair, Susie must not be told. Barbara would have to brave her mother's wrath. "Barbara, listen to me," she said sternly. "You must go to your mother, she'll have to help you. There just isn't anyone else. My sister—well, I won't go into that, but I don't want her to know."

"Well, she's sure to know the moment my mother does," Barbara said practically. "She won't waste any time. I know my mother. She'll tell all of Clarkston, probably Philadelphia, too."

Eliza cast around wildly. It was probably true that Barbara's parents, once they knew, could make things worse. Wait. She hadn't explored this thoroughly. "Barbara," she said. "How do you *know* you're pregnant? I mean has anyone told you?"

"I haven't had my—you know—since." The sudden intrusion of modesty into this bizarre conversation made Eliza feel the onslaught of hysteria. Trying to control herself, she said, "But you haven't been to a doctor?"

"Who? Dr. Grunig wouldn't . . "

No. Dr. Grunig would be impossible, Eliza had to agree. And who indeed could she turn to? She was definitely hysterical now. She had a sudden vision of herself, Barbara at her side, trying to explain the situation to the rigid and totally humorless town doctor and shook with repressed laughter.

Barbara eyed her with alarm.

"Oh, forgive me, Barbara," Eliza said quickly. "It's just that I can't seem to think . . ." She spread her hands helplessly. "I really don't know what I can do to help you."

"Maybe I should go to your sister," Barbara said.

"Oh, no, no, you mustn't do that, Barbara. Promise me, you have to promise me you won't."

Barbara looked desolate. "Well, what can I do?"

"We have to find a midwife, someone who can take the baby," Eliza said firmly. Then her eyes filled with pity and she shook her head. "I don't see any other way. I'm sorry."

"I suppose I'll just have to endure it," Barbara said and began to sob.

"Barbara, Barbara, please stop," Eliza said frantically. "My husband—he might come home any minute, and if he finds you here in this condition . . ." Barbara stopped instantly.

"Now," Eliza said, "you had better go home. I'll try to think. Hard. Come back tomorrow morning. At ten."

By nine thirty the next morning Eliza was on the train to Philadelphia. She had had a difficult time justifying her trip to Fred but told him that a sudden toothache made it essential that she see the dentist immediately. She had given Nellie a note for Barbara explaining that she was on her way to see her doctor, the family physician. She hoped he would be able to give her good advice. She had spent a tortured night, wondering how she had managed to get into this in the first place and how she could get out of it in the second. She reminded herself wryly that she had thought she was quite worldly but now that she was suddenly faced with trying to save a young girl's reputation, her sister's health, the family honor, and a major scandal in Clarkston and Philadelphia, her self-possession seemed to have deserted her.

It was one thirty on the afternoon of Wednesday, September eleventh, when Eliza arrived in Philadelphia. She had sent Dr. Penwood a telegram saying she would get to the station before one and take a cab directly to his office. The last of the summer still lingered in the city's dusty streets, but Eliza's apprehension made her unaware of anything except the urgency of her problem. Even so, she had taken time, in preparation for seeing the doctor, to put on a new blue-green "walking dress" of corded silk with a simulated bolero made especially for her by a fashionable Philadelphia dressmaker after a design by Worth. The front of the bolero was buttoned tightly over the bust from the snug little collar to the V-shaped point over the stomach. The tight-fitting sleeves ended three inches above the wrists, revealing cuffs of figured brocade in bright yellow.

Eliza fidgeted nervously during the ride to Dr. Penwood's office. Once there, she gave the driver a quick nod and plunged up the front steps. Dr. Penwood opened the door himself and ushered her directly into his office.

Books were crammed into the long shelves that flanked the fireplace at the room's end, some of them lying haphazardly on one side. The eight globes of the gas chandelier were brilliantly reflected in a wide mirror that reached to the ceiling from the mantel. Autographed cabinet photographs of William Osler, Weir Mitchell, and William Pepper, the doctors who had made Philadelphia without medical rival in the nation, stood in front of the mirror. It was a room whose atmosphere suggested stability.

Eliza had brought her anxieties about Danny here many times in the past. Out of habit, she sank down in the low rocker upholstered in green velvet. Waiting to see if she was comfortable, the doctor moved to the opposite side of his desk, adjusted a standing kerosene lamp on his left and seated himself in his revolving mahogany chair. He had noted Eliza's lunge up the front steps and sensed that something out of the ordinary was bedeviling her. "I trust you have been well since I saw you last. Your visit is—ah—a bit precipitous and you look a trifle distressed. Is Danny—?"

"It's not about me or Danny, Dr. Penwood. You see—oh—I have something dreadful to tell you. I didn't think of you until the middle of the night. I—I hope you can help me."

"Oh. Well. The middle of the night. I am flattered." The doctor had his little ways, but he was kind. He had been understanding as well as tenacious in the past. Other doctors had either found Danny's illness inexplicable, "an unknown malady," or had suggested he might be suffering from syphilis caught from a wet nurse. Eliza remembered gratefully that Dr. Penwood had refused to accept either diagnosis. He had persisted long after she and Fred had given up. "Europe," he had said. "Still think we have a chance of finding out something more there. Better research. Asked every doctor I know going abroad to look up research on bone and muscle deficiencies." Finally one of his students had come back with the answer. The student had discovered a paper written in 1849 by a Dutch anatomist, Willem Vralik. It described a disease of the connective tissue called Osteogenesis Imperfecta. Danny's symptoms exactly matched the description: the brittle bones, the blue sclera of the eyeball, and the impaired vision. Vralik's studies indicated that while nothing could be done to cure the condition, acute discomfort would lessen after adolescence.

A wave of gratitude for the man across the desk swept over Eliza. "You've never failed our family, Dr. Penwood." She hesitated, drew off her gloves, and glanced at her wedding ring. She wished now she had told Fred. "This—this is about other people, young people, very young people. One is Barbara Shipley and the other is my nephew, Griswold Frazier. You know how I feel about his mother, Susie. She's always been my favorite and now she's in trouble with that baby. Griswold, he's made her pregnant, doctor, and we've simply got to see she doesn't have the baby."

She had rehearsed this over and over on the train and in the cab, but there was something wrong with it and it hadn't come out with any delicacy at all. There really wasn't any way to glide over these gruesome facts.

The doctor smiled. "It's a little difficult to tell which baby you're referring to, Mrs. Clark, but I assume Griswold has made someone called Barbara Shipley pregnant and that's the baby you—er—want to get rid of?"

Eliza was crimson. "Yes, please. It's absolutely essential."

"Now, Mrs. Clark, hold on a minute. These acts of nature—not so easily undone. Why shouldn't she have the baby? Why can't the boy marry her?"

"We didn't even discuss that," Eliza said before she had time to think and then went crimson again as she saw the doctor's look of disapproval. "Oh dear me," she fumbled on. "I mean there are lots of reasons. This is so horribly complicated. I'm making a terrible mess of it, but you see, first of all Griswold is actually only seventeen years old, she's eighteen, and it would ruin their lives. Then her family—they would disown her and let her be disgraced. You have no idea how straitlaced they are. I don't know what would become of her and I'd hate to have her downfall on my conscience. Griswold was visiting us when it happened, so in a way I feel responsible. And finally and terribly important to me is the reaction Susie might have if she knew. I'm so afraid that Shipley woman—Barbara's mother, that is—will tell her if I don't help. Doctor, you've been taking care of Susie. Don't you think it would have a terrible effect on her if she finds out her son behaved this way?"

He nodded. "Um, suppose it might. Better not to have your stepsister know, upset at this time. She's—well—old to be having this baby. Forty when it's born. To be candid, with her history, I was not pleased to learn she was pregnant. Shouldn't divulge this to you. Appreciate it if you would keep it to yourself."

"Oh, I won't tell a soul, doctor," she said quickly. "Susie herself told me she was having trouble. But, please, can you be very honest with me? Wouldn't it be disastrous for her to have such a bad shock just now?"

"People have survived worse. However, if possible, better to keep it from her."

Eliza took a deep breath. Her poor stepsister. "Dr. Penwood, this is a terrible thing to ask, but under the circumstances, considering the good of everyone, couldn't you take the baby?"

"No, I could not," he said firmly. "Do you know how many months pregnant she is or when she thinks the encounter occurred that made her pregnant?"

"On the second of June," she said. "They were on a picnic and they wandered off by themselves. They found a ravine, below Pulpit Rock, protected by banks of laurel. She was almost poetic about that."

"Then, if she's to be believed, she's over three months along. Under no circumstances should that baby be disturbed. You'd be risking the girl's life. Only a charlatan would consider it. Have you—has the girl talked to anyone else about this—a doctor, that is?"

"No, not anyone, not anyone at all. There isn't anyone I could—I came straight to you," Eliza blurted out. She was throwing herself on his mercy and she hated herself for doing it. "I'm sorry," she added faintly.

"That's all right." He seemed to understand. "You aren't exactly used to this sort of thing." He looked thoughtful. "I think I'd like to talk with the girl."

"Can I bring her down to you?" Eliza asked timidly.

"Yes. Of course." He consulted his calendar. "Nothing here I can't rearrange. Would day after tomorrow at the same time be all right?"

"Yes. Fine," said Eliza, wondering how she would explain going to Philadelphia twice in three days.

"Now, assuming she is pregnant, what do you propose to do?"

"I don't know. What does anyone do under these—?"

"I would suggest that someone take the girl away, far enough so that she won't be tracked down, let her have the baby, and put it out for adoption. Such things have been done before—for a price."

"How does one go about—where would she go?"

"Oh, I'd say either Europe, or if this country, I think I'd suggest California." He toyed with the Tiffany shade on the lamp. "There's one pretty good foundling hospital in San Francisco. Been going for nearly twenty years. Used to know Howard Sloan, one of the doctors there, classmate of mine in medical school here, went West a couple of years after graduation. Useful man to know at a time like this. But you can't very well go to a foundling hospital. Hardly the place for this girl." The doctor had a way of delivering unpunctuated sentences. Eliza was listening intently, afraid of missing something. "Hardly the place for anybody actually, eighty-percent mortality, understaffed, babies who don't have much of a chance to begin with and less after they get there, miserable conditions—" The doctor brought himself up short. "In your case, or rather Barbara's case, I believe Howard Sloan might arrange an adoption in advance and find a private home in San Diego, where the winter climate is warm and where the girl could be confined."

"What was that about eighty-percent mortality?"

"Oh. Well. You see, girls who have to go to foundling homes are mostly servant girls," he said, shrugging, "farmers' daughters—no education, no money. If the infants live, they mostly go on to orphan asylums or almshouses until they're adopted."

"What happens to the ones who are adopted?" Eliza asked. She was ashamed. She had never given a single thought to any of this before.

"These children are adopted for one reason only," the doctor said matter-of-factly. "Work, add to the family income." He stopped as he noticed Eliza's stricken expression.

"But it's wicked," she said slowly, "to make children the victims of such a system."

He looked at her appraisingly for a moment. "The working man and his family are not supposed to have as sensitive feelings as the rich do."

Eliza was uncomfortable. "I've never thought much about children—children who are orphans," she said.

"Oh, it's not as bad as it used to be," he said cheerfully. "Don't worry too much about Barbara's child," he persisted. "A baby who comes from a good background won't have much trouble finding a good home—perhaps with parents who may be in the same sort of circumstances that you are."

"But that's disgusting," Eliza said, trying to fight off the wave of relief his statement brought. "I mean just because a child is better born than someone else, he had a better chance than the rest of those unfortunate—"

"Way of the world, my dear," the doctor said philosophically. "If we're discreet, I'm sure it will be possible to place the baby with a fine family."

She shrank down in her chair. She had been put in her place.

The doctor continued, "By the way, who is going to take the responsibility for this girl? Anyone who does will have to be gone a long time."

Eliza's "I don't know" was barely audible.

He looked at her keenly. "Are you thinking of doing it yourself? I really don't see how you can keep this from the mother. She should be the one to go, you know."

Eliza shook her head. "The poor girl is terrified of her mother, and, in a way, so am I. Besides the Shipleys haven't any money."

"It certainly doesn't sound good," he said, "and she'll obviously have to go immediately if you don't want anyone else to know. Once she begins to show, it's all over. Meanwhile, bring her here day after tomorrow and go back now and talk it over with your husband. Have you told him?"

"No."

"I thought not. I've noticed most wives keep this sort of information to themselves."

"I've never kept anything from Fred in my life. It's just that—"

"I know." He sounded faintly apologetic, as though he had

made an unscientific and uncomplimentary remark. "Try not to worry too much. Would it make you feel better if I wrote to Howard Sloan? There isn't much time, and he'd have to find a private home first where either he or a competent midwife can deliver her. That's the first thing to arrange, even though, if the date you gave me is correct, she won't be needing either the place or the services until February."

February. That was after January, after Christmas, the begin-ning of next year. She felt trapped.

He tinkered with the shade again and for a moment was absorbed in watching its multicolored pattern. "Eliza," he said, "are you seriously thinking of accompanying the girl yourself?"

He had shocked her into an unexpected awareness of the man himself. He had never before used her Christian name and its use combined with the gentleness of his tone had turned him into a fellow human being, an intimate friend.

"I don't know how I can go or not go," she said. "Or what might happen if I don't. If I thought there was anyone else who could go with her or help her . . ." she said, looking up at him, "but there isn't. At least I don't think so now or can't think of anyone or maybe I'm just not thinking straight."

"The only good thing about your going," he said, "would be getting you out of Clarkston and into a warm climate for three months of winter. After your bout with pneumonia last year, I would welcome that. You could stay in San Diego, where the weather is mild. Dr. Sloan could come down from his foundling hospital for the confinement. First thing you'll have to do, Eliza, is talk it over with your husband."

"He'll hate the thought of my going."

"No doubt." He stood up, came around the desk and placed a hand on her shoulder. "You're a very brave lady," he said.

She got up hastily, preparing to go. She could feel the sting of tears under the bridge of her nose. He took her arm, saw her to the door, and helped her into the waiting hansom. "Take care of yourself. I'll see you the day after tomorrow. I'm sure everything will work out." He stood there a moment, watching the cab as it started on its way to the station.

The letter was giving him difficulty. He couldn't seem to get beyond "Dear Howard. An old patient has come to me with a problem . . ." He knew she would go to California with the girl, and he was afraid of what it would do to her marriage.

For the first time in her life she felt the force of Fred's anger directed at her. "Why, why, why, Eliza?" he had railed at her. "The girl is probably a slut and very well able to take care of herself."

"Fred!" She was outraged.

"Oh, come on, Eliza. Face the facts."

He had never talked to her like that. "You," she said acidly, "have not seen her. She is terrified—like an animal who doesn't know where to hide. And it is not her fault as I've told you. Griswold *forced* her."

"I very much doubt that, Eliza. He's only seventeen, and I've never seen any evidence of his being uncontrollably passionate. If I remember Barbara correctly, she damned well may be."

"That's totally unfair and you know it."

"All right. I'll withdraw the point, and it doesn't matter much anyway, since the pregnancy seems to be a fact, but I do wish you'd wait and see what Griswold has to say. I want to make sure he was the boy."

"Fred! How can you?"

"Don't be ridiculous, Eliza. You're filled with sympathy for this girl to the apparent exclusion of everything else. What about your responsibility to Anna and our six-month-old grandson? What if they should need you in Philadelphia while you're three thousand miles away? Really, Eliza, it's not too much to ask you to be sure you have the facts."

"All right," she said coldly. "I'll question her thoroughly tomorrow. Or perhaps you'd like to?"

"God, no. Leave me out of this. Just make damned sure you know what you're doing before you even think of going to California with her." He got to his feet. "I've had enough for one night. I'm going to bed." He went out of the room without a backward glance. This goddamned place, he thought. If we'd been in Philadelphia, Eliza would never have got mixed up in such an unpleasant mess.

On the train to Philadelphia Barbara was pale, nervous, and

silent. It was clearly not the time to question her. Once they were in the doctor's offices, greeted this time by the nurse who led them to a small, stuffy waiting room, Eliza began to relax a little. Here, at least, she would find someone who wasn't furious with her. Before she could sit down, the nurse asked Eliza to come into the doctor's study.

"I hope you don't mind if I see Barbara alone," Dr. Penwood said.

She noticed he had gone back to calling her Mrs. Clark. "Oh, please do. And please get as much information as you can. That's what Fred wants."

"So you've told him?"

"Yes."

The doctor nodded. "Please show Miss Shipley into the examining room," he called to the nurse, and then said to Eliza, "I won't be long."

When he came back, he said, "I think everything confirms my original assumption that mid February is the date."

It took Eliza a minute to grasp the significance for her of this, then unable to control her curiosity, she said, "Doctor, what did you ask her?"

"You mean how did I go about approaching such a delicate subject?" The doctor laughed. "Well, Eliza, may I call you that?" She nodded gratefully. "I simply said, 'Miss Shipley, Mrs. Clark tells me you're going to have a baby, and to be sure you will be all right and plan for the baby properly, I must ask you some questions.'"

"I believe the only time I caused her any embarrassment was when I asked her if this was the first time she had had relations with Griswold and if he had been the only one. She protested strenuously. In fact, she tends to blame the whole episode on the boy. I wonder. Perhaps he enticed her, but I doubt that he forced her. Now the question is, how involved should you get? What did your husband suggest?"

"He doesn't want me to have anything to do with it."

"I would agree with him completely, except as you know, I don't want you to spend the winter in Clarkston. I've also thought more about your stepsister."

"That part of it worries me too."

"You're quite right. If she finds out about Griswold, it certainly won't help her coming confinement. But what about confronting Griswold with this?"

"Griswold isn't due back until the end of September."

"That's too late. It's lucky she shows as little as she does now."

"You mean she must get away as soon as possible?"

"That's right," the doctor answered. "The thing that bothers me most is Barbara's family. I'm not in favor of keeping this from them. Barbara seems hysterical on that score, though. Has it crossed your mind that if they find out, they may cause the Clarks a lot of trouble?"

"What do you mean?"

"I mean they may be after what they can get. Money," he said bluntly.

"Oh no. They couldn't. She's a conventional prig and he's completely under her thumb."

The doctor rose. "Well, look. Nothing can be done for a week or two until I hear from Howard Sloan. I wrote him yesterday. If you like, you can tell Fred the San Diego climate would be a help to you. I'll telegraph when I hear from Sloan. Meanwhile, try not to worry."

Ten days later the telegram arrived. "SLOAN ABLE TO ACCOMMO-DATE. SUGGEST IMMEDIATE ARRANGEMENTS FOR MISS SHIPLEY'S DEPARTURE BE MADE. HARRISON E. PENWOOD. M.D."

Tension had been building between Fred and Eliza since her visit to Dr. Penwood. Searching desperately for some way to keep her at home, Fred had gone to see Sumter Frazier and in a thoroughly unsatisfactory meeting told him about Griswold and Barbara. Frazier, already nervous because of his wife's condition, greeted the news with disbelief and then truculence. He pointed out that there was absolutely nothing he could do about it while Griswold was in Europe; he didn't want to hear anything more about it now, and why, for heaven's sake, didn't the girl's mother take on the responsibility for what was undoubtedly a wayward daughter? Fred then asked how Sumter would like to have the whole affair exposed in Philadelphia, not to mention Clarkston. Sumter said coldly he doubted his son's role could be proved and why should the Shipleys expose their daughter to the disgrace in the first place? Utterly frustrated, Fred came away determined to make Eliza see that she should never have become involved with the girl. But she was already deeply embroiled, he realized. Barbara had become a daily visitor; she was complaining now of not feeling well, and one day, according to Eliza, she had even fainted. Barbara had succeeded in extracting every ounce of Eliza's sympathy. When Fred told her about Sumter's reluctance to take any responsibility for Barbara and her unborn baby, Eliza accused all men of being irresponsible hypocrites. It was as though she was the victim of some kind of spell. She had become completely unreasonable.

After several bitter arguments the subject of Barbara was scrupulously avoided. Now that the telegram had arrived, it would have to be brought up again.

Clutching the telegram in one hand and a dish of after-dinner mints in the other, Eliza walked over to Fred's chair. "Here," she said grimly, offering both.

"No, thanks." He barely looked up from his evening paper. She tried again. "Fred, you'll have to read this."

"Oh." He glanced at her apologetically. "I'm sorry. I thought you meant the mints." He reached for the telegram. He was silent for a moment and when he spoke, his voice was gentle. "You know, Eliza, I fault myself in all this. I never should have allowed my father and Dexter to persuade me to bring you here. We should have stayed in Philadelphia, where such a grotesque mishap probably would not have occurred—and certainly you would never have been involved." He reached for a cigar in the humidor beside him, cut off the end, lit it, and inhaled deeply. "Eliza, let's discuss this as rationally as possible," he said.

"That's all I've ever wanted to do."

"All right. Now, if you can, please tell me exactly the reason you think it's your duty to take this girl to California."

"Oh, Fred, we've been over it so many times. She hasn't anyone else to turn to; besides, my nephew Griswold is responsible. Unless the whole thing is handled right, that baby like so many other poor infants may die, wind up in an almshouse . . ." She shook her head. "I don't know, Fred. There's a lot I never knew before."

"My God." Fred was on his feet. "Don't tell me you're getting a social conscience. That's Jessie's bailiwick, not yours."

Despite herself she blushed. "Let's not fight, Fred, please."

"You don't expect me to let that pass, do you?" His face softened as he saw her turn away to hide another blush. "All right, Lady Bountiful. It seems to me that come hell or high water, you're bound to go, and nothing I can say will stop you. Perhaps that's the trouble. As my brothers say, I spoil you. I'll get the tickets tomorrow."

She felt deflated. She had been braced for a long, fierce argument, and without warning he had capitulated. Uneasily she remembered his remark about spoiling her. It was unfair; this was the one time in her life she had tried to do something unselfish, to help someone else. Oh Lord, was she as bad as that? Her mind darted around, remembering the way she had spent her days before the advent of Barbara, moping, bewailing the fact that she was stuck in Clarkston, living only for trips to Philadelphia, the Assembly, the opera, her dresses, her jewels, never giving a thought to "helpless orphans" or anybody else either, she supposed, including the man in front of her, whom she thought she loved so dearly.

"Oh, Fred," she said brokenly. "I'm sorry—I'll make it up to you, I promise." She turned away again, this time to hide the tears.

He walked over to where she stood and took her in his arms. "It's all right, Eliza. I don't think the trip is going to be much fun, unfortunately, but I'm very glad to have you go to a good climate for the winter. Danny and I will try to survive without you."

He smiled bleakly and drew her close.

CHAPTER 7

Philadelphia and San Diego
October 1890

DESOLATION SWEPT OVER ELIZA as she watched his retreating figure. She waited until she saw the top of his derby disappear through the iron gates at the end of the track at Broad Street Station, noting dismally that he never looked back. She had left Barbara in their drawing room so she could walk to the platform and say good-bye to Fred. It had not been a happy moment. She had made the mistake of starting to apologize again for the trip.

Almost immediately he cut her off. "There is no point in talking about it further. I think you'll find your accommodations comfortable, and I hope the trip goes well." He glanced at her miserably and noticed for the first time she was wearing a new dress of gray wool and a new gray felt hat with a wide brim. It was turned up slightly all around and decorated with a stuffed bird "in flight." Its smartness only added to his irritability. Then he saw the beginning of tears in her eyes and relented a little. "I'm sorry. I guess you have to do what you have to do. Take care of yourself, please. I won't stay to see the train pull out."

A brief hug and a kiss and he was gone. When she lost sight of him, she turned and started back to the drawing room. The conductor caught up with her halfway there. "Mr. Clark has asked me to take special care of you and the young lady, madame. We'll be leaving in five minutes. The hotel car is forward and just two away from your drawing room. May I make a reservation for you with the steward and at what time."

Eliza nodded numbly and murmured, "In an hour." Then she fled, determined to get herself under control. In the drawing

97

room Barbara was sitting huddled next to the window, staring out.

Eliza swallowed the lump in her throat and said as cheerfully as she could, "We're just about to leave."

Barbara sighed heavily and said nothing. She seemed curiously indifferent to everything about her.

Eliza tried again. "The dining car is two cars away. I told the conductor we'd dine in an hour."

Barbara pressed her face against the window. The train had started to pull out. "I don't want any dinner."

It was a remark best ignored. Later, when they reached the dining salon, Barbara seemed a little less listless, even somewhat impressed by the elaborately decorated car. Half a dozen kerosene lamps swung from the ceiling as the train wound around the gently curving hills and valleys of the open farmland fifty miles west of Philadelphia. Outside, the sun was setting behind occasional groves of deciduous trees—maple, sycamore, oak, chestnut, and walnut, all much more friendly than the stark evergreens on the mountains of Clarkston. Inside the car the tables seating four on one side of the red-carpeted aisle and tables seating two on the other were irresistible, with their glistening white linen tablecloths, folded white napkins, sparkling crystal glasses, and highly polished silver. A gay little bunch of chrysanthemums decorated each table and set off the green-bordered, cream-colored china with the matching emblems of the Keystone State and Pennsylvania Railroad.

Eliza, studying the bill of fare, said, "What would you like, Barbara? The choice is grouse, beefsteak, and mutton chops, vanilla or peach ice cream for dessert."

"Chops, please."

"Grouse for me, please, and chops for the young lady— although everything is tempting," Eliza said to the waiter. She was determined to sound gracious.

"Thank you, ma'am. After Chicago we'll have buffalo, elk, and antelope. Tonight it's the New York and Philadelphia meats." The waiter bowed and left to place the order.

There was an awkward silence, and Eliza could feel herself growing angry as she watched Barbara staring fixedly at the floor.

"Barbara, it's a beautiful train and the scenery is lovely. Let's try to enjoy it, shall we?"

"You can enjoy it if you want. I can't enjoy anything. All I can think about is getting rid of your nephew's baby."

The remark was as appalling as it was insolent, but Eliza decided to let it pass.

Each time the train stopped to take on water or fuel, Eliza got out and walked vigorously up and down the platform. The two days in Chicago had been a time to be endured, not enjoyed. Barbara's preoccupation with herself blinded her to any new sights.

Eliza's mounting boredom with her roommate drove her to conversations with other passengers. Mr. and Mrs. Strong, middle-aged, rich, and friendly, were going to southern California in search of a better climate for Mr. Strong's lungs. They had traveled up and down the Riviera on the same quest but finally decided they wanted to finish their days in America.

"And you, Mrs. Clark, are you and Miss Shipley going for the winter?"

"No, just four or five months—the early part of the winter," Eliza said. "I was ill last year with pneumonia and my doctor said I mustn't spend another winter in the East. I'll go back in February as soon as—I mean—" She bit her tongue in panic. Since the beginning Barbara's whole miserable affair had been riddled with pitfalls. "—in time to go to Florida with my husband and son. We always go then for a month to get away from the cold. . ." She left the sentence unfinished, preoccupied with the thought that she must learn to avoid traps like these.

Mr. Pusey, a clergyman and the first friend Eliza had made on the train, spoke up. She had picked him at the start as safe. "I'm sure you'll find San Diego ideal," he said. "Whenever I've been there, the sunshine has been constant." Mr. Pusey, who had something cheerful to say about almost everything, was leaving the East permanently and had accepted the ministry of the San Diego Episcopal Church.

"The shops are excellent," Mr. Pusey said, eyeing Eliza's stylish figure. "The old, or Spanish, part of the town is extremely picturesque, the beaches stretch for miles, and Mexico is only a short distance away. I think Miss Shipley will enjoy herself. You're lucky to have such a young woman traveling with you, Mrs. Clark."

"Yes." Eliza hoped her smile looked genuine. "I persuaded Barbara to come with me because, of course, my husband can't get away now, and I thought it would be nice for her to see the West." Eliza started to relax. She felt she had carried that off nicely.

"Perhaps she can meet some young people through the church when we get there. We must be sure to keep in touch," the clergyman said hospitably.

"Yes, indeed," Eliza wanted to run, to disappear completely. A web was closing around her.

"Where are you staying, Mrs. Clark?"

She was prepared. "For just a few days at the Hotel del Coronado in Coronado Beach. After that our plans are very indefinite."

By the time Eliza and Barbara reached the Union Station in San Diego, the Spanish mission architecture and the crowds of Indians on the platform were no longer a novelty. All through Arizona and New Mexico they had appeared with monotonous regularity.

Eliza climbed into a waiting carriage, beckoning Barbara to follow. In five minutes they had left the railroad and its ugly tracks behind them. For sheer beauty, Eliza had never seen anything like the surroundings of San Diego. It was situated on a crescent-shaped bay, with the snow-capped Jacinto Mountains in the background; she could understand why it was known as the "Naples of America."

The coachman delivered them at a dock, where porters piled their luggage on a ferry bound for Coronado. They crossed San Diego Bay on the ferry, disembarked, and climbed into a small railroad train that made Eliza think yearningly of Danny. They were carried across the beach, past hundreds of cottages and tents to an immense building in the center of a green park. This was Eliza's first glimpse of the Hotel del Coronado.

"Do look, Barbara," she said. "I don't believe you've ever seen anything like that before."

The building with colored banners waving from three turrets stretched across the lawn in a series of uneven galleries. From the front door a bellboy led them down a long corridor to their bed-rooms. Barbara's overlooked San Diego Bay, Eliza's the Pacific. As soon as she was unpacked, Barbara found and established as hers an easy chair in the corner of a small nearby sitting room. Eliza, who had been glued to the window, turned to speak to her.

"I'm going to walk in the gardens for a few minutes. I need a little exercise." She did not add that Barbara, too, could do with some exercise. "You can meet me in the dining room when it's time for dinner."

Eliza stopped at the desk on her way out to ask if she had any mail. Dr. Penwood had told her that probably a letter of instruc-tions from Dr. Sloan would be there either on her arrival or shortly thereafter.

"Eliza Clark."

Startled, Eliza spun around. It was Diana Struthers, an old friend from Philadelphia.

"What in the world are you doing here?"

Eliza started to stutter. "D-D-Diana. Where—?" She stopped, realizing she had been thrown completely off balance. It had not occurred to her that she would ever run into anyone from Philadelphia. "—did you come from? I'm—I'm here because of my health. Dr. Penwood insisted . . ." Eliza swung into the much practiced lie.

"Oh. I'm sure the climate will do you a world of good. And Fred—is he here, too?"

"Oh, no. He can't leave Clarkston and the business. Poor Fred."

"Anyway, I'm delighted you're here, and George will be, too. We're only going to be here for two more days, but do let's get together."

"I'd love to." Eliza was relieved. If it was only for two days, she could manage.

"How long are you staying?"

"I don't know—there's so much to see. We'll probably move on soon." They'd have to, Eliza thought. She was too apt to run into acquaintances at the Coronado.

"Could you join us for dinner tomorrow night?" Her friend was oblivious of Eliza's panic.

"Yes. Fine." Eliza wondered what she'd do with Barbara.

Let her stay in her room and have her dinner on a tray.

"A letter for you, Mrs. Clark." The clerk handed it to her. After she arranged a time to meet the Struthers for dinner, Eliza went to the garden with the letter, praying it would suggest a place to hide. She walked into the courtyard of the Coronado Hotel and found a bench in a secluded corner beyond a grove of oranges. Her hands were shaking a little as she ripped open the envelope containing Dr. Sloan's letter.

It was brief and to the point.

. . . I have been in touch with an excellent midwife in San Diego. She is Mrs. Eleanor Holmes, widow of a pharmacist who moved to California years ago. She lives in a small house at 922 Carroll Avenue. She has two rooms, which she would rent to you and Miss Shipley. If you decide to stay with her, you will not be as likely to meet any tourists from the East as you would risk staying at a hotel.

Whether you choose to stay with her or not, I have suggested to Mrs. Holmes that she keep in touch with you and Miss Shipley, especially as the pregnancy advances, and I have asked her to let me know when the birth is imminent. She is skilled enough to see the young woman through the birth alone, but if it is possible, I would like to come down from San Francisco to deliver the baby myself so that I would take it away immediately for adoption. This is largely for the good of the mother. Don't worry about a home for the baby. It will not be hard to find a couple who will provide for it well.

Dr. Penwood also said you wanted to know about a contribution to our foundling hospital. Any contribution you wish to make will be greatly appreciated and the amount is entirely up to you.

Let me know your plans after you speak with Mrs. Holmes.

Eliza was enormously relieved. No matter how small and shabby Mrs. Holmes's rooms were, she was prepared to accept them.

She must get letters off to Fred and Danny right away, Eliza thought. Writing to them would relieve the tedium of Barbara's company. She was missing her husband badly.

Back in Clarkston, Fred had been feeling he should keep Eliza up to date on the trouble Barbara's family seemed intent on causing them. He was still upset with Eliza and not inclined to be affectionate or gentle with her. In his first letter he wrote that he had already been summoned to Philadelphia by Griswold's parents and had been a party to an extremely disagreeable interview with Mrs. Shipley. It certainly didn't augur well for the future, and she had turned out to be an even more dreadful woman than he had realized.

In point of fact, Fred had arrived back in Clarkston the night of the visit to the Fraziers exhausted and out of temper. He was surprised and not particularly happy to see that Danny had waited up for him. Hoping he wouldn't betray his feelings, he barely managed to muster a smile as he walked into the living room.

"Father," Danny said, waving a letter in greeting, "I waited up to tell you the first letters from Mamma came today. One for you and one for me. Mine says she's fine, the gardens at the Hotel Coronado are beautiful and she misses us, but we shouldn't worry about her." Danny held out the letter addressed to Fred. "Here."

"I'll read it carefully later," Fred said, stuffing it in his pocket. "Did she say anything else important?"

"No, but she sounded all right and really enthusiastic about the California scenery."

"That's good."

"I think Barbara must be a wonderful companion for her. I've always liked her. She's very pretty," Danny said awkwardly.

Fred resisted the impulse to blurt out the truth and got up. "Well, I've had a long day and I'm tired. I'm going to turn in. How about you?'

Danny nodded and reached for his crutches and together they went up the stairs.

"Good night, Danny. See you in the morning." Fred went off to his bedroom. Whe he got there he sat down on the bed, unlaced his shoes and pulled the letter from his pocket. He waited for a moment before he opened it.

"Dearest Fred," Eliza wrote.

I miss you more than I ever dreamt possible. And although I cannot resist being interested in my surroundings, I look at all of them with many pangs of loneliness. The Hotel del Coronado is not like anything I've ever seen in this country. Its style is Spanish with a dash of Queen Anne and Elizabethan.

It's a huge place with a race track, a museum and an ostrich farm. But the part I like best is the inner court filled with fruit trees. There are almonds, figs, loquats, limes, lemons, oranges and a lot more. I cannot tell you how ironic it seems to me to be here with Barbara instead of you. The only thing that makes any impression on her is size and quantity and I must admit there's enough of both in this hotel to satisfy anyone.

The beach is magnificent and at low tide, there are plenty of horseback riders and carriages. There's also swimming in the surf or at the natatorium. Oh, how many things we could do if you were here!

I am learning to manage somehow with Barbara although she exasperates and puzzles me. The truth is that in spite of the beauties of the climate and the place, I miss you terribly.

All my love,
Eliza

Fred put the letter down. So far she seemed to be having a nice time but not as nice as she had anticipated with that impossible girl. When they left Clarkston, Eliza was still convinced of Barbara's injured innocence. Maybe it was because Eliza had not been exposed to some of life's harsh realities. She was used to being protected, but it was difficult to see how she could be blind to the motives of such an opportunist. He wondered if he should also worry about his son. Danny had always been especially perceptive, seemingly born with an instinctive knowledge of his fellow man, but he'd had no chance to learn about women. Lacking all experience, he would keep his illusions, Fred thought sadly.

Would it have been different if they'd stayed in Philadelphia, where Danny would have been exposed to boys and girls of his own background, Fred wondered. Once again he felt himself the prey to ever-recurring doubts at having imposed Clarkston on his wife and family, and all because of the tyranny of his father. It was too late to change anything now. As for Danny, perhaps his illness and deformity would have set him apart more in Philadelphia than in Clarkston. Here, at least, he had the mines and his railroad and Dexter's shops, where he could spend hours working on increasingly ambitious plans.

The morning after Eliza heard from Dr. Sloan, she made Barbara get up at seven o'clock.

"Please get up at once," Eliza said crisply. "I want to be at Mrs. Holmes's house by eleven. And we won't be able to catch the ferry unless you start right now."

An hour and a half later, they were on the ferry. Eliza looked ahead at the feverish activity on the docks and at the wide curve of the bay beyond, melting into distant marshlands. She was struck by the paradox of so much man-made activity taking place within a few hundred yards of wild lagoons and quiet inlets where snipe and duck and other water fowl were feeding and swimming unconcernedly.

She looked at Barbara standing by the ferry rail and frowned. The view should have been provocative enough to arouse anyone's interest, but Barbara, elbows on the rail, chin in her palms, was as usual preoccupied with her own troubles. Something demoralizing had happened to Barbara; her natural animation had been smothered by her self-absorption.

As they left the ferry they saw a variety of carriages drawn up at the dock. They engaged a hansom and asked the driver to take them to Carroll Avenue.

Mrs. Holmes, white haired, plump and cheerful, opened the door. "Come in, come in," she said. "The living room is on the left," and she led the way briskly.

"Sit down, sit down," said Mrs. Holmes, pointing in the general direction of a settee. Ignoring amenities, she came directly to the point. "Now, young lady," she said, looking at Barbara,

"Dr. Sloan says your baby is due in early February?"

Barbara shrugged.

"So that means you have four months to go. If you and Mrs. Clark decide to stay here, we'll work out plenty of things to keep you and the baby healthy." Mrs. Holmes turned to Eliza, jerking her head in Barbara's direction. "It's hard on them. They're generally used to a gay life and young folks. It's hard," she repeated and paused. "But it passes with time."

Eliza hoped she could avoid any long conversation with Mrs. Holmes, but said, "It's kind of you to take us in, Mrs. Holmes."

"Let me show you the guest rooms." Mrs. Holmes rose and started for the stairs. Eliza and Barbara followed her. The rooms each held a fourposter bed, a rocker, a dressing table and a washstand.

"I'm sure we'll be very comfortable," Eliza said, looking around. The rooms were larger but not much better than the ones the maids used in the Clarkston houses.

"I do the cooking," Mrs. Holmes said with a trace of nervousness, glancing at Eliza. "It's just plain food, but we have plenty of fresh fruit and vegetables.

"The charge is eight dollars a week per person, Mrs. Clark, and for the confinement one hundred dollars, unless we have to call in Dr. Sloan. His charge would be between you and him." She turned to look at the moping girl. "As for you, miss, we'll find plenty for you to do. Dr. Sloan and I agree that work and activity are extremely beneficial to women in pregnancy. Do you know how to cook?"

Barbara shook her head.

"Garden?"

Another negative shake.

"Make beds, wash dishes, sweep, scrub floors?"

Eliza's eyes widened and then, as she saw Barbara shrink back, she smiled. She might have underestimated Mrs. Holmes.

"I'm sure," Eliza said, turning to Barbara, "that we will be very comfortable here. I love being out of doors and I'd love to try some gardening."

"Good." Mrs. Holmes smiled brightly. "I'm glad to think you'll be happy. When would you like to move in?"

"Tomorrow," said Eliza.

CHAPTER 8

Philadelphia and Clarkston
November 1890

THE PLANS FOR THE RAILROAD were occupying Fred so completely that his resentment toward Barbara and her mother was fading. He even managed to get along without Eliza with less pain than he would have believed possible. He made plans for financing the railroad by day and discussed the plans for building it with his son by night.

Danny was, in fact, responsible for filling the void Eliza's absence had created. Initially, Fred had planned to go to the New York and Philadelphia banks alone. Then, one day, when he was in Danny's office, he realized that if Danny came along with his drawings and talked to the bankers about the specific plans for the D. S. and S., they might be less concerned about the soundness of their investment. Danny combined an unusual talent for getting on with people, no matter what their occupation or class, with a quiet confidence in his knowledge of mining, engineering, and railroading. Fred sometimes wondered how his delicate son, whose lack of health had deprived him of a formal education, could have developed into such a thoughtful and mature man.

Fred smiled. "I've arranged it so that we see Morgan last," Fred said. "I hope to get the really substantial money from them in New York and I'd like the chance to practice on the lesser banks."

"Who will you go to first in Philadelphia?" They were sitting in Danny's office, a monument of order in comparison with other Clark offices. Danny's chair, especially upholstered to fit his misshapen back, was a high swivel that put him within easy reach of all his charts. Beaverboard, well pockmarked by thumb tacks used

107

to keep working drawings in place, covered a wide desk. Within arm's length were dozens of blueprints tidily rolled up and stacked in one corner; Danny's crutches stood in the corner opposite. Conspicuously placed beside the desk was a cuspidor. Once Eliza had complained to Danny about it, but he silenced her, saying, "Mamma, the workmen are my friends. When they come here, I want them to feel at home."

Fred paused before giving Danny an answer. "I guess I'd say the Bank of North America. But we can't count on the Philadelphia banks for much."

Danny picked up a pencil and toyed with it. "Father," he said, "you shouldn't count on me too much—with the banks, that is. I'm—oh—I'm not very social—and I get along better with workmen than bankers."

"That's nonsense, Dan. You know everything there is to know about the railroad. You'll be invaluable to me."

Danny smiled in polite disbelief. Fred thought Danny had the most engaging smile he knew—straight white teeth, red lips turned up at the corners. Even his eyes behind the thick glasses shone with penetrating intensity and his ears, reminiscent of a faun's, lifted almost imperceptibly when he was amused.

With parental pride, Fred continued, "Besides you're a Clark."

"Even the Clarks can't get away with everything," his son said quietly.

Oh God, Fred thought, how could I have said that? Before he could reply, Norman Bentz came in. Danny waved and half rose from his chair. Gone was the tentative, shy boy and in his place, a man sure of his prerogatives.

"Come in, Bentz. What can I do for you?"

"Danny, I'm having trouble with the steel axles. I think the balance is off. Can I check the design for the journals?"

Danny reached toward the stacked blueprints and drew one out. He spread it on the beaverboard, deftly tacked it in place. Bentz leaned over him as he traced a line in the drawing with a forefinger. The two men were totally absorbed. Fred knew he had been forgotten.

"Oh, Christ, here it is." Danny picked up a pencil and jabbed it at a point on the board. "Now why in hell didn't I see that? I should have changed the lousy diameter when I was experimenting with the length." He ripped a sheet of blank paper from a pad on the side of his desk and began a few rapid calculations. "There. Jesus Christ, that was stupid of me, Bentz. Sorry as hell. Take a good look at this. Think it's all right?"

Silently, Fred began to laugh. The bankers, no more than crass money lenders at heart but priggish New York and Philadelphia snobs on the surface, would be more apt to raise disapproving eyebrows than money if they were exposed to Danny's language. It was, he thought, probably Danny's way of manifesting masculinity. He cast another glance at his son, hunched over the drawing board in a position that accentuated the cruel hump on his back, and, without saying good-bye, left the room.

The nine o'clock train from Clarkston arrived in Philadelphia a little before noon. Fred and Danny planned to meet Jasper Brown, president of the Bank of North America, for lunch. Dexter said he would go to the office. He had more than enough to do.

When Fred and Danny reached the office after lunch, Fred was jubilant. "You won't believe it," he said to Dexter. "We actually got half a million from the old Quaker and I was sure he'd balk at one hundred thousand dollars. Danny was magnificent—confined himself to using just 'hell' and 'damn' and by my count only used 'hell' five times and 'damn' twice."

Danny made a face. Fred laughed. "My boy, you can swear as much as you like when you get back to Clarkston. Just see that you put on the same kind of performance when we call on Morgan. Seriously, Dex, he made that damned railroad come alive— you could practically see the locomotives steaming along the sides of the mountains. He had Brown mesmerized."

Danny shook his head. "Please, Father. That's enough—and I'm dead."

"I know and it's been a long day. We had to wait hours in his office with the close-fisted old gent while he had the papers drawn up. You ready to go, Dex?"

"No. I want to do some more work—I may be quite late. You two go along, and I'll see you at Spruce Street later this evening or in the morning."

"You won't be in for dinner?"

"No. I'll— Don't worry about me. I'll just see you later."

Fred looked at his brother curiously. The brusqueness in Dexter's tone was unusual. He almost sounded evasive. Fred shrugged. Probably he was caught up as he often was in a spasm of work.

"All right, then," he said. "We'll go along and hope to see you later."

Half an hour after Fred and Danny left, Dexter closed his desk, said good night to Wilmer Jackson, the clerk, and walked out the door. One block north of the office he stopped and waited for the trolley.

At ten minutes before seven o'clock Jessie was sitting in front of the fire waiting for Mary to announce dinner. Her setters lay in their usual position at her feet. She heard the pantry door swing hard and looked up to see Katie Malloy hurrying toward her. Startled, Jessie rose.

"Katie, what is it? One of the children—?"

"No, no, mum." Katie was out of breath. "It's you."

"Me?"

"Yes. The men—I'm afraid. Oh, mum, Stephen didn't want me to tell you, but John Murray stopped by. They're just gone with five others to Hanley. I came as fast as I could." The exertion was too much for Katie. She had to stop to cough.

"Katie, Katie, slow down, please," Jessie said. "You'll just bring on more coughing. Now when you get your breath, tell me slowly. John Murray stopped at your house and he and Stephen have gone to Hanley. Is that it?"

"Yes. They're meeting a group from Buck Mountain and Hanley and two foremen from Stockton. Then they're going to Freetown to meet with the rest of the men from all over. And you know, ma'am, they'll be drinking beer up there. They always do. Murray said after they all get together, they'll march on down to Clarkston—to—scare the hell out of Schlenker now that the—the old man's—that's what Murray said—is in Philadelphia."

"Katie, let me think." Jessie walked back to her chair and sat down. "At least Schlenker isn't any more popular with the men

than he is with me," she said, allowing herself a moment's satisfaction.

"Mr. Schlenker, ma'am, John said he heard he got wind of it
and had called the sheriff for help."

He would, Jessie thought. If Schlenker tried to use force
against the men, someone was bound to be hurt, perhaps killed.
She would have to try to reach Dexter and have him talk to
Schlenker.

As the clock on the mantel struck seven, Mary came in to
announce dinner. Jessie shook her head. "Thank you but I'm
afraid I can't come just now, Mary. Perhaps later." Mary went
back to the kitchen.

"How much time do we have, Katie?"

"Stephen told me they planned to leave Freetown after eight
thirty and be in Clarkston at nine o'clock."

"That gives us two hours. Katie, do you know anything more
about it?"

"Well, mum, I hate to tell ye this, but Murray says he wants to
scare yourself as well as Mr. Schlenker. He's been saying for weeks
that he was going to put a crimp in the Clarks' high and mighty talk
about being so good to the men. He says the reading and sewing
classes and Mr. Clark's night school was just an excuse to make the
men forget the Clarks was handing out starvation wages. He used
awful bad language, mum. He says what the men need is a living
wage—not charity doled out to them."

Jessie brushed a strand of hair away from her face. "I haven't
time to worry about that now," she said, aware of a fleeting sense
of guilt. "Katie, do you think they're liable to do any real harm?"

"I don't know." Katie remembered only too vividly what
Stephen had told her about Murray's talk to the miners. That was
two nights before, and she had wanted to go to Jessie then but
Stephen had prevented her. He persuaded her that perhaps the
whole thing would blow over. When the march became a reality,
Katie knew she had to try to warn Jessie.

According to Stephen, Murray had said, "Next time the old
man goes on one of his trips, we'll scare the living bejasus out of
that bastard Schlenker, and after we get through with him— By
the way, boys, if ye find he's resisting ye, there'd be no harm in a bit
of a shove here and there. Mind, I don't want ye damaging him too

bad—just a mite, ye might say, around the edges." There was a roar of approval. "Next, we'll give a little lecture to the Madam, tell her a thing or two about her sainted husband and his charitable ways."

Silence had greeted this. Perhaps that was the reason Murray had shied away from suggesting that any actual harm come to Jessie or her house, or perhaps he realized that, among the men, there were many who were grateful to her for her kindnesses. But Katie was deadly afraid of the combined effects of liquor and passion on some of the men, especially Murray.

"After they get to Clarkston, they're marching on to Stockton to keep the colliery there from opening tomorrow."

Jessie groaned. Dexter's new iron breaker modeled on Clarkston Number 2 was in Stockton. It had taken two years to complete, and Dexter was prouder of it than of anything else he had built. "That's the new breaker, Katie," she said sadly.

"That's why, mum. Everything there is new and most of the Hungarians and Poles coming in don't know anything about it or even how to speak English. The older men there don't want them coming in—they want to keep all the jobs for themselves, but Schlenker says he'll train the Hungarians in no time and they'll work harder and for less money than the Irish."

"The same old story," Jessie said wearily. "The Hungarians and the Poles against the Irish and all of them against Clark Brothers. Where does Stephen stand in all this?"

"I—it's hard to say. I think—I hope he's trying to calm John down. I don't think he knows how much I heard, though I'm certain he didn't want me to come here. But I had to, mum. Stephen's a good man." Katie turned her head away to hide the tears. "But it's the truth, I don't know what gets into his head when he's around John."

They both stiffened as they heard a sharp knock on the front door. Mary came through the hall to open it and Schlenker burst in, brushing past her without ceremony. Katie shrank into a corner as he walked over to stand in front of Jessie, hat in hand.

"Excuse me, Mrs. Clark. It's a serious situation I am here to report. We must be ready for a riot. The county sheriff has appointed me special deputy sheriff. I have power to appoint my own deputies."

"You know how Mr. Clark feels about using force against his men," Jessie said stiffly.

"Ja. But we have no choice."

"Mr. Clark has told you that we will use force only as a last resort." Jessie tried to keep the anger out of her voice.

"That is what we have here. A very last resort." Schlenker paused to weigh his words. With Clark out of the way he could for once have the freedom to deal with the situation as he wanted. He was master now and he was not going to let a woman interfere. "I have had reports that the men are going to march on Stockton but they will come here first. They intend harm, Mrs. Clark. They will do terrible things if they do not know I am in control of all situations. Riot—bloodshed will come. Mr. Clark is in Philadelphia. I have to keep order and I will. I have named Emerson Untermeyer and Philip Clark, Jr., as my personal deputies. That shows the family is involved."

"But they're both useless." The words escaped before Jessie could stop them. "I'm sorry, Mr. Schlenker, but I do wonder if they are qualified to be effective police. Philip is a charming boy, but he's always been delicate and—well—sheltered." Emmy, vacationing in Charleston, would be aghast if she knew her pampered son had been called out to help put down a riot. "And Emerson isn't really a very likely policeman. He's always done desk work—I don't believe he's ever been near a mine—or a miner."

"I do not believe Philip, Jr., is as delicate as his family thinks. And it will not hurt Untermeyer to learn about the miners first hand."

Schlenker wasn't even bothering to hide the fact that he was enjoying his power. She must get in touch with Dexter immediately.

"And you, Mrs. Clark. Right away, you must have the maids close all the shutters. I am directing two deputies to your porch. These are men from the shops and completely trustworthy."

Jessie stood up, putting a hand on one of the setters, who was growling softly. She noticed absently that the hackles on both dogs were up. "Mr. Schlenker, I do not want any police on my porch and I will not close my shutters." Her tone softened. "Mr. Schlenker, these men and their families have been my friends for twenty-five years." She smiled faintly and took a step toward him. "I couldn't possibly conceive of using force against them. Have you been able to get in touch with Mr. Clark?"

"Naturally, as soon as I got the details of the scheme, I tried immediately. I called just after five thirty. The Philadelphia office said he left five minutes before."

"You telephoned him?"

"Of course." Schlenker had been at the colliery when he first got news of the march. A Pinkerton man had rushed into his office shortly after five. He had heard rumors of Murray's plans two nights before, but since they did not seem definite, decided to wait for further details before informing Schlenker. He took the precaution, however, to stick close to the bar and the bartender. This afternoon, pretending to be on a drunken spree, he discovered that the men were to meet in Freetown and march to Clarkston around eight thirty. He reported all this to Schlenker, and after a few careful questions, Schlenker dismissed him and sat silently at his desk, plotting his course. It would be foolish not to go through the motions of informing Clark. He glanced at the clock; more often than not when Dexter Clark was in Philadelphia, he left the office promptly at five thirty. It was now five twenty-six. Schlenker decided to wait a full ten minutes, then telephone. At precisely five thirty-five he rose, reached into his pocket, pulled out a cigar, removed the band, and walked into the adjoining room and over to the wall telephone.

He got through to Wilmer Jackson at five thirty-eight. Jackson told him that Mr. Clark had left to take the trolley about five minutes before and asked if there was any message.

"No," Schlenker said slowly. "There isn't any way to reach him, then." It was a statement, not a question.

"I guess not, sir," Jackson answered, "unless you want me to try—"

Schlenker interrupted him. "Tell him his superintendent called," he said and hung up.

The memory of that conversation was making him faintly uncomfortable. He drew his shoulders back farther and trusted that Mrs. Clark would not sense anything hesitant about his manner. "I assure you, Mrs. Clark," he began.

Jessie interrupted. "Whom did you talk to in the office? Was Mr. Fred there or Danny?"

"Nobody. I left a message with Jackson."

"Then, if they sent a messenger to the house and Mr. Clark comes back to the office, they will telephone you at the Clarkston office?"

Schlenker nodded noncommitally. He wished the woman would leave him alone.

"Please try the Philadelphia office again, Mr. Schlenker," Jessie said sharply. "Meanwhile, I will telegraph Mr. Clark at home."

"Yes, of course," Schlenker stopped worrying. There wasn't any way the mine owner could get here now unless they put on a special train, and he doubted that Dexter Clark would demand that from the Lehigh Valley even if his wife did send him a telegram. "I will post ten men around the shops and the library and twenty across the road at the colliery. You should allow me to post men here, too, Mrs. Clark."

"No," said Jessie firmly. "I'll be better on my own. Tell the office to let me know the minute Mr. Clark telephones." She walked to the front door and showed him out. Once he had gone, she gave a sigh of relief.

Katie came forward from her corner. "It's easy enough to see why the men hate him," she said.

"I didn't exactly hide my own dislike, I'm afraid," Jessie answered. "Good, there's Mary—Mary—"

"Your dinner, ma'am," Mary sounded distracted.

"Never mind that now. What men are on the place?"

"Eroh left at six, Mrs. Clark, and Janos and John went home about five thirty since Mr. and Mrs. Fred and Mr. Danny are all away."

Even Emmie's coachman was off, Jessie thought, and felt a little shiver of fear at the idea that the miners had perhaps realized this. She must at all costs get hold of Dexter. The clock struck the quarter hour. Seven fifteen.

Jessie said, "Katie, you'd better go home to the children. You were very brave to come and tell me, but I don't want you to be found here. Mary, you and Sarah stay in the kitchen. I have some things to attend to that will take me an hour at least and I'll have to go to the office. I'll have some supper when I get home. The front door is locked and I'm sure nothing will happen."

Katie ran to Jessie and gave her a shy little hug. "May the good Lord protect you, ma'am! I hate to leave you."

"Thank you, Katie, I'll never forget it." For a moment Jessie felt close to tears, realizing how much Katie meant to her. "Run along, now." She patted Katie's thin shoulder and looked after her with affection.

There were ten blocks up and two blocks across from the Clark Brothers offices in Philadelphia to the family house on Spruce Street. If the messenger receiving Schlenker's telephone call took a horse car up Walnut and Dexter caught one down Spruce, the relay would take about forty minutes, Jessie calculated. That is supposing that Dexter was at 1512 Spruce. There had been times after his Philadelphia trips when he had seemed less than candid in accounting for certain hours spent away from the office. Jessie remembered pressing him once until he had turned on her savagely and said, "For God's sake, Jessie, can't you understand that I sometimes have to relax and spend an evening at the Club." She had suspected he was not telling the truth, but an instinct for self-preservation warned her not to go further.

She brushed the past out of the way and turned her attention to the task of finding him now. She went into his study and reached behind the French dictionary for the key to the drawer containing his private papers. She had never used it before, but years ago he had told her where it was hidden. Underneath some bills of lading, she found the Clark telegraph code book. It had been deliberately compiled without the usual key for decoding and was often employed for private communications to the partners and the agents. Of course, Schlenker had access to the code, so Jessie would have to be careful not to let him see her telegram. She sat down at her husband's huge desk and laboriously wrote out: WYETH YALLOP WALLPAPER WEISHOFF ZEALOT SCHLENKER WAPITI WYBLIN WALES WEIDNER WALDON WAINRORE JESSIE. Translated the telegram said, "Vital you come immediately. Men uneasy. Schlenker determined to use force. I fear bloodshed. Jessie."

Across the road Schlenker was marshalling his forces. Each of his recruits was given a Coal and Iron Police badge and a gun. Each was told not to fire unless the miners attempted to enter the shops or the colliery. In the office a clerk walked nervously up and down, waiting for the telephone to ring. By now Schlenker was sure Mr.

Clark would not call back, but he had asked the clerk to stay in case he did. Down the hall the telegraph operator, always on duty twenty-four hours a day, lounged in his chair, chewing the battered end of a cigar. He jumped to his feet when Mrs. Clark walked briskly through the door, holding in one hand a folded paper, and in the other the leashes on her setters. She had come in through the back entrance, hoping to avoid Schlenker.

"I want to get this telegram off to Mr. Clark immediately," she said, handing it to the clerk.

She waited until he was through tapping out the syllables and asked him to give the original message back to her. With a quick, "Thank you," she hurried home.

It was five minutes past eight when she opened her front door. Mary came into the hall to meet her.

"I'd just like some poached eggs, toast, and tea, Mary," Jessie said. "Could you please bring me a tray to the living room so I can sit by the fire?"

"Wouldn't ye be better off in the dining room, Mrs. Clark? You can be seen from the road in the living room."

"Nonsense," Jessie said firmly. "So much the better. None of the men I know would hurt me, and I'm certainly not going to act frightened."

It had been more than two hours since Schlenker had telephoned Dexter. Where could he be? She wondered if he had called back and the superintendent hadn't told him she wanted to speak to him. She sat down next to the fire, in a chair that faced the windows; her hand fell on a volume of poetry by John Dryden lying beside her on the table. She fingered the pages absently, leafing through them until the line, "A daring pilot in extremity;" caught her eye. Nothing could be more fitting, she thought to herself grimly. She went on reading: "Pleas'd with the danger, when the waves went high/ He sought the storms; but, for a calm unfit,/ Would steer too nigh the sands to boast his wit." Was that what she had been doing, she wondered. But she had no choice— certainly she had had to send the telegram and what good would it do her to hide?

Mary came in and put her supper on a small table in front of her. Jessie nodded thanks, picked up her fork, and went on reading Dryden's "Absalom and Achitophel." The coal fire in the grate was glowing comfortably, and she had almost finished supper when the clock struck nine. Simultaneously she was aware of a heavy rumbling noise and the sound of tramping feet. On Saturday nights she had often heard a crowd of miners coming back from Freetown singing with boisterous good humor. She hated these weekly excursions and had protested to Dexter. There must be something Clark Brothers could do to prevent the men from spending their hard-earned money on drink.

"Nothing," Dexter had said matter-of-factly. "As you know, all the Clark towns are dry. They can't get a drink in Clarkston, Hanley, Oneida, Shepton, Buck Mountain, or Stockton. But we don't quite own all the region and we don't own Freetown."

Tonight the men sounded neither boisterous nor gay. Jessie listened intently. There was something sinister in the steady, even, restrained murmur that swelled and died. She put her book down but stayed quietly in her chair. The murmur was now an angry roar, mounting in crescendo. Then abruptly, there was the sound of glass shattering and she was shocked into fury by the sight of a brick splintering a pane in one of the living room windows. It landed on the floor five feet away from her chair. The dogs sprang up, barking.

Jessie hurried to the front door, flung it open, stood at the top of the porch steps, and looked down into a blur of faces lit by an occasional kerosene torch. The dogs, trembling, stood on either side of her.

"You cowards." Jessie's voice quivered with disdain. "Attacking a woman alone."

"Oh, hell, you're not alone. We saw the police up there by the shops."

"There are no police here on this place or in this house," Jessie said. "I wouldn't allow them and you should have known that. Is this your way of repaying Mr. Clark and me for the things we've done for you?"

There was a roar from the crowd, and to Jessie's horror a second brick crashed through the other living room window. Above the noise she heard a man's voice say, "Take that for your goddamned charity."

Jessie stood stock still. She could not have moved if her life depended on it. Then she realized someone was trying to speak.

"Leave her alone, men." The voice was not familiar to Jessie. The crowd quieted. The next voice she recognized. It was John Murray's. "That's right, men. She'll learn soon enough that we don't give a damn about her charities. We hate Black Creek Hall and all your lousy handouts at Christmas and the Fourth of July. Save your good works for them that appreciates them, lady, and tell Mr. Clark he'd better agree to bargain with us or his beautiful new breaker in Stockton won't start next week. We want justice and a living wage."

There was silence for a moment. Then, murmuring among themselves, the crowd turned and shuffled out the gravel driveway, down toward Clarkston and the road to Stockton. Jessie started to pray aloud, "Please, dear Lord, don't let the police show themselves." Apparently her prayer was answered, and after a few minutes the sound of tramping feet faded in the distance. They said they were on their way to Stockton. Did Schlenker have police posted there? And what good would a few hastily gathered raw recruits do against that mob of angry men? They could only inflame them further. She turned back to the house. Mary and Sarah were standing in the hall, shaking. "Glory be to God, Mrs. Clark," Mary said breathlessly. "Are ye all right?"

"Certainly, I'm all right, Mary," Jessie said impatiently. It would never do to let the maids know she had been terrified. "Please pick up the mess on the floor. I don't want the dogs to cut their feet on the glass. And see if you can find some cardboard to patch the windows until morning."

She glanced at the clock and wondered how many times she had looked at it during the evening. Nine twenty. Possibly the walk to Stockton might work off some of the men's anger. Meanwhile, if they confined their violence to smashing windows, everyone should be grateful. They had a good deal of right on their side and Dexter must be made to see it. Why, oh, why hadn't he called?

"I'm going to bed, Mary," she said. "You and Sarah had better go, too. There won't be any more trouble tonight."

Jessie slept fitfully. Once she thought she heard a shout but ignored it. Some time later she had just fallen into a really deep sleep when she was wakened by five unmistakable shots and several screams. Jessie turned over and listened anxiously. When she heard no more, she put it all down to a bad case of nerves. She heard the clock strike ten thirty, then eleven o'clock. Just after that the colliery whistle blew, sounding the fire signal.

After the destruction of Clarkston Breaker Number 2 three years before, Dexter had set up a system that would alert the Freetown Fire Department as quickly as possible.

Bert Drummond was on duty the night of Murray's march. When the colliery whistle blew, it took him just twelve minutes to reach Freetown, bang on the firehouse door, and rouse the firemen asleep upstairs. It took the men another five to slide down two poles to the engines and horses and set off at breakneck speed for Clarkston.

The front doorbell chimed as Fred and Danny were lingering over their coffee in the drawing room. They had had a good dinner, and Fred, although he missed Eliza, was luxuriating in the comforts of the family home and the knowledge that his contacts in the city were as important to Clark Brothers as Dexter's engineering skills.

Fred pulled out his watch. Eight thirty. He looked at Danny questioningly and got up to answer the bell. The maids were upstairs clearing the table.

"Never mind, Nellie, I'll go," he called as he went into the hall.

A Western Union messenger was standing outside. Fred took the telegram and walked back into the drawing room. "It's for Dexter—from Clarkston." He tore the envelope open. "From Jessie."

"Jessie?" Danny asked.

"But it's in code," Fred said. "And the code book's at the office."

"We'd better go right away." Danny reached for his crutches. "Something drastic must have happened to make Aunt Jessie send a telegram—and in code."

"I don't understand this at all. Are you sure you're up to going back to the office?"

Danny nodded. Fred started toward the front door and called back, "I'll go round the corner and get Patrick."

They arrived back at the office at nine o'clock. When they saw a light in the rear, they assumed Dexter was there, still working. They were surprised to find only Wilmer Jackson.

"Jackson, you still here?" Fred said. "Is Mr. Dexter—?"

"Yes, sir—I mean, no, sir. Mr. Dexter left just after you did," Jackson said.

"Oh, well, I need the code book." Fred walked into his office to the right and unlocked the middle drawer. "You hear anything from Clarkston today, Jackson?"

"Yes, sir." Jackson followed Fred into his office at a discreet distance. "The superintendent called. Around five thirty—just after Mr. Dexter left. Didn't leave a message. Just to say he called."

Fred was sitting down transcribing the telegram. "Danny, look here. Jessie says to come immediately. Wait until I get the rest of the thing decoded."

Danny swung in and faced Jackson. "Jackson, you sure the superintendent didn't say anything else?"

"No sir. That's all."

"Listen to this, Danny. 'Vital you come immediately. Men uneasy. Schlenker determined to use force. I fear bloodshed.'"

"I hope to God she's stopped him," Danny said.

Fred turned to the clerk. "Jackson, have you any idea at all where Mr. Dexter went?"

"I don't know, sir. He took the Walnut Street horse car like most nights when he leaves the office."

Fred looked at Danny and bit his lip. With one exception, nobody in their circle lived in West Philadelphia. He tried to still his suspicion and found he couldn't. "I'm afraid I'd better try and find him," he said to Danny. "Uh, why don't you stay here with Jackson and I'll drive out Walnut Street with Patrick."

"I'm coming too, Father," Danny said and, to Fred's acute discomfort, added, "How old do you think I am?"

Fred, nonplussed, answered, "All right. Of course."

"If we find him, shouldn't we get a special train put on?"

"Yes," Fred stopped to consider. Unfortunately, he was positive they would find Dexter. "I'll call right now and save that much time." He walked to the telephone in the main office, cranked the handle, and asked Central for the Lehigh Valley Railroad. He told the clerk who answered that he had an urgent message for William Fisher, the president of the road. He said there was a chance of bad trouble at Clarkston. He and his brother must get there before morning. He hung up feeling relieved and confident that Fisher would supply transportation. No matter how much they fought over rates, heads of railroads and coal companies had a habit of sticking together in times of trouble.

After they settled themselves in the brougham, Fred gave Patrick the address, 4031 Walnut Street. He glanced at Danny, imperturbably looking out the window. It was impossible to sit there in silence until they arrived.

"Danny," Fred said tightly, "there are facets of things in a man's life that aren't very easily explained. I'm afraid this is one of those times that, well, it's going to be damned awkward."

Danny looked at his father.

Hedging, Fred asked, "You know where we're going? To Mrs. Robinson's," he said, lowering his voice and instantly thinking how unnecessary that was. The man on the box couldn't hear them, and anyway he probably knew precisely where they were going and why. But Patrick was a good servant and could be counted on to say nothing. Nothing to the family at least. What he might say to the other servants was a matter for uncomfortable conjecture.

To Fred's vast relief Danny spoke. "But," he said deliberately, "she's a widow, isn't she?"

"Yes."

Fred said no more for the moment. The clip-clop of the horses' shoes on the road filled the silence inside the carriage. Then finally, Danny spoke. "Don't worry about it, Father. What Uncle Dexter does when he's away from Clarkston isn't really any of our business, is it?"

"No," said Fred. My God, he thought, he had certainly under-estimated Danny. Perhaps in spite of his illness Danny knew more than Fred realized. He was, after all, twenty-four years old and must be aware of his own growing maturity. Fred cursed his inability to discuss such things with his son. I'm every bit as inhibited as my father was with us, he thought. But then we were lucky. There were five of us brothers and no subject taboo.

Danny stole a sidelong glance at his father. He was as amused as he was annoyed that his parents seemed to think he was some sort of eunuch. He looked at his watch. It was nine fifty as they drove into the shallow crescent driveway in front of Gertrude Robinson's house.

Patrick reined the horses in, and Danny said briskly, "I'll wait here, Father. No point in my delaying you."

"All right," Fred said gratefully and stepped onto the ground. Danny was perfectly right, he told himself as, pulses pounding, he walked to the door. What business was it of theirs? After all, if he had been married to Jessie, he too might— Impatiently he cut off the thought and put his mind to the task ahead.

He rapped on the front door three times and stepped back to wait. After an eternity he heard Gertrude's voice call out, "Who is it?"

"Fred. Fred Clark," he called and wished his heart would stop jumping.

The door swung open immediately. "Fred!" Gertrude gasped.

Involuntarily, Fred was aware of the stunning impact of her beauty. She was dressed in her favorite color green, the light behind her silhouetted her graceful figure and the hall chandelier shone down on her gleaming red hair, accentuating the delicacy of her sculptured face. The sensuous woman behind the brilliant eyes and generous mouth could not be denied.

"Something's wrong—" Gertrude started and stepped back, motioning Fred to follow her.

"I really don't know," Fred said vaguely. He didn't want to alarm her. "We have—that is, Dexter has a telegram from Jessie that sounds urgent. And I wondered if by any chance Dexter could be here?" You fool, he thought to himself furiously for the third time that night. Why didn't you just ask the question outright instead of trying to put a conventional frame around it? He felt himself blushing.

"Yes, he's here, Fred. Come in." Gertrude led the way to the living room. Dexter was standing in front of the fireplace looking anxiously toward the door. He came forward the moment he saw Fred. "Fred! Good God! What's happened?"

"I don't really know, Dex," Fred said again, feeling like the second lead in a drawing room comedy. "We have—that is, you have—" What on earth was wrong with him? Couldn't he say anything straight? "There's a telegram from Jessie. Here." He pulled both copies of the telegram out of his pocket and handed them to Dexter. "I called the Lehigh Valley Railroad. They'll try to have a car and an engine ready by midnight to take us straight up."

"Yes." Dexter turned back to the fire, read the telegram carefully, then put his elbows on the mantel, and let his glance search the red coals. He looked sick and Fred saw that his shoulders were trembling. But in thirty seconds he managed to pull himself together and wheel around.

"What about Schlenker? Have you tried to reach him?"

"No, damn it," Fred said. Why hadn't he thought of telephoning Schlenker while he was still in the office? "Jackson said he called earlier, at five thirty, but that you'd just left. He didn't leave any message. I'm sorry. I should have tried to call him when I went back to the office to decode the telegram. It didn't occur to me then. I wanted to reach you as quickly as I could."

Dexter made an obvious effort to concentrate. "We'll have time to try him when we go to the office now—and we'd better telegraph Jessie that we're coming." He turned to Gertrude. "Jessie says the men are up to something and she's afraid Schlenker may use force. If he does, all hell is apt to break loose. I'll let you know as soon as I can what's happened." He walked to the hall and took his overcoat off one of the hooks beside the big mirror. "Come on, Fred." And then, glancing through the door at the waiting brougham, he saw his nephew. "I'm glad Danny's here, too."

Fred was reassured. Dexter was a captain who had regained, after a moment's faltering, complete command of his ship. "He can be a big help with the men," Dexter continued. He walked over to Gertrude and took both her hands in his. "Good-bye, my dear," he said in a voice barely above a whisper.

Together the brothers went out the front door and climbed into the waiting carriage.

The Lehigh Valley was remarkably efficient about putting on a special engine and car. It was waiting for them at the Ninth and Green Street Station when they drove up at a quarter to twelve. It left five minutes after the passengers boarded and arrived at Clarkston at 3:02 A.M. It was an interminable three hours for Dexter. His brother and nephew dozed fitfully as the engine hurled its single passenger car around the curves with more than usual violence. The engineer was making the most of his instructions to get them to Clarkston as fast as possible. When they left Bethlehem and started up through the mountains, the car lurched so that Dexter had to hold onto the arms of his seat in order not to be thrown on the floor. How can Fred and Danny sleep, he thought enviously. He must put Gertrude out of his mind until he'd settled Schlenker and the men.

God damn the miners. Dexter nearly said it aloud. They were responsible. For everything. For the loss of Gertrude—and he thought again with renewed agony of his whispered good-bye. He had known then that the end had been decided for them and had wondered what it would be like to die. The miners—blast their souls!—had taken away the only solace he had ever known.

He moved restlessly in his seat. The train was emerging onto the plateau beyond Hazleton and Fred and Danny were stirring.

"Uh, where are we?" Fred mumbled, stretching his arms. He opened his eyes and stared out the window. "Good God!" he said and pointed a trembling finger.

The horizon was suffused with pink.

"There aren't any more wooden breakers around to burn," Dexter said wearily.

"It's not in the colliery or near the shops," Danny said, peering through the windows. The train was slowing to a stop "It's in the center of town. It's on Main Street." He looked at Dexter appalled. "Black Creek Hall."

"My God, let's hurry!" Fred had his overcoat on and was halfway to the door of the car.

"You two go on ahead of me. I'll be along." Danny motioned to his father and uncle to go quickly. Both men hesitated. "Please," Danny said urgently. "The conductor will help me off, and after that I'll be fine. Go on now. Hurry. I'll wait in the shed until you send someone. The stove there is always going."

This time Jessie knew she could not remain frozen by anxiety and fear as she had when Clarkston Breaker Number 2 had burned. Then Dexter had insisted he wanted her to stay home, and she had obeyed him. Tonight she must make her own decisions. She jumped out of bed at the colliery signal. Four long and two short blasts. She stood at the window long enough to see the guard gallop past on his way to Freetown. She would have a few minutes before the fire engines reached Clarkston.

Jessie ran to her wardrobe and tore a plaid wool dress off a hanger. Her stays were neatly laid out on a chest. She stared at the laces for a second. She had never been outside her bedroom without a corset. She thought briefly of the women who had crossed the plains to go West with their men and had fought the Indians. At that moment Dryden's lines flashed warningly through her head. Never mind. She couldn't worry now about coming close to danger and those pioneer women would not have bothered with stays at a time like this. She pulled her nightdress over her head, flung it in the direction of the bed, drew on her flannel drawers that were lying beside the abandoned stays, pulled a camisole off a hook, ripping a seam in her haste. With a supreme effort of will she ignored the tear and refrained from stopping to pick up the crumpled nightdress that had slipped from her bed to the floor.

Once she had pulled on her black lisle stockings and knotted them just below the knee, she laced up her oxfords. At the sound of the fire engines clattering down the hill, she rushed back to the window. The three horses pulling the forward engine were galloping full tilt, the driver using all his strength to hold them back. Jessie could see the fireman on the back platform, hanging on with one hand while he stoked the engine with the other. They turned the corner by the colliery and dashed out of sight into Main Street. Jessie held her breath. The fire must be in the village, perhaps close to the stables. She started for the stairs. On her way she automatically turned up the gas. She stopped in the hall, grabbed Dexter's ulster off a hook and put it on. The coat overwhelmed her, making her look ridiculously small. Impatiently she turned up the sleeves, wrapped the ulster around her as best she could and headed for the door. Outside she crossed the road toward the colliery gates, where two deputy police were on duty.

One of them was Boris Lotsky, a foreman who worked in the shops. "Mrs. Clark!" He stared at her in astonishment.

"Boris. I'm glad you're on duty. I must alert Mr. Welles—the horses."

"Horses?"

"I'm afraid the stables may catch fire—if they haven't already."

"We hear it's Black Creek Hall."

"Oh." The stables were next to the Hall. "We can't waste a minute," Jessie said. "You must come immediately." She turned and started down the hill, half running, the foreman following her in a daze.

It was past twelve when she reached Black Creek Hall. The two-story structure would shortly be reduced to rubble. The firemen seemed to have abandoned it and were playing their hoses to right and left on two nearby houses and on the stables. So far they had managed to limit the fire to the hall, but the sparks coming from it were terrifyingly large. Jessie pushed through the townspeople, all of whom made way for her the moment they recognized her. She asked each person she came to if they had seen George Welles, the Welsh stable manager, in charge of all horses and mules. Finally a carpenter told her he had seen Welles with several of his men about an hour ago, evidently on their way to the horses. Jessie pushed on in the direction of the stables. Beyond them a quarter of a mile down the road, she saw a collection of horses and mules huddled together in the pasture. The horses from the fire engine and tender were tethered nearby.

"I see them. They safe, Mrs." Boris had spotted the horses at the same moment.

She turned with a sigh of relief to speak to the company storekeeper, who was standing beside her. "When did it start?"

"About nine thirty, they think. Must have been smoldering before it broke out. Broke out all over about eleven."

When Jessie realized they had started it right after they came to the house, she wanted to weep. Curiously, she felt no anger—only pity for the men and an infinite sadness for Dexter, who would once more be crushed that his men, who should be grateful to him, had caused such devastation.

"At least the horses are safe," Jessie said, staring at the Hall, still in flames.

"Welles, he here now." Boris was tugging at her sleeve. The stable manager came up behind her. As she turned to greet him, he said, "It's a bad job, ma'am, but all the horses and mules are out—and now it may not spread to the stables."

"I'm relieved they're safe," Jessie said. "That's the main thing I was worried about. When did you first know about the fire, George?"

"The whistle blew at eleven. I found two of my men right away and we came to the horses. They must have set the fire in several places. Everything—all at once—went up like a fire-cracker."

Jessie was beginning to feel sick. "Will you be able to take care of the horses for the rest of the night?"

"Yes, ma'am. Three of us will be on duty all night. We'll tether them at the far end of the field when the fire engines leave."

"Then I may as well go home, I think. There's nothing I can do here."

"No, ma'am. I'm going back to my horses and mules."

"Yes." Jessie turned to Boris. "Would you take me back now, please?"

Mary was waiting for her at the front door. Realizing the maid must have been terrified by the noise and the smell of smoke, Jessie said, "It's Black Creek Hall, Mary, but don't worry. I believe they have stopped it from spreading and the horses are safe."

"Black Creek Hall. I'm sorry, mum." Mary knew how much the Hall meant. "I was scared half to death, mum, but I didn't know what was on fire until the telegraph boy came a few min-utes ago." She handed Jessie a telegram.

"It's from Mr. Clark," Jessie said, opening it. "It says they're leaving around midnight. That means they should be here—" Jessie broke off and walked into the living room to look at the clock on the mantel. "It's just after one now," she said returning to the hall, "and if they left at twelve, they should be here about three."

Mary looked at her with compassion. The strain was begin-ning to tell. Jessie's face was tired and drawn and her peculiar getup made her seem pathetically vulnerable. "Hadn't you best go back to bed, mum?" Mary asked.

Jessie shook her head. "No—I'll wait up. Mary, here, take this thing"—she shrugged off the ulster—"and hang it up. Thank you I'll wait in the living room."

The fire had taken its toll. By the time Dexter and Fred arrived at the scene, one fireman was suffering from bad leg lacerations received soon after the fire started, and a second fireman had suffered third-degree burns.

It took no more than fifteen minutes for Dexter and Fred to decide there was little they could do at the scene of the fire itself. They were told about the injured men and took a grim satisfaction that the first aid classes Dexter had added to the curriculum of his night school in the Hall were probably responsible for saving the firemen's lives. Fred talked to a man from the Construction Department who thought the horror of the fire might stop any further sabotage on the part of the miners. He suggested the troublemakers might have overreached themselves. Schlenker, who was at the scene giving directions, had characteristically assured Dexter that he personally had everything under control. It was tacitly understood by everyone that some miners must have set the fire. That, by itself, was probably the most powerful deterrent against future violence for the time being.

But neither Dexter nor Fred had yet suspected that it was Schlenker's hastily assembled police force that had goaded the arsonists into action. Murray, a past master at stirring up men's passions, had shrewdly realized the superintendent was playing into his hands. Marching down the hill, his men became increasingly furious at the sight of the deputy police posted twenty feet apart, guarding the colliery. The crowning indignity was that two were stationed in front of the Hall. Murray waited until the crowd was assembled. Then he walked up the steps leading to the front door of the Hall, and as he reached the top, he turned to face his followers. Holding up an arm, he shouted, "Is there a man among ye who goes armed?"

"No," the crowd roared back as one.

"Yet ye've noticed every twenty yards, the Clarks put a man with a gun to guard their stinking mines. And two here to guard the lousy place they use to justify the starvation wages they hand out. Men with guns all over the place. And the Clarks, always saying they don't mean us no harm and don't want no bloodshed. What do they want, then? What say we teach the Clarks a little lesson?"

Another roar of approval went up.

Murray held up his hand for silence. "Wait a bit, boys. It so happens ther's some of us is not surprised at this. Quiet now. 'Tis entirely possible we'll be doing no more marching this night. Back in the shadows, all of ye." The men drifted back to stand under the trees.

Murray walked down the steps and over to one of the guards. "Now, me lad, I don't believe in people being hurt. It's your gun I'll be having before ye do any damage." Murray held out his hand. The guard was Philip, Jr. Because Black Creek Hall seemed the safest possible place for a guard to be, Schlenker had posted him there.

Philip, Jr. drew back nervously. "No—no." He was stammering.

"Come on now, lad. Give it here." Murray moved forward menacingly.

"D-d-d-don't. I'll shoot." Timidly, Philip, Jr., raised the gun. He wasn't exactly sure how it worked.

Murray dropped to the ground as one of his men attacked the deputy from behind. In the shuffle, Philip, Jr., accidently fired two harmless shots. His fellow guard, a clerk from the store, fired three more to alert the deputy police at the colliery. But the warning came too late. While Murray was holding everybody's attention two men stole around to the back of the Hall. They were Jamie and Tim O'Neill.

Two weeks before at McShane's Bar in Freetown, Murray had taken the O'Neill brothers aside. Jamie, the older O'Neill, worked as a foreman in Hanley and his younger brother, Tim, as a miner's laborer in Oneida. Both were loyal members of the Knights of Labor and, in Murray's eyes, trustworthy.

"When we make the march," Murray had told them, "I want to be prepared. Mind you, no violence unless they force it."

The brothers had kept their eyes trained on Murray.

"This is what we'll do." Murray had leaned over close to them and kept his voice to a whisper. "You know the professor who's at the small building at the rear of Black Creek Hall and his daffy new assistant—it's the little chemistry building I'm speaking of."

The brothers had blinked their eyes, visualizing the rear of Black Creek Hall. There was a door in the middle with two windows on either side and to the right a smaller building, the office of Professor Oswald Freulich, where classes in mining and civil engineering were held during the day. When these classes were over, the professor and his assistant usually left to go home to supper. They returned to Black Creek Hall at seven P.M. to hold additional classes for those men unable to attend during the day-time.

"Now, as you probably know, the Professor and his assistant leave at five thirty and come back to the Hall at seven. While they're gone, a can of kerosene will be placed just inside the door of the chemistry building."

Murray had looked around the bar. Neither brother moved a muscle.

"Now, you're well acquainted with the Hall itself?"

The brothers had nodded solemnly.

"This is what we'll do if it comes to it. You both know where the newspapers are stacked—on the big table in the library."

Again the brothers had nodded. A large classroom took up the center space on the ground floor of the Hall. There was a library to the right and smaller classrooms to the left.

"Now the instant the first shot is fired, the both of you run like billy be damned to the chemistry building in back of the Hall, pick up the kerosene, go into the Hall through the back door, get the newspapers, soak them, and leave them at opposite ends of the classroom."

Murray had paused thoughtfully and scratched his chin. "After you get them lit—" A smile spread over his face. "You know that looney new assistant of the professor's almost blew up the chemistry building once. Who's to say he won't be blamed for this? That is, indeed, if it happens. But you've got to remember—you don't make a move until the first shot is fired We don't want the wrong people getting hurt this time."

Neither Dexter nor Fred found out that night exactly what had happened; they learned only that there seemed to be no chance of the fire being accidental. After Dexter finished talking with Schlenker, he looked around for Fred and found him with the stable manager.

"Hello, George," Dexter said, addressing Welles. "I gather the horses and mules were led out right away."

"Yes, Mr. Clark. It is that I attended to immediately. Mrs. Clark, she came down the hill to see also that they were safe."

"Jessie!" Dexter turned and stared at Fred.

"Perhaps we'd better go and see how she is," Fred said.

"I'll go alone," Dexter said, feeling his heart begin to pound. "Have you sent anyone for Danny?"

"Yes. I spotted Janos and asked him to get the buckboard and go for him. I think they'll be home any time now."

"All right. I'll go along."

Dexter walked up the hill. He came to his front door and resolutely pushed it open, wondering as he did why it wasn't locked. Jessie was sitting by the dying fire, asleep, her head resting against the side of the wing chair. Something had happened to the windows; two of the panes were covered over with cardboard. He had known all along that Jessie would stay up, waiting for him. She looked cramped and very tired. He would have to wake her up and hope that whatever questions she had could wait until tomorrow.

He walked to her chair and stood looking down at her. She was awake instantly. "Dexter! Thank the Lord you're here! I didn't hear—but I left the door unlocked for you."

He stared at her. She looked small and wounded and he was suddenly filled with a sense of tenderness and guilt which obliterated temporarily his desolation over Gertrude.

"Are you all right, Jessie?" he said quietly.

"Yes. And you?"

Dexter nodded. "When did it start? Schlenker said something about the men coming to the house."

"I think it was nine o'clock. Katie warned me—that's why I sent the telegram."

Dexter gestured toward the front of the room. "What happened there?"

"They hurled bricks through. I told them they should be ashamed of themselves."

"You what?"

"Oh, Dexter, you have to do something for them. You see, now I know how they feel. When they threw the first brick, I was furious. They were all on the driveway, so I went out and spoke to them, and then they threw a second one. That was when I got frightened. It was horrible. I felt angry, trapped, and helpless all at the same time. And that's the way they feel, and that's why they have to have some way to bargain, to be able to state their case for higher wages. Don't you see?"

Her plea was startlingly reminiscent. Gertrude had said something like that to him years ago. Was it impossible for women to understand the difference between right and wrong? He looked at her helplessly. "What do you want me to do?"

She took a step toward him and put her hand on his arm. "You look tired. And so am I. First, perhaps we'd better get some rest."

"All right. Jessie, do you know that they burned Black Creek Hall to the ground?"

"Yes." Jessie started for the stairs.

"And you still want me to bargain with men like that? Arsonists. Lawbreakers?"

"Yes I do," said Jessie firmly, continuing up the stairs. "But first I want you to fire Schlenker."

By the time she got to bed, Jessie was numb with fatigue. Her whole body ached, but sleep for which she longed eluded her. Her legs, her arms, her brain felt as taut as though she were stretched on a rack. Schlenker would be dismissed, she thought with grim satisfaction. But there was something else to worry about—the long gap between her telegram to Dexter and his to her, saying he was on his way.

With a sudden flash of intuition, she guessed: Dexter had been with Gertrude. For years she had refused to admit a tiny suspicion that lurked in the background every time Dexter went to Philadelphia. Now, at the end of this terrible day, she was as certain as if he had confessed it to her himself. How could she have been so blind? I've been a fool, she thought.

Of course, he had always liked talking with women, so perhaps it wasn't surprising that he had apparently had some kind of a flirtation with Gertrude. Jessie was able to tell herself this after wrestling with a fear that was both new and nebulous.

Then with sudden insight, she asked herself why he had never mentioned that he was seeing Gertrude. Wouldn't it have been normal for him to have said something about it? Come to think of it, Dexter had often been evasive about how he spent his time in Philadelphia.

Was it impossible that anything more than a good friendship had been between them? Her thoughts crept back to her own wedding night and the days and nights that had followed. She had been afraid of the passion in Dexter then: He seemed to have feelings he couldn't control. But, by now, all these years later, those feelings seemed to have been tamed with age and responsibility. He hadn't the time or the energy for them. Why, it had been—Jessie bemoaned an accurate memory and sat bolt upright in bed, her heart in her throat. It had been just eight years since Dexter stopped trying to enter her bedroom. And it was just eight years ago that he found the library job for Gertrude. He told her about that. As a matter of fact, that time when he came back from Philadelphia he told her about Gertrude and the details of what he had accomplished for her with considerable satisfaction. He also said several times that she had a wonderful mind, that he thoroughly enjoyed talking to her.

After that first time he rarely mentioned Gertrude. What a fool I have been, Jessie thought. Of course he wanted more than talk, and I was so stupid I never caught on. There was a pounding in her ears as she tried to imagine Gertrude responding to Dexter's embraces. How dare she! Jessie thought, and how dare he? It's my fault, I guess, she thought in despair. I've rebuffed him every time he came near me. Is there something wrong with me? She threw herself down on the pillow in a paroxysm of jealousy. Dry, wracking sobs shook her body. Tomorrow, she thought, I'll try to figure out what to do.

Finally she turned on her side, exhausted. The spasms in her arms and legs subsided and she slept.

Four days after the fire, on the pretext of having to attend a business meeting, Dexter went back to Philadelphia to see Gertrude. In the few days he had been away from her, he managed to overcome his sense of guilt and convince himself that it made no difference that Fred knew. He had told himself unrealistically that Danny was probably too inexperienced to understand what it was all about. In any case, both Fred and Danny would be discreet. The real task would be to convince Gertrude that they should go on as before.

Armed with a bottle of the same burgundy he had taken to her on that first night, Dexter arrived at her house in the late afternoon. When she opened the door she looked more beautiful than ever.

"Come in, Dexter." She smiled but with sadness. She led the way silently to the living room, took the proffered bottle with a nod of acknowledgment, and put it on a table.

Dexter knew then it was going to be very bad. Unsure how to begin, he said, "Gertrude, I—"

She held up a hand to stop him. "Before you say anything, I want to tell you what I've done—or rather arranged. I resigned from my position on Monday, and I've put the house up for sale."

"Good God, Gertrude, what are you saying?"

"Just that, my dear," she said gently. "I'm going to New York. I've been promised by the library here that I won't have any trouble securing a position as a librarian there, and I've written Alicia Cummings—you remember? she was a good friend of mine in school—and I asked her if I could stay with her temporarily. I'll just rent something at first—at least until the house is sold."

"You can't—you can't do this." Dexter's eyes were filled with pain.

She stood up and went over to him, placing her hands lightly on his shoulders. "I must. We've known always, haven't we, that we couldn't allow ourselves to go on forever."

"No!"

She shook her head and drew him to her. He put his arms around her hard and buried his head on her shoulder. Silently, he began to weep.

"Don't," she was scarcely breathing. His arms were holding her in a vise.

He released her and stepped back, quickly brushing his hand across his eyes. "Gertrude," he said brokenly, "my darling, I can't—" He stopped and made a desperate effort. "Look, you're being overly sensitive. Fred—it doesn't matter, you know." He couldn't bring himself to say more.

"Dexter, it does matter. I—we have to, well, start over. I've thought about this very hard. It was too easy to relax, to let you love me and to let myself love you. I've thought about Jessie, too. You know, my dear, she's the perfect wife for you—"

"Never mind Jessie," he said impatiently. "She's, well, Jessie."

"I know. And underneath you love her. But let's not talk about it anymore." The sparkle came back into her eyes. "Let's have the most wonderful evening on earth." She came across the room and kissed him lightly on the cheek. "Would—would you take me out to dinner—to a place we've never been?"

"Of course," he said dully.

They said good-bye the next morning. All during the evening Gertrude had teased, cajoled, and argued with him and made him forget that when this time together was finished, they might never see each other again. They spent the night in each other's arms, breakfasted together, and then said good-bye.

"I'll send you a letter at Christmas every year," Gertrude said at last. "To your office, marked personal, and I'll tell you everything I've done during the year. Will you do the same for me?"

He nodded, unable to speak. Then he pulled her to him, kissed her hair, and fled, forcing himself not to look back.

Dexter plunged into his work with an intensity that startled even Fred and Danny. In an effort to kill his yearning for Gertrude, he forced himself to concentrate on an equation for an improved traveling grate. He was frequently so absentminded that Jessie had to send to his office to remind him it was lunchtime. A strong instinct of self-preservation told her not to question him or let him know she noticed that his trips to Philadelphia were less frequent. Certainly she never mentioned Gertrude's name. Maybe it was all over—whatever it had been. In the future she'd better take a leaf out of Eliza's book. With all her faults she had managed to keep Fred as much in love with her today as he had been when they were first married.

One Sunday sitting beside Jessie in church, in the middle of the sermon, Dexter slapped his knee and with a loud "By God, I've got it," stalked down the aisle, along the road, and back to his shops. That evening his triumph was so great, Jessie had not the heart to rebuke him for his impiety.

Little by little Dexter acknowledged to himself Gertrude was probably right. Since his break with her Jessie seemed to be making brave efforts to please him.

Brought up in a family of teetotalers she had always preached abstinence, but one night he was astonished to find a bottle of claret sitting in a silver wine coaster in front of him. Quickly he checked the places at the table. Only two, and they never had wine when they were alone. "Is there something special about today, Jessie?" he asked, pushing her chair in.

"No. You're wondering about the wine, I suppose. You seem to enjoy it so much when we have guests that I thought it might be a good idea to have it more often," Jessie said airily.

"That's—that's wonderful." He sat down wondering what had come over her.

He noticed that she almost managed to finish her glass. Perhaps she discovered that she liked it. Conversation during dinner wasn't strained, but it wasn't entirely natural, either. The bottle of wine seemed like a sentinel. Somewhat uneasy, Dexter followed Jessie into the living room for after-dinner coffee. He had just begun to relax when Jessie stood up. "Dex, how about taking a walk around the garden. It's such a beautiful night." She looked timid as she said it.

"Why, all right, Jessie, if you'd like to." He was mystified. Then a sudden, terrible thought struck him. Could she possibly suspect anything about Gertrude? It would be easier for her to talk about her suspicions in the dark.

He looked at her warily as he followed her out the door. They walked a few steps, and to his astonishment Jessie slipped her hand into his. "We—we have had a pretty good life together, haven't we, Dex?" Her voice was faint.

"What? Why, uh, yes. Of course." What was this? he thought. Had the wine gone to her head?

"I've liked being your wife, Dexter." Jessie whispered it.

Good God! he thought and tightened his hand on hers. Was it

really possible that she knew? But how could she? Then he realized that if by some unlikely chance she did, there would be no recrimination, no questions. Instead she was reaching for his affection and he thought leadenly, I cannot respond, not now, not so soon after—and he looked at the woman by his side and realized how much courage these innovations, and that was what they were, had taken. Jessie had finally perceived his need, and now that she had, there was no way in the world for him, at the moment, to reciprocate. Time, he thought, he must have more time.

"We'd better start back, Jessie." He said it as gently as he could. "It's a nice idea to take a walk after dinner. I feel pleasantly sleepy and relaxed." He turned to smile at her and hoped he sounded convincing. His heart was pounding and he was having difficulty breathing. "So much so that as soon as we get back to the house, I'm going straight to bed and to sleep."

In the days following, Jessie continued to make a few tentative gestures of affection. She seemed less sure of herself, more open to compromise, and finally months later when the pain of separation from Gertrude became less acute and desire began to be a part of his life again, Jessie even permitted him into her bed. Her heroic efforts to respond touched him. This was not duty on her part, he thought; it was love. Now it was he who must overcome his reluctance. He took her tenderly and, afterward, held her gently in his arms. For the first time in their lives, she slept there briefly. When she woke, he kissed her forehead, murmured, 'Thank you, Jessie," and was gone.

CHAPTER 9

San Diego
November 1890–February 1891

BY THE END OF HER SECOND DAY at Mrs. Holmes's Eliza had acquired a series of aches and had discovered the existence of muscles she had never before thought about. By the end of the first week, she was so exhausted she had lost all desire to sightsee. It seemed to her now that the housework she had always taken for granted when someone else had done it was a necessary evil but that a garden had a soul. She was astonished to find one day that she got much satisfaction from a well-grown fig or peach.

Barbara made a minor effort to help around the house, but as soon as she could, she would escape and bury herself in a romantic novel. The girl had changed alarmingly. In Clarkston she had always been well turned out. Now, as the months wore on, her blond hair lost its life, her lovely complexion turned sallow, and the luster in her blue eyes disappeared. She continued to look at herself frequently in the mirror, but Eliza could see that she did so with increasing disgust. One day, she turned to Eliza, snarling, "I hate this damned baby. I hate myself and my body, the way I look. I hate Griswold for what he did to me. I hate that stupid old Mrs. Holmes, and if she doesn't stop telling me what I should do for the good of the baby, I'll hit her."

"Barbara, don't—you'll just make things worse. I know it's hard. It's hard on me, too; I don't like being away from my family."

"It wasn't my idea to come here." Barbara flung herself on the bed sobbing. Eliza watched her coldly.

"Stop it. Immediately. This is an ordeal that has to be gone

139

through, and self-pity isn't going to help. You'll have to learn to bear it." Eliza walked out of the room.

After that Barbara made no more complaints. She merely endured her confinement with bad grace. Eliza couldn't bring herself any longer to feel affection for her, only a distant sort of pity.

At five thirty Monday morning, February third, Eliza woke up. Across the hall she could hear the sound of moaning. She got out of bed and crossed to Barbara's room. Mrs. Holmes was standing in the doorway.

"How long have you been having pain, Barbara?" Mrs. Holmes asked.

"I don't know. But it's awful. I can't stand it."

"I think you'd better go for Dr. Sloan, Mrs. Clark," Mrs. Holmes said.

Eliza nodded and went to dress. Dr. Sloan and his wife had been in San Diego for the past week. After Mrs. Holmes had alerted him that Barbara's time was approaching, he decided this was a good moment to take a brief vacation. They were staying at Horton's, and two nights ago Eliza had mustered the courage to go to the hotel to have dinner with them. She was relieved not to run into anyone she knew.

It was six-fifteen A.M. when she started walking briskly through the early morning fog. At the hotel she sent a message to Dr. Sloan to come immediately. Then she left to go straight back to Barbara.

"I'm going to ask you to help me," Mrs. Holmes said. "I want to take one of the leaves from the dining room table upstairs. I can carry it up myself without any trouble, but I do need help to get it under Barbara's mattress. It will make her labor easier later."

Eliza helped Mrs. Holmes carry the board upstairs, and together they slipped it on top of the springs, replaced the mattress, and remade the bed. Barbara was sitting in a chair moaning. Mrs. Holmes hurried downstairs and came back carrying two heavy cords, each with a loop at one end.

"What on earth are those for?" Eliza asked.

"For the contractions," Mrs. Holmes answered. "I tie them to the bedposts, and she can ease her severe pains by pulling hard."

"The pains can't get any worse than this." Barbara had heard her and was frightened.

"If you try to relax and go along with them, they'll hurt less," Mrs. Holmes said to Barbara without sympathy. The doorbell rang. "That'll be Dr. Sloan." She came back two minutes later followed by the doctor.

He walked directly over to Barbara, who was huddled in her chair in the corner. "Pains coming regularly?"

"Yes." Barbara looked at him beseechingly.

"Now, don't worry. That's a good sign—not a bad one. I want you to get in bed and if you'll help us and do what I say, the ordeal shouldn't be too long."

Two hours later Barbara's forehead was covered with sweat and her mouth was dry. From time to time Mrs. Holmes told her to pull on the ropes.

Soon the pains were following each other in rapid succession.

"I feel as if—it's like—beaten with—a fence rail," Barbara groaned.

Eliza came back into the room after a short walk. Mrs. Holmes was giving Barbara occasional whiffs of chloroform. The doctor, standing opposite, was trying to prevent the emerging head from tearing his patient. Eliza noticed the expression of dismay that came over his face with each of Barbara's pains. It was wonderful, Eliza thought, to find such a sympathetic doctor. Only later did she realize that Barbara, in desperation, had dropped the loop and lodged her right hand in the seat of Dr. Sloan's trousers. With each severe contraction she had given him an excruciating pinch.

Eliza heard the baby's first cry at the same time that Dr. Sloan said with relief, "A fine, healthy boy."

He handed the child to Mrs. Holmes, who wrapped him in a Shetland shawl. Mrs. Holmes asked Eliza to carry him in the next room and put him into a waiting basket. Eliza looked down at the tiny wrinkled face. It was a caricature of Griswold. Without a doubt it was his child. The words in a letter of Fred's crept into her mind. The letter arrived early in her stay at Mrs. Holmes' and she had put it aside in anger. Fred had said, "Griswold has admitted to his part in the affair. However, I gather his attentions were not discouraged. I would like to warn you again. I do not trust Barbara or her family and I want you to be very careful."

She looked down at the infant cradled in her arms. My sister's grandson, she though in awe. She put the baby in the basket as Dr. Sloan came in.

"Mrs. Clark. My word, you look shaken," the doctor said cheerfully. "You're taking this harder than the mother. She's gone off to sleep. It's all over now, and she'll forget about it in a couple of weeks and go back to living a normal life."

He picked up the baby. "He's a pretty nice little boy and he's going to make my childless couple in Santa Barbara very happy."

"I suppose I should be glad." Eliza's voice was low. "But— it's just that I didn't know I'd care so much. You see—he's my sister's—my great-nephew."

"Yes, of course, I understand. But hasn't your sister just had a baby of her own? Hard as it is, I think this baby will be much better off with a couple who is longing for a child than with a mother who, I'm afraid, might resent everything about it."

Eliza nodded. "But at least, do you think I could hear about the baby from time to time?"

"No. In these cases, Mrs. Clark, you have to cut the ties completely, right from the start. If you don't, it might destroy the parents' peace of mind and, as a result, the infant's."

His words were final, but she felt compelled to add, "You mean when you take him away tomorrow or the next day, we'll never know what happens to him, whether he gets sick or is badly treated or . . ." Her voice trailed off.

"Never," the doctor said. "And the baby's parents will never know anything about you or Miss Shipley or the baby's antecedents. It's a case of both sides having faith in my judgment." He paused, looking apologetic. "But I feel confident this baby's a lucky one."

Eliza went to her room where she took five hundred dollars in bills from her bureau drawer and put them in an envelope. She came back to the doctor and handed it to him. "If we can't do anything about this baby's future," she said, "at least we can make a small contribution to your foundling hospital. Perhaps this will help you find homes for others. It's—it's my husband's gift."

"That's extremely generous. Thank you, and thank your husband for me. This will be used entirely for children in my care and I am grateful." Still holding the baby on his left arm, the doctor slipped the envelope into his waistcoat pocket. Then he put the baby back in its basket and turned to Eliza. "Good luck to you, Mrs. Clark. And don't worry about the baby's future. He'll be all right."

Two weeks later the Santa Fe bound for Chicago and the East pulled out from the San Diego Station. Eliza and Barbara were in a drawing room.

"Well, that's over," Barbara said. "I don't care if I never set foot in California again."

She was looking better, less sallow and plump. The last thing Mrs. Holmes had shown her was how to bind up her breasts to help dry up the milk.

She looked at Eliza appraisingly. "I guess this has been hard on you, too, Mrs. Clark."

Eliza felt old, tired, and mean. "From now on, Barbara, don't count on me to get you out of any more scrapes. You can't plead ignorance any longer."

"No use your getting upset now that it's all over, Mrs. Clark," Barbara said firmly. "Anyway, no one's going to have to worry about me in the future. I'm going to get a husband one of these days. He'll be rich and he won't be Griswold."

She settled back in her chair and gazed out the window, looking almost contented. Eliza, watching her, repressed a sharp, unexpected sense of foreboding.

CHAPTER 10

Clarkston and Chicago
Summer 1893

BY THE TIME DR. HERBERT ARRIVED, the Stavniki child had strangled to death. The doctor took a smear of the dead child's throat and would take it to Hazleton to the laboratory to be analyzed, but there was no doubt in his mind about the cause of death. He felt too much pity for the parents to be angry with them, but why hadn't they called him five or six days ago?

The mother's face was drawn and still. She stood by her dead son's bed, her chin jutting forward, her fierce gray eyes staring straight ahead. Her only gesture was to bow her head on hearing the pronouncement of death from the doctor. The miner, Stavniki, was equally stolid until without any sound he began to weep. Tears dropped down his cheeks, accentuating the careworn traces on each side of his face, its gray, unhealthy hue, and stubbly beard.

"I must ask a few questions," the doctor said gently. "How many days, how long has the child been sick?"

The parents looked at each other.

"This is Saturday," the doctor said. "Can you tell me what day of the week you first noticed he didn't feel well?"

"I think Monday," the mother said. "But"—she lifted her hands helplessly—"it ws only sore throat. He come to me then and said throat tickled."

"Did he complain again Tuesday? Did he cough?"

"No. He didn't cough until Wednesday. Then I gave him medicine. Syrup. It helped."

"What about fever? Backache?"

144

'I noticed fever Thursday. He ached, too. But"—she closed her eyes—"he had this many times. He always got well"— she drew in a sharp breath—"until now."

"What day did he begin to vomit? Do you remember?"

The miner's wife nodded. "Friday, yesterday in afternoon. Then all during the night—"

"Was he having trouble breathing?"

"Yah. Very bad all night. I put on the croup kettle and stayed up all night."

"I think that's all I need to know, Mrs. Stavniki. Except which of your children have been with other children recently? This is terribly important. You see I am quite sure your child died of diphtheria."

Stavniki's eyes widened. He spoke for the first time. "Diphtheria. What is it?"

"It's an infection in the throat," the doctor answered, "and children can catch it from each other. That's why I want to know where Billy and your other children have been lately."

The doctor knew all six children, including the three eldest, who were in their early teens. They were beyond the age of greatest susceptibility to diphtheria, but there was always a chance that one of them might be a carrier. Billy was four, and his five-year-old brother and six-year-old sister were particularly vulnerable. The doctor must find out what other children had been exposed to them. He prayed it would not be very many, or the town would be in for an epidemic. He looked at the broken parents and felt wretchedly futile. If only they had called him right away.

"Mrs. Stavniki, do you know if any of your children have seen other children within the past week?"

"I kept the little ones home since Monday because Billy sick. Both big boys go to mines and Theresa helps me here."

"All right," the doctor said. That at least was something to be grateful for. "Now, I must ask you all to stay in the house or yard until I let you know. I think we can get your food and whatever you need delivered. We—we will take Billy away as soon as I can arrange it."

Stavniki and his wife looked at each other like frightened animals. The doctor took the woman's hands in his. "God will take care of Billy," he said gently. "As soon as I leave, I'll ask Father Aust to come. Now, listen, please, very carefully. We must try everything possible not to spread this, and you both can help. If anyone else in the family shows a sign of fever or sore throat or stomach upset, put the sign in the window and I will come immediately."

The doctor left the culture at the Hazleton laboratory with instructions that the results of the test be sent immediately to Clarkston. In twelve hours it would be possible to make a diagnosis.

Diphtheria, he realized, if it struck in force, could result in the death of a third or more of the town's children. On his way back to Clarkston the doctor was thinking with frantic urgency about the measures he must take to prevent disaster. He flicked his horse with the whip. He was so sure the Stavniki child had died from diphtheria, the analysis was a mere formality. He must set up an examining clinic as soon as possible, and he would have to enlist the help of Jessie Clark immediately. From whom, he wondered, had the dead child caught the infection?

The maid ushered the doctor into the parlor, and Jessie, who had been sewing upstairs, came down in a few minutes.

"Dr. Herbert," Jessie said cordially. She was always glad to see Francis Herbert. Two years ago Dr. Grunig, tired of the limitations of Clarkston, had decided to move to Philadelphia and extend his practice. When he was replaced by Francis Herbert, Jessie was delighted; she found him more cooperative than the rigid German. She smiled at the doctor and said, "It's always nice to—"

He interrupted her. "I'm sorry to arrive so unexpectedly, but I'm afraid I have some bad news."

"What—?"

"A little while ago the youngest Stavniki child died, and I have taken a culture of his throat to Hazleton, so my diagnosis is not yet confirmed, but I am positive it was diphtheria."

"Oh no. Not diphtheria." Jessie sat down. "What must we do? Are you really sure?"

"Yes. The false membrane strangled him."

"The false membrane?"

"Yes, you see, the diphtheria bacilli enter through the mouth and infect the tonsils, the palate, and the back of the throat. The bacilli spread into the windpipe and the blood vessels and grow into a false membrane. This can ultimately strangle the victim. The only cure, once the disease has progressed this far, is tracheotomy—but in this case the parents didn't call me even in time for that."

Jessie, listening intently, nodded. "But if the Stavnikis had called you in the very beginning, couldn't you have given the child the diphtheria antitoxin?"

"Yes," the doctor said sadly.

"And that child might be alive. That's almost more than I can bear."

"I know," the doctor said. "But very few people suspect anything at first. This means we must set up a clinic instantly in Clarkston and examine all the children. It means also we should get an immediate supply of antitoxin. I'm sure they have it in Philadelphia at the Pennsylvania Hospital if Mr. Clark can persuade them to part with at least fifty units."

"I'll get in touch with Fred immediately," Jessie said, "Dexter's in Chicago."

She stopped and turned. Mary was standing in the living room doorway looking frightened.

"What is it, Mary?" Jessie said.

"It's Pat O'Meara, mum. He's outside and he saw the doctor's buggy. He wants Dr. Herbert to come right away. He says Jimmy—that's the three-year-old—can't breathe right."

Jessie paled. "The Fourth of July picnic. Last Saturday. Every child in the town was there."

"Of course." The doctor rubbed his eyes. "I'd forgotten. Can you get notice to every family in town to come to the miners' hospital at ten o'clock tomorrow morning? I'll have to set up a special clinic. The first thing I want to do is take a throat culture of every child under six. Later we'll do the older ones as a precaution." He stared at Jessie. "What did they have to eat?"

"At the picnic? Why, it's always the same. Lemonade and ice cream."

"No more effective way of spreading the disease," the doctor said and went out.

By three that afternoon four new cases had been reported. By nine the following morning there were a total of thirteen, most of them severe. Dr. Herbert stayed up three nights running, going from one family to the next.

Immediately after the doctor left, Jessie sent for James Smith, the superintendent who had replaced Schlenker. She gave him a notice to be copied and posted everywhere. The notice required all parents to bring any children under six to the clinic the next morning. Then she set out to recruit Eliza for extra nursing help. She found her on her knees, weeding. Ever since her visit to San Diego, Eliza had been an avid gardener.

"Eliza," Jessie said. "We are facing an epidemic. Of diphtheria. All of us must help. I would like you to be at the hospital at ten in the morning."

Eliza rocked back on her heels and looked up. "Diphtheria! Oh God. When—?"

"The Stavniki child died this morning. And then while Dr. Herbert was talking to me about him, Pat O'Meara came to fetch him because little Jimmy was ill. That makes three cases so far, and I'm afraid there may be many more before tomorrow. I must go now. I haven't yet told Emmy and we'll need every bit of help we can get."

"Jessie, wait." Eliza scrambled to her feet. "I can't help you. Anna is here with both children. I'm sorry, but the children mustn't be exposed."

"Oh. I forgot Anna was here. I'm afraid," she said slowly, "that Freck may already have been exposed at the picnic."

"My God, Jessie, of course."

Eliza's three-year-old grandson, on whom Fred positively doted, had been allowed to go to the picnic, but his baby sister was kept at home.

"I'm afraid that's where the diphtheria began—on the Fourth of July. I'm afraid the damage is already done."

"Jessie, I'm sorry. I'm certainly not going to take any more chances."

"Perhaps you should send the children home with Anna."

"I don't know what I should do—particularly when you tell me Freck's already been exposed."

Jessie's face froze. "You'll have to do as you think best, of course, but your grandchildren are not the only ones in danger."

"They're what matter to me," Eliza said as fear tightened the muscles around her stomach. "And I'm certainly not coming to the hospital."

"As you like." Jessie shrugged her shoulders. The future of the town was at stake, and Eliza was unable to rise above her anxiety about her own grandchildren. With an exasperated shake of her head she turned and marched out of the garden.

Eliza moved her cramped legs and stood up. The tightness in her stomach contributed to a paralyzing sense of panic. I must talk to Anna and Fred immediately, she thought. This would be a frightful blow for Fred. He idolized their little grandson and was already dreaming of the day when he would become a member of Clark Brothers. That hateful Jessie. She can't order me around. It's lucky she hasn't any children of her own. Always busy with the hospital and the miners and Sunday school and playing God in this wretched place. I wish to heaven I hadn't let Freck go to her old Fourth of July party. Eliza walked toward the house. It will be Jessie's fault if Freck catches diphtheria, she thought despairingly. Please, God, don't let him catch it.

It was twelve noon when Jessie's telegram arrived in Chicago. Dexter was in his room at the Grand Pacific Hotel writing letters. He gave the bellboy a nickel and waited until he shut the door to pen the envelope. After he read it, he shook his head and muttered an oath. Why did telegrams from Jessie always have to augur disaster?

Just an hour ago he had left Danny and Tommy Malloy at the Exposition in the Transportation Building. The purpose of the Chicago trip was twofold: Dexter had come to report on his new automatic stoker before the meeting of the Mining and Mechanical Institute, and Danny was there to supervise the showing of his two model engines.

Three years before, Danny had finished building his train, described in trade papers as "the smallest locomotive in the world." It had a tiny engine capable of doing considerable work. With its tender, it weighed 618 pounds and had seven flat cars. A reporter for the trade paper, *Locomotive Engineering*, who had ridden on the train with Danny, wrote, "With 140 pounds of steam, the engine started from a dead stop and ran 2,500 feet to a dead stop again in one minute and 40 seconds, over 20 miles an hour."

Danny had Tommy Malloy in Chicago with him to help set up the train. Tommy's aptitude for engineering had earned him a scholarship at Lehigh University the following September.

All three men were overwhelmed by their first sight of Chicago. The monstrous grain elevators that Dexter pointed out worked in almost the same way as the breakers in Clarkston and the bridges swinging on their turntables, complicated substitutes for the more commonplace drawbridge. But it was the Exposition that made the city a special paradise for engineers this year.

Until Jessie's telegram arrived, Dexter and the two young men had four days left—time enough to see almost everything they wanted. Dexter walked through the crowd. Soon he spotted Danny and Tommy talking with a mechanic at the Small Train Exhibit. Without ceremony Dexter pulled Jessie's telegram from his pocket.

"I'm sorry to interrupt," he said curtly, "but this just came." He read it. "'Four cases of diphtheria here. I fear epidemic. Can you cut short your stay? Jessie.'"

For a moment Danny said nothing.

"I'm sorry," Danny said finally and looked at Tommy. "Our work's just about finished anyway, Tom?"

"Yes," Tommy said reluctantly. "Everything's in order. I've checked the engine and all the cars—side, top, and bottom. They look fine."

"How soon do you want to leave, Uncle Dex?"

"I think we could manage tomorrow—three days ahead of schedule."

Dexter had been exhausted at the end of every full day of sightseeing and had fallen into bed at night and gone solidly to sleep. But that night when he went to his room, after dinner, sleep eluded him. Jessie's telegram had triggered a host of memories.

It was three years since he had seen her, but the picture of Gertrude remained as vivid as the first night he made love to her. Terrible as the pain of their separation was for him, he had kept his promise and they exchanged nothing more than a note at Christmas.

He lay in an agony of longing, frustration, and resentment.

He almost felt that Jessie rejoiced when she could summon him home with bad news. His mind told him he was being unjust, but he was awash with self-pity and loneliness.

By the time Dexter reached Clarkston, Jessie and Dr. Herbert had established an almost military medical routine. Jessie had collected the most competent of the employees' wives, organized regular visiting rounds, arranged to have food and supplies brought to the stricken families, and set up extra beds in the hospital. No one who was ablebodied got much sleep.

On Monday the nineteenth of July Mary brought Jessie's breakfast tray upstairs to her as usual. To her astonishment Mary found Jessie still in bed.

"Mrs. Clark, are you all right?" Mary put the tray on the table and went over to Jessie's bed.

"I don't know. I tried to get up, but I felt dizzy."

Mary noticed that Jessie's eyes were bright and her face was flushed. It wasn't surprising, considering the fact that she had been on the go day and night. Mary stared at her and wondered what she should say next.

"Would—would you like me to help you up, mum?"

"Yes. I mean no. If you'll just stay here while I try again—" Jessie's voice trailed off and she shut her eyes.

Mary suddenly realized Jessie was seriously ill. "Mrs. Clark," she began and clutched the Virgin's medal around her neck. "Mrs. Clark," she said again firmly. "I am going for the doctor. I'll send Sarah up to stay with you. And you're not to move from that bed."

"Yes." Jessie opened her eyes for a brief moment and whispered the word.

By now Mary was thoroughly frightened. She hurried downstairs and sped through the hall to the kitchen, told Sarah to go upstairs immediately and see that Mrs. Clark stayed in bed until she came back with the doctor. Then she ran down the road to the hospital.

Dr. Herbert came back with Mary half an hour later. Jessie's fever was very high. "Mrs. Clark, when did you first start feeling ill?"

Jessie blinked. "Oh, I guess I felt a little tired yesterday."

"And the day before that?"

"I don't re-mem—know," Jessie answered.

The doctor turned to Mary, standing nervously at the foot of the bed. "Have you sent for Mr. Clark?"

Mary shook her head. Because of the town crisis Dexter left every morning very early to meet with his superintendent.

"Please get someone to go for him now. And then come right back. I'm going to give Mrs. Clark an injection when you return."

All through the week the doctor and Jessie fought for her life. She had spasms of terrible coughing and vomiting. She gasped for breath, and on Friday her lips were blue and every breath was a struggle. On that day the doctor never left her side. He would be just about to do a tracheotomy when her gasping would ease a little and she would drift off to sleep.

Dexter spend the day in her room, sitting in an easy chair by her bed, remorseful that he had thought so harshly of her when she summoned him from Chicago. When a fleeting thought of Gertrude insinuated itself during his long vigil, his anxiety for Jessie rejected it guiltily.

At seven Friday night Jessie coughed and brought up a piece of the loosened membrane that had been strangling her. The doctor, who had been afraid he would lose his patient, looked at Dexter encouragingly for the first time in days. By eight o'clock Jessie's muscles began to relax and her lips regained their normal color. During the days and nights of fever Jessie drifted in and out of sleep, and in retrospect it seemed to her that she had managed to relive the better part of her life. Her childhood, spent in the huge Jenkintown house just outside Philadelphia, the lessons: French from Mademoiselle; piano lessons from Mr. Altschul, the German master; singing lessons from the Italian, Aurelio Giorni; drawing lessons at the Academy of Fine Arts in Philadelphia, where she and her sisters had gone one winter; learning to school her horse in the meadow with her father ("You have the best hands I've seen, Jessie"); posture or the importance of dignified carriage ("Stand straight, Jessie, balance the book on your head"—her mother talking); art appreciation (Giotto is the father of art); the training in social custom (at home calls with Mamma, cards left on the silver salver); instruction on becoming a wife ("Submit, Jessie, you must submit, but in time . . ."); the fire; her wedding night (the blessed hoop skirt that eased an agony of embarrassment); the garden where the wedding took place; the fire ("Where, oh where, is Dexter?"); the sound of the screaming fire engines; Black Creek Hall in ruins . . . Then she was awake to dream no more.

The toll the diphtheria epidemic took in Clarkston was severe. Out of its population of 2,500 adults and infants, the town lost 137 children and 3 adults. Jessie was ordered to stay in bed for five weeks after the crisis and it took her until after Christmas, a full six and a half months, to recover. As a result, Dexter's burdens almost overwhelmed him. He did his best to delegate Jessie's duties to other women, but he found nobody as skilled as she in running the hospital, the Sunday school, sewing classes, children's classes, and countless other activities.

By the week after New Year's Jessie was once more back on her feet and Dexter full time in his office. He tried once haltingly to tell her how impressed he was by the devotion the miners' wives and families had shown her, but she was embarrassed and changed the subject. Finally he said gruffly, almost as embarrassed as she, "Well, Jessie, you've made me feel very humble. I guess like everybody else in Clarkston, I don't know what I've done to deserve you." It was the greatest compliment he had ever paid her, and Jessie had to make a valiant effort to hold back her tears.

CHAPTER 11

Clarkston
March 1894

DEXTER WAS IN HIS OFFICE trying to catch up with long neglected European correspondence when his superintendent knocked.

"Sorry to interrupt you, sir," Smith said, "but I have something I think I ought to report to you."

"Oh, what is it?" As Dexter motioned to Smith to sit opposite him, he had a fleeting memory of that day many years before when he had first learned from Schlenker of trouble among the miners. There was something about Smith's appearance that gave him a sense of foreboding.

"Well, sir, you remember you've always told me to keep an eye on John Murray and to report anything he did that seemed out of the way."

Immediately Dexter stiffened. "Yes?"

"Well, after that, I spread the word around—just to a couple of miners that I knew I could trust and I swore them to secrecy like you told me—"

"I don't believe I told you to tell anyone, Smith."

"Uh, no sir, I guess maybe you didn't, but I know I can trust these men, and frankly you made quite a point of watching Murray, and I didn't see how I could do that alone. God knows he isn't going to confide in me."

Dexter grimaced. "I suppose you're right. Go on."

"Well, one of these men, that I spoke to, came to me and he said he thinks Murray acts suspicious. Murray and Malloy are drinking buddies and whenever Murray gets a couple of beers in, he talks about the small pay and long hours at Clark Brothers.

154

Like—well, the rest of the country, he's all in favor of the eight-hour day."

"Damn the man, anyway! I hope to God Malloy's not involved. It would kill Mrs. Clark if I'm forced to discipline him."

"I don't think so, sir. My man indicated that Murray just uses Malloy as a listening post to rave and rant to, and that Malloy tries to quiet him down."

"Malloy's a decent man but a weak one," Dexter said. "He always seems to be down on his luck. I wish I could be as sure of his loyalty to me as I am of his wife's to Mrs. Clark."

"His leg gives him a lot of trouble and he's not as strong as most. Anyway, to get back to Murray, I think he's got to be watched—"

A knock at the door interrupted Smith. Danny pushed the door open, looked at both men, in particular at his uncle's angry expression and said, "Damn, I'm sorry, guess I'm interrupting— I'll come back later."

"Wait, Danny," Dexter said, "maybe you'd better stay and hear this."

Danny hobbled over to a chair at the side of the room.

"It's about Murray—John Murray," Dexter said. "You know how I feel about him. Smith tells me he's agitating for an eight-hour day."

"No law says a man can't agitate for what he wants, Uncle Dex," Danny said cheerfully and watched his uncle's expression harden.

"Go on, Smith," Dexter said.

"Well, it's hard to put my finger on it exactly, but evidently Murray got a lot of inside information from the Iron and Steel Workers Union about the Homestead strike. He must have friends in that union and he's looking for ways to bring that sort of trouble here."

"Let him," said Dexter grimly. "Frick smashed that union completely."

"Maybe," said Danny, "but you remember there was a lot of blood spilt."

Dexter nodded. The Homestead strike was the bloodiest in history. When the members of the Amalgamated Association of Iron, Steel and Tin Workers refused new wage cuts at Homestead they were supported by the rest of the Homestead labor force. Henry Clay Frick, the company's general manager, instantly shut down the plant and refused to negotiate with the workers entrenched behind a barricade of steel bars. Frick filled two barges with three hundred armed Pinkerton men, had them towed up the Monongahela River, and for thirteen hours a battle raged on the plant's waterfront. The strikers temporarily overcame the Pinkertons, who, in return for safe conduct, gave up their arms. But Frick would not accept defeat. Six days later, he appealed successfully to the governor of Pennsylvania to mobilize eight thousand state militia and take control of Homestead. Under this military protection Frick imported scabs, and the Carnegie Company filed charges of rioting and murder against the union leaders. The cost was seven strikers and three Pinkerton detectives dead.

"Homestead, thank God, is a long way from Clarkston and we still have no union here," Dexter said.

"But that's the point, Mr. Clark. Murray—and I don't like to tell you this—but he keeps comparing you with Frick and he is constantly reminding Malloy and the others that there already is a union in the bituminous mines in the western part of the state, and he keeps preaching that unionism is the only way the workers will get what they deserve."

"Oh, I know, I know," Dexter said wearily, "but it won't reach the anthracite miners. If we can just keep outsiders from stirring up our men, we'll be all right."

"I think that's what Smith is trying to tell you, Uncle Dex," Danny said quietly.

"Yes, sir, I'm afraid I wouldn't put it past Murray to bring in an outsider. He talks a lot about a man called John Mitchell in Illinois. He was president of his local lodge of the Knights of Labor, but when the United Mine Workers was organized three years ago, he joined them, and Murray says he's one of the strongest organizers in the country."

"Oh, for God's sake!" Dexter's patience had given out. He was on his feet and shouting. "Murray says, Murray says. I don't give a damn what Murray says. That man is nothing more than a goddamned agitator, and I want him out of here, out of

Clarkston. He's a rabble-rouser and dangerous. Smith, fire him. Immediately."

Smith paled. "But I—"

"No ifs, ands, or buts. Fire him. Right now." Dexter sat down. He was shaking.

Smith, who plainly was frightened, hadn't the faintest idea how to defy Dexter's authority, but he knew he should not fire Murray. He looked at Danny imploringly.

"Smith," Danny said, "what would happen if you fired Murray?"

Smith took a deep breath. "There'd be a strike."

Danny said, "He's right, Uncle Dex. You see, you'd be firing a man without cause."

Dexter's hand slammed down on the desk. "Like hell I would! You know who was responsible for burning Black Creek Hall."

"But," Danny said calmly, "you can't prove it."

Dexter said nothing for a moment. His anger seemed to evaporate. He turned his chair and stared out the window. Then finally he said, "No, I can't. I can't even say it. It was Katie, of course, who told Jessie and Jessie made me promise I'd never betray her." He swung his chair around and faced Smith. "Smith, I'm sorry—let's just forget this conversation ever existed. But I want you to continue to watch Murray, and I want you to report everything you learn to me. I don't know what the country's coming to, but I do know I'll fight the unions until the day I die."

CHAPTER 12

Clarkston and Philadelphia
July–October 1894

DANNY TOLD THEM ABOUT HIS ENGAGEMENT on the way back from the church. He watched his parents carefully, eager for a reaction. To his astonishment, they appeared to be stunned into silence.

"Aren't you going to say something?" he asked.

Eliza looked at Fred's stony face and knew it was up to her. She had a sick feeling that Danny's course was irrevocable. Her mind dashed back to the picture of Barbara sitting on the train as they left San Diego and saying complacently, "I'm going to get a husband one of these days. He'll be rich and he won't be Griswold."

"I'm sorry—it's such a surprise. I had no idea that you— Danny, I'm sorry I didn't—and, of course, congratulations are in order." Eliza reached across Fred for Danny's hand.

"They are not. I'm sorry. We'll discuss this when we get home."

"What?" Danny looked at Fred in bewilderment. He had never heard his father sound so outraged.

"We will discuss it later," Fred said, giving each syllable equal importance.

The ride home took eight minutes. In the minds of the occupants of the carriage the time stretched out interminably.

"I think you and I had better go to my study, Danny," Fred said.

Eliza opened the front door. Her mind was racing. She must stop Fred. If there was a rift between father and son, it would be more than she could bear.

158

"Fred, I want to talk to you a minute. Danny, darling, go on ahead to the study. I'll only be a second."

The parents were silent as they watched their son swing along the hall on his crutches. After Danny closed the door behind him, Fred said, "What is it, Eliza? He'll marry Barbara Shipley only over my dead body." The coldness in his voice went through Eliza like a shaft.

"But, Fred. Oh, please God, at least listen to him. Didn't you feel his happiness when he told us? Fred, Fred, he's in love, I think— Don't hurt him. Maybe all we can do is to pray that it wears off."

"I think you'd better stay out of this, Eliza." Fred wheeled around to stride toward his study.

Danny was seated in a chair by the fireplace, staring at the flickering coals. Fred took the chair opposite, reached into the humidor on the table beside him, handed one of his best Infanta cigars to Danny, and took one himself. That done, he rose to stand in front of the fireplace, feet apart, looking down at the deformed figure in the leather chair.

"I'm sorry, Dan," Fred said. "You cannot marry Barbara Shipley."

"Cannot? Exactly what does that mean?"

"Simply that your mother and I are unable to allow it." Fred was careful to make his tone civil.

"Father, we're living at the end of the nineteenth century. You can't forbid me and Mother wouldn't. I'm of age, you know."

"That doesn't make any difference, Danny," Fred said and instantly regretted it. For God's sake, keep this reasonable, he told himself. "Look, I'm sorry, but what you have to understand is that this would be a completely unsuitable marriage."

"Because Barbara's normal and I'm not." The words hit Fred like a bullet.

"Oh, my God, no." Fred was close to shouting. "It's not you—it's her. She's—she's impossible. Danny, she's just out to get a Clark. She—"

"Even a cripple, eh?"

Fred walked over to the window at the opposite side of the room. This was much worse than he could have imagined possible.

"Danny, please, please believe me. You're worth fifty of her. That's what I'm trying to tell you. Barbara Shipley is hard, ruthless, and unscrupulous. She would make you utterly miserable." He chanced a look at his son. Danny was staring at him through thick glasses, his upper lip curling.

"You seem to think I don't know what I'm getting into. I know all about the trip to California—and Griswold. Poor Griswold. I wondered at the time why Aunt Susie and Uncle Sumter shipped him off to the navy. I must say I didn't lose much sleep over it. I sort of gathered they were both more interested in their new baby than in him and that he was rather in the way."

"Wretched little squirt. Never did like him." Fred said.

"Anyway, Father, all that is ancient history. Barbara told me everything ages ago."

Of course she had told him, Fred thought. No fool, Barbara. She wasn't going to risk having either of Danny's parents spring an unpleasant surprise on her captivated fiancé.

"Of course, she told you," Fred said. "Better she than your mother or me. Oh, I'll grant you she's not stupid. She probably also told you that she was too young and too innocent to know what she was doing."

"Well, she was. Good God, Father, she was only eighteen at the time. She still blames herself, and she told me Mother was wonderful to her in California."

Fred winced. "All right, Danny. But, well, you haven't had much experience with the opposite sex and I—"

"I don't know what you mean by experience, Father, but I'd rather that you didn't go around thinking I'm completely unaware of what goes on between men and women because I'm not. And to be even more blunt, I am not inexperienced."

A muscle in Fred's left cheek twitched. It had cost Danny a great deal to say that. Looking at him now, covertly, Fred could see that he was deathly pale. Danny's so-called "experience" must have been with Barbara. It would be fatal to say anything more against her. "Danny, I'm sure Barbara has many fine qualities." He hesitated as he gagged over the words. "And I certainly don't think that Barbara's adventure when she was young and innocent should be held against her all her life but—"

"But what, Father?"

"Danny, there's such a thing as being too unworldly—maybe too idealistic."

"Father, I've been in love with Barbara for over a year, and I think I know her pretty well. And by the way, I've noticed that when you and Uncle Dexter get in a tight spot with the men, you think I'm worldly enough to handle things. Now, when it's a question of my own life, you treat me like a child."

"It's not exactly that," Fred answered slowly. He felt he was floundering and he damned the day that Barbara had been born.

"Danny, you know as well as I do that Caldwell Shipley has never been much use in the business. Your uncle and I have tried him in a dozen different positions, but he never really measures up. I'm not blaming the man for that because he's quite content with his place in the firm and I suppose he's decent enough, but his wife is—forgive me, but the only adjective I can apply to her is vicious."

Danny looked away. "I'm not planning to marry Mrs. Shipley," he said.

"I know that, Danny," Fred said. "But you see you've just fallen into the trap she laid for you. Mrs. Shipley has already arranged to have two of her daughters marry Clarks and without a doubt she's been planning your engagement to Barbara for months. If you marry Barbara, she will have accomplished exactly what she wants. She is very shrewd about making up for her husband's incompetence. For a long time she has wanted to have each of her three daughters called 'Mrs. Clark' with everything that means in Clarkston and Philadelphia."

"Father, you—" Danny stopped. His voice was barely audible, and Fred noticed with pain that he had curled his legs up under him and was clenching the sides of the chair with his hands to keep from shaking. "I fail to see what the hell is so wonderful about the Clarks that they should set themselves above other people."

"Well, the Clarks have a pretty well earned position, Danny," Fred said. "I think even you would have to agree that the Clark record of breeding, education, ability, and industry is a good one. And an old one. Up until now each generation's tried to follow the precedents set by a Clark many years ago—in the eighteenth century."

"You sound more like my grandfather than yourself, Father,"
Danny said acidly. "I should think you'd suffered enough personally for that precious Clark tradition without wanting to pass on
the chains to your children."

"Danny, you're forgetting yourself," Fred said softly.

"Sorry. But I don't see what the stinking ambition of an old
eighteenth-century ancestor has to do with my right to marry the
girl I love in 1894."

"Maybe nothing," Fred said. "But the point is you are being
used to further a contemptible woman's ambition. Danny, I know
you've suffered a lot in your time, but now you're a man and
you're growing stronger every day. As Dexter and I get older,
you'll be taking on more and more responsibility. Eventually, and
this is my dream, you and Freck"—he spread his hands—"will
run all this. To this day I have terrible doubts as to whether I
should have brought you and your mother and Anna here. Only
one thing can ever make the struggle worthwhile and that's when
you and Freck take over and I can sit on the sidelines and watch
you."

Danny cut in. "I'm sorry, but nothing—I mean nothing—is
going to keep me from marrying Barbara, Father. Neither
threats, nor bribes, nor rosy pictures of a great future with myself
and my four-year-old nephew running the wonderful Clark
Brothers Kingdom nor—nor you—nor Mamma."

It was a statement of finality.

"All right, Dan. I guess you'll have to know everything."
Telling it as accurately as he could and in detail, Fred poured out
the story of Mrs. Shipley's attempt to blackmail the Fraziers.

"It happened when your mother was in California. As soon as
she and Barbara were on the train, Mrs. Shipley wrote your Aunt
Susie saying she had to see her immediately but to tell no one.
She did not realize, the fool, that the first thing Susie would do
was tell Sumter and the first thing Sumter would do was tell me.

"When Mrs. Shipley arrived on the appointed day and was
shown upstairs to Susie's room by the butler, she was confronted
by Sumter and me on either side of Susie's couch. She was a
grotesque sight—all in black and draped in veils. Susie invited
her to sit down, and it took her no time at all to confirm my
suspicion she intended to blackmail Susie."

"Oh come, Father."

"Danny, you must believe me. She said Griswold had ruined her daughter's life and reputation. Sumter pointed out she had no proof."

"Father, for God's sake! This is like a dime novel."

"Would you like to know how Mrs. Shipley answered your uncle? She said the fact that your mother had taken Barbara to California was proof enough."

Fred stole an uncomfortable glance at his son. "Forgive me, Dan. I've stored this up for a long time. I'm not angry at you. It's just that that damnable woman is getting everything that she wants, and when that includes you, it's more than I can stand. To finish this off, I told Mrs. Shipley to go ahead and tell all of Clarkston and Philadelphia. I pointed out that spreading the story about Barbara would only break up Barbara's younger sister's engagement to Alfred Clark. That brought her up short. She was speechless. Then, with considerable dignity, Susie summoned the butler to show her out."

Fred was silent a long time, waiting for his son's reply.

"I'm sorry," Danny finally said. "I'm sorry if you feel my marriage means some sort of humiliation for you and Mamma, sorry you had such a disagreeable experience with Mrs. Shipley, sorry Mamma had such a bad time in California, and sorry I haven't turned out to be the conventional handsome son who could fulfill his parents' and grandparents' social and breeding ambitions. But I did not ask to be born this way. I've known humiliation, too, with my twisted legs, my pigeon chest, my goddamned hunchback, and my rotten eyes. I've had to face myself in the mirror every day and wonder how any woman could look at me without shuddering. And now—" He stopped. Then, in a voice that was almost a shout, "Can't you understand? A miracle has happened to me, and I am not going to be deprived of marrying Barbara."

Fred walked over to Danny's chair and put out both his hands. Danny looked up and reached toward his father. Fred pulled him to his feet and held him in his arms as gently as he had done when he was a little boy.

"Oh, son," he whispered. The ominous cloud receded and Fred's compassion for the man in his arms obliterated his bitterness.

It had been, Eliza realized, eight days since Danny had told them he was engaged to Barbara, and she could no longer put off calling on Mrs. Shipley and Barbara. She glanced at Fred across the table from her, scraping up the last bit of tapioca pudding from his dessert bowl. As soon as he started back to the office, she would order the carriage. Conversation during lunch had been desultory, but so had all communication since Danny had announced his plans. The coming marriage, it was tacitly understood, was forbidden territory, but since neither Eliza nor Fred could think of much else, any spontaneous exchange between them had vanished.

"Fred," Eliza said, "I think perhaps I ought to go to Philadelphia toward the end of the week. I hate to leave you, but I need to do some shopping."

"To shop, eh? For what? The happy couple's wedding present?"

Eliza flushed. "Fred, darling, sarcasm isn't going to help. You said yourself we have no choice but to accept it. Besides, Barbara, the Shipleys aren't really as bad as all that."

"Don't say that to me, Eliza. You have no idea what you're talking about."

"I think I have, Fred. After all I was the one who spent four and one-half months with Barbara and under pretty strained circumstances."

"And how much time have you spent with Barbara's mother?"

"Oh, for heaven's sake, Fred. You know perfectly well I avoid her because she's a priggish, sanctimonious woman whom I consider a bore."

"Priggish. Sanctimonious. Like hell. Is that the description you'd apply to a blackmailer?"

"Fred." Eliza reached for her finger bowl. "You're making things twice as bad as they are by refusing to—"

"I am not making things twice as bad as they are. Listen to me, Eliza, and listen carefully. The minute you and Barbara were on that blasted train to California, your 'sanctimonious' Mrs. Shipley—"

"Fred darling, if you mean her visit to Susie, I've known all about that for ages."

Fred opened his mouth in disbelief and took a long breath. "You mean Susie told you?"

"Of course. I was just as horrified as you. But it seems to me, you all made short shrift of her." Eliza allowed herself the suspicion of a smile. "I must say, though, I felt frustrated when I realized that my elaborate efforts to spare Susie not only were in vain but that she rather relished the confrontation."

"Well, I'll be damned." Fred was resigned. "Maybe you're right—maybe the best we can do is to hope that this isn't a case of like mother like daughter. I suppose I'll have to give Barbara credit at least for not being a party to her mother's schemes."

But, Eliza thought, she *was*. Barbara had lied to her that first day. She had given the impression that her mother would kill her if she found out she was pregnant, while all along Mrs. Shipley had known. Mother and daughter had worked together as a successful team. Eliza could feel her anger rising. She had believed Barbara's lie at the time, and Fred now, thank God, in his fury at the mother, had apparently forgotten the daughter's role in the deception.

"Fred, darling, I am as appalled as when I first learned about it," Eliza said.

"I'm sure you are—and perhaps I shouldn't have brought it up again. I never intended to any more than I intended to tell Danny. But I did. It was a last resort to try to persuade him not to go through with this."

Shock wave was following shock wave.

"You told Danny?" Eliza asked.

"It didn't make the slightest bit of difference to him. Barbara is clever. She had already told him about Griswold. My guess is that Danny's probably put the business about Mrs. Shipley out of his mind. And maybe you should, too. If we have to go through with the blasted wedding, we'd better do our best to forget the past. I'm sorry, Hodie. It's an unholy mess, but I guess we'll survive." He got up, came around the table, and kissed her. "I have to get back to the office. I'll see you later."

As Eliza watched him walk out of the room, she wondered if they would indeed survive. For the moment she knew only one thing. She would have to postpone today's call on the Shipleys. She couldn't possibly face either mother or daughter today.

The following afternoon Eliza settled herself in the carriage. She was still shaken by yesterday's revelations and the drive to the Shipleys took much too short a time. She stepped out of the carriage and walked up to the front door, came to a dead stop, and eyed it, making a supreme effort to compose her expression.

Mrs. Shipley's maid came to the door. "Mrs. Shipley will receive you, madame," she said, leading the way down the hall.

Will receive, indeed, thought Eliza, following her.

"Mrs. Clark, how nice to see you," Mrs. Shipley said, holding out her hand.

"I've been looking forward to this," Eliza said and choked slightly. "And I hope Barbara is home."

"Yes, indeed she is, and she will be delighted to see you." Mrs. Shipley tripped across to the stairs. "Barbar-a, Mrs. Clark is here," she called and turned back to Eliza. "Oh, dear me, do sit down." She walked over and patted an ornate gilt armchair covered in needlepoint.

Eliza went to the chair and sat down.

Mrs. Shipley seated herself on an equally elaborate gilt sofa. "Barbara has been spending every minute on her trousseau. She's really very clever with her needle."

"Oh, yes," Eliza said politely.

At that moment Barbara walked in and over to Eliza. "How do you do, Mrs. Clark. I'm so glad to see you." Barbara sounded almost shy.

"Hello, Barbara. How are you, my dear?" Eliza said.

Awkwardly, Barbara withdrew her hand and went over to sit beside her mother. Eliza, watching her closely, realized the girl was embarrassed. She was somehow changed from the irritating companion in California.

"Mrs. Clark, this is such an exciting occasion, and I am absolutely overjoyed by the coming union of our two families," Mrs. Shipley said with enthusiasm.

I bet you are, Eliza thought. For the first time she recognized the shiftiness in Mrs. Shipley's face. The eyes too close together that never missed a trick made a mean triangle with the thin compressed lips and jutting chin. Barbara, on the other hand, had never looked better. Her light golden hair, drawn back and held with a blue velvet ribbon, framed a delicate oval face. Barbara's wide china blue eyes were her best feature. Eliza studied her intently. Only the mouth betrayed her. Small and round, it drooped at the corners. But there was grace in the way she sat on the sofa and beauty in the gentle curve of her bust that narrowed into a tiny waist. It was easy to see the appeal she must have for the opposite sex.

"We are very much looking forward to the wedding and reception," Mrs. Shipley announced. "With all your Philadelphia friends and acquaintances, I expect it will be the biggest wedding Clarkston has ever seen."

How stupid of her not to have been prepared for that, Eliza thought. It was a problem she would have to deal with immediately.

"Mrs. Shipley, that's terribly generous of you," she said, "but it simply isn't possible. You see, my son, Danny—isn't capable of standing too long, and this means we must make the receiving line as brief as possible."

"But—but—" Mrs. Shipley floundered, "I had certainly hoped to give Barbara the same kind of reception as Margaret and James, only bigger." She brightened. "Perhaps we could arrange a way for Danny to sit."

"No, mother." Barbara's answer was abrupt. "The wedding is going to be exactly the way Danny wants it."

Eliza was immediately relieved.

"Thank you, Barbara," she murmured.

Encouraged by Eliza, Barbara went on. "You see, I asked Danny how he wanted the wedding. He said he would like his family—that is, just those in Clarkston, all his railroad crew, and some men from the shops to come. Then after—"

"Railroad crew—you can't be serious, Barbara." Mrs. Shipley's voice had risen.

"Oh, but I'm sure she is, Mrs. Shipley," Eliza said and couldn't resist adding. "Danny has many friends among the men."

Barbara, her confidence reinforced, said, "Yes, he has. In fact he has asked Bentz to be his best man and Tommy Malloy to be an usher."

"That's marvelous, Barbara," Eliza said. What had happened to this girl?

"And James and Alfred will be the other ushers."

"Who will you have as bridesmaids, Barbara?" Eliza asked.

"Just my sisters."

"That's nice. And what time are you planning to have the wedding?"

"At noon. Then afterward Danny feels he can stand at the back of the church long enough to speak to the men. There are seventy-five of them, he told me."

"I hadn't realized there were so many," Eliza said.

"And after the wedding we'd like to have a simple luncheon here, just for the family."

"Oh, good. That sounds like the absolutely perfect wedding," Eliza said. She guessed that Barbara, once she knew she had Eliza's support, jumped at the chance to communicate her plans to Mrs. Shipley. "Danny abhors a lot of fuss and formality," Eliza said, as it broke over her that they would all be spared something she had been dreading. Barbara had arranged it so that Griswold's family would not be included. Eliza looked at her son's fiancée if not with affection with a determination to put the past behind her.

During the conversation between Eliza and Barbara, Mrs. Shipley had glanced from one to the other, jerking her head like a child's diabolo. The maid brought in the tea tray and set it down in front of Mrs. Shipley with a clatter. Mrs. Shipley glared at her.

"One lump or two, Mrs. Clark?" she asked.

"One, thank you."

Mrs. Shipley poured the tea, dropped the sugar in, and handed the cup to the maid. "Do you really think the reception should be kept so terribly small, Mrs. Clark?"

"Absolutely," said Eliza, knowing perfectly well that the idea of a miner's son being an usher and Danny's men being the largest company of onlookers at the wedding must be repugnant to her. "I think Barbara is being most considerate, and having the wedding this way will make Danny very happy."

"Thank you, Mrs. Clark," Barbara said and Eliza began to feel as she once had felt when Barbara came to her. Perhaps Danny had made a better choice than she and Fred had thought.

Tommy arrived home jubilant late the afternoon before the wedding. He and the men on the railroad and in the shops had combined to give Danny a wedding present. Danny had made each man he thanked for it feel like a prince who had given his kingdom away.

Katie, as usual, was in the kitchen. She was at the stove, her back to the door, and she hadn't heard Tommy come in. Tommy crept up behind her and in one swift movement wrapped his arms around her.

Katie shrieked, dropping the wooden spoon she was using to stir the beans. "Tommy! You're a rascal, scaring the daylights out of me. Now, let me go, you devil."

He did and Katie turned to look at him. "What happened today to make you look so cheerful?"

"We gave Danny his present. Remember? I told you they asked me to give it to him myself."

"Ah, yes. And did he like it?"

"Did he ever! It was the greatest present he ever got, he said. He thanked every single one of us."

"He's very happy, isn't he, Tommy?"

"That he is." Tommy frowned. "I guess it's good he's getting married."

"Sure and it is, Tommy. Be glad for him." She watched him intently. "And you'll be as close as ever. You'll see."

"Tommy, you home?" It was Stephen calling from the bedroom. He had been asleep since eleven in the morning and it was time for him to get up and go to work.

"Yes, hello, Dad," Tommy shouted back.

"Tell him it's time to have breakfast," Katie said.

"Time for your breakfast," Tommy yelled.

As Katie bustled around the kitchen, Tommy watched her thoughtfully. She was very thin, her frailty more apparent than ever. Her hair, once thick and inky black, was sparse and streaked with gray. She wore it drawn into a knot at the nape of her neck; the way it was pulled back emphasized the prominent cheekbones, the lines in her forehead, and the shadows under her eyes, which were still deep blue. Tommy remembered sadly that her cheeks were once full and pink and her arms round and sturdy.

"Where's Moira?" he asked. "I thought she was supposed to help you. She's upstairs resting, I suppose?" He was proud of Moira, who had become Clarkston's leading seamstress, but she was lazy as far as helping her mother was concerned.

"Yes, she is resting and you leave her alone, Tommy," Katie

said. "You're always picking on Moira and you let your brother do anything he wants. He's upstairs, too, on my orders and he'll have his supper there alone." Katie turned back to the stove.

"All right, what's he done now?"

"Go take a look at him," Katie said shortly. "And mind you tell him to stay put."

Tommy found Stevie huddled in a corner of the upstairs bedroom, chin on his hands, head down. "Stevie, what's happened?"

Stevie looked up. His right eye was purple and his lips were swollen.

"Fighting again?"

Stevie nodded.

"Who was it this time?"

"Carl Platz. He said we were a bunch of Irish micks."

Tommy laughed. "And so we are." He went over and sat down by his brother and put an arm around him. At twelve, Stevie was both sensitive and belligerent; as a result his days in school were always in jeopardy. "Why do you mind so much?" Tommy said to his brother. "Pay them no heed, Stevie."

"That's—that's not all, Tommy." Two tears started rolling down Stevie's cheeks. The fight had evidently been a rough one.

"What else?"

"That we take charity from the Clarks. That Dad is no good—and the Clarks just handed him the job as night watchman because of Mom, who is Mrs. Clark's pet. And that—you, you got where you are on account of Danny."

Tommy swore and drew Stevie closer to him. There was just enough truth in what his younger brother said to make him uncomfortable. Tommy knew he had done his job well, but Danny had given him his start. As his father grew older, the injured leg became more troublesome, and it was obvious that he could no longer do heavy work. Tommy was pretty sure that the sought-after position as night watchman had come about through Jessie Clark.

"Still pay it no mind, Stevie," he said aloud. "Platz is a lousy German anyway, and he's just jealous. Mom says you're to stay up here for supper."

Stevie nodded miserably. He felt abused.

"I'll see if I can't get you out of it. After all, you've just been defending the family honor."

That was what he told Katie, careful not to let his father hear. After resisting halfheartedly, Katie relented. Tommy's final argument had persuaded her.

"We're supposed to be happy tonight," Tommy said, "because of tomorrow. Tomorrow is Danny's wedding day."

Eliza sat in the front pew watching Barbara come up the aisle on Caldwell Shipley's arm. She could not avoid looking at Fred out of the corner of her eye. When Danny came in with Bentz to stand in front of the altar and wait for his bride, it seemed to Eliza that Fred was making a heroic effort to conceal his feelings. He was squeezed into a ten-year-old cutaway kept exclusively for formal occasions. Even Danny wore a morning coat, stiff wing collar, and gray silk cravat. Eliza was struck for the first time by his resemblance to Fred. Such superficial differences as Fred's baldness and Danny's shock of auburn hair, Fred's black moustache and Danny's clean shaven face could not conceal the similarity in their round Clark heads, brown Clark eyes, and full lips. No one could mistake that they were father and son, each of them handsome and stubborn, Eliza thought indulgently.

The church had never been more lovely. Sprays of red, white, and gold chrysanthemums had been tied on the end of every third pew; two large vases of the same flowers arranged against a backdrop of autumn leaves stood on the chancel steps. Barbara's dress had been made for her in Philadelphia and was the height of fashion. Its material was a heavy silk poplin lined with crisp taffeta that rustled as she walked. The skirt was wide and stiff with a white silk bow just below the waist as reminder of the now vanished bustle. The silk bodice had balloon sleeves overlaid with a coarse but effective lace. A chiffon jabot lent softness to an otherwise rigid corsage and a large lace veil fell just short of the heavily gored skirt.

The ceremony was over; Eliza glanced sideways at Fred. Even he could not fail to be moved by Danny's shining happiness. Fred returned his son's smile. Then his eye fell on Mrs. Shipley and Eliza saw his mouth tighten.

Eliza, Fred, the Shipleys, and the rest of the family went, according to plan, directly to the Shipleys'. Danny and his bride, after greeting their wedding guests, followed in what seemed an eternity to Eliza but was actually only an hour.

At the reception Fred was making a superhuman effort to act like a happy guest. Eliza watched him nervously and noticed that while he avoided Mrs. Shipley, he was trying to talk cordially to her husband. Anna, aware of how her father felt, stuck close to him, doing her best to help him through.

Hours later, or was it days? Eliza thought, as she walked into her own house, the wedding was over. They had seen Danny and Barbara off on the special train Fred had arranged to take them directly to Philadelphia, and Fred had unbent enough to kiss the bride good-bye, but he looked as though he'd bitten into an unripe persimmon. He had drunk glass after glass of champagne during lunch, but it had nnot had the slightest effect on the rigidity of his mood. Eliza wondered if anything ever would.

When the bellboy thrust open the door of their suite, Barbara gasped. Filled with flowers, it looked like a bridal bower. It was the hotel's spacious Colonial Suite; sunlight streamed through the long windows that looked out on the street, highlighting the blue and gold brocade of the curtains and upholstered gilt chairs.

"It's beautiful, Danny," Barbara said. "Let's stay here forever."

"I wish we could, but we will stay long enough to find you some little trinket—a souvenir of our honeymoon. We'll start tomorrow."

"What kind of trinket, Danny?"

"You have only to name it, darling. Emeralds, rubies, diamonds, sapphires—whatever pleases your fancy, my love."

"Um." Barbara crossed the room to place her cheek against his.

The next morning they were at Bailey, Banks, and Biddle— according to Eliza, the best jewelers in Philadelphia.

"What would you like to look at, Mrs. Clark?" Mr. Sherwin, one of the partners asked. "Necklaces, brooches, rings, or a smattering of everything?"

"Just necklaces," Barbara said. "Is that all right, Danny?"

Danny smiled at her. "Everything is all right with me, darling. You know that."

Mr. Sherwin retreated and returned with a white kid box lined with white satin. "Here is an exquisite diamond necklace," he said as he opened the box.

"How lovely!" Barbara exclaimed. "May I put it on?"

"You certainly may." Danny picked up the slender string of diamonds and fastened it around her neck.

"Ooooooh! Dan, I love it."

"So do I." He looked at her admiringly.

"I'm afraid that for all its simplicity, the value of the individual stones makes that necklace quite expensive, Mr. Clark."

"Never mind," Danny said, coloring. "This is my wedding present to my wife."

Barbara looked at herself in the standing mirror on the counter. "It *is* beautiful, Dan." She stroked the necklace with the thumb and forefinger of her right hand. Then, in a supreme effort to resist temptation, "But Dan, it's *much* too much."

Danny took advantage of Barbara's preoccupation to move to the end of the counter for a rapid consultation with Mr. Sherwin. He turned back to his wife. "It's all right, darling. And there's nothing I would rather do than give it to you."

"Are you sure, Dan? I don't want your mother to be shocked and disapproving."

"My mother. Don't be silly. You don't realize how much she loves beautiful jewelry herself."

"Yes I do, Danny. But I also know your mother pretty well."

"This time I'm the boss, not my mother," Danny said proudly.

"Oh, Danny, darling, thank you, thank you, thank you." Ignoring Mr. Sherwin, she threw her arms around Danny and hugged him. "May I wear it home?"

"In the daytime?" Mr. Sherwin stammered.

"Right now," said Danny and he and Barbara left Bailey, Banks, and Biddle hand in hand. Mr. Sherwin remained at the front door staring after them.

Barbara took the necklace off only when she went to bed at night. Then she placed it carefully on the table beside her so that she could look at it the moment she woke in the morning. Danny was delighted.

The three weeks Danny had allotted for their honeymoon sped by; they went to the theater or the opera almost every night;

they dined out with some Philadelphia friends of Danny's; and they spent their days doing a little sightseeing and a lot more shopping.

Danny's Aunt Jemima had conveniently gone off to Europe for a year's stay one week after their marriage and had offered Danny and Barbara the family mansion until they built one of their own. Since her parents' deaths, Jemima now ran both the Philadelphia and the Clarkston houses. Aunt Jemima had thoughtfully assured Barbara that the house more or less ran itself and that Bridie, the cook, could easily take charge of things. Barbara had smiled politely and immediately realized who would rule in the kitchen.

Aunt Jemima's maids were lined up at the front door to greet them on their return to Clarkston. Maria, Danny's old nurse, had come down the hill from Danny's parents' house to join the welcoming group. Danny kissed her affectionately.

"Hello, Maria," he said. "How do I look? Like an old married man?"

"You look wonderful, Dan, and welcome home to you and your wife." Her nod in Barbara's direction was cool. Maria, like Eliza and Fred, had deplored the marriage.

"Let's go in, darling, and get unpacked." Danny broke the stiff silence. "We're tired and later we'll be famished. But I bet you've got the usual wonderful dinner for us, Bridie."

Bridie beamed. "I hope so, Mr. Dan. I tried to remember all your favorites. A barrel of oysters from the Reading Terminal Market came up on the train with you and I got a fine pair of ducks from the farmer in the valley. And I hope you still like vanilla ice cream and white mountain cake?" Danny groaned with satisfied pleasure. "I thought maybe Mr. and Mrs. Fred would like to come to dinner with you, but Mrs. Fred said she was sure you'd rather be alone the first night. She said she wanted to give you time to settle in."

Danny frowned.

"Well, perhaps they'll stop in for tea," he said and started into the house.

After they were unpacked by the chambermaid, Barbara went down to the kitchen.

"I've sent Janos with a note to Mr. and Mrs. Clark, asking them to tea, Bridie," she said.

Bridie, standing at the sink preparing the dinner vegetables, turned around at the sound of Barbara's voice. "Yes, ma'am, I—" She stopped abruptly. The diamond necklace had caught her eye.

"We'll have tea at four. I hope that's all right," Barbara said, sounding tentative.

Bridie's "Yes" was without enthusiasm. "Miss Jemima Clark always has bread and butter sandwiches and sponge cake. Will that suit you and Mr. Danny?" She was still staring at the necklace.

"Certainly, Bridie." Now that they were back in Clarkston, Barbara realized she could ill afford an enemy, even among the servants. She turned and went to the living room.

Eliza came to tea alone. Barbara's invitation had arrived after lunch just as Fred was about to go back to his office. Fred looked at it, grunted, and said shortly that he had much too much work to do to consider going.

Eliza threw her arms around Danny when he opened the door. Barbara was standing slightly behind him. Eliza held out her arms and kissed her on the cheek. Then she stood back and said, "Let me look at you, you look—" She hesitated for a second. The necklace had momentarily caught her eye. "—just marvelous. Especially you, Danny. I've never seen you look better."

"I've never been better, Mamma. I'm walking a lot without crutches now. That's what marriage to Barbara has done for me. Come on into the living room."

As she sat down, Eliza took a deep breath. "That's quite a handsome necklace, Barbara."

Barbara gave her mother-in-law a brilliant smile. "It's Danny's wedding present to me. I love it more than anything in the world."

"It's very lovely, Barbara. Breathtaking, in fact."

I was right, she is shocked, Barbara thought.

Eliza turned to Danny, "What did you do all the time in Philadelphia?"

Just then the tea arrived. Barbara slid sideways into the high-backed chair behind the polished silver service. She heated the teapot with boiling water and skillfully emptied it into the silver slop bowl. The waitress passed the teacups, removed the silver tops from two serving dishes, one holding bread and butter sandwiches, the other sponge cake.

"I envy you your hearing *Othello*," Eliza said. "Did Emma Eames sing Desdemona?"

"She did—and beautifully. But Mamma, the program said that Melba and Plançon were going to sing *Faust* in January. You must make Father take you."

"I'd love it," Eliza said.

"We had a wonderful time," Danny said. "Now I guess we'll have to start settling down." He smiled wistfully at Barbara.

Barbara interrupted him. "That's all right, Danny. We have this house 'til your aunt comes home and we'll be busy building our own place."

"You certainly have plenty to do, Barbara," Eliza said. "Danny's father and I are anxious to have you two for dinner. How would next Friday be?"

"That would be lovely."

"Fine." Eliza eyed the necklace. "It will just be a simple dinner—with us, alone. Don't dress up. Delicious tea, Barbara. Thank you so much." She got up to leave.

"I'll see you to the door, Mamma," Danny said.

"Oh, Dan, you don't have to do that."

"He wants to show you what an athlete he's becoming, Mrs. Clark," Barbara said.

"All right, then, and thank you again." Eliza nodded at Barbara and walked down the hall with Danny.

At the bottom of the steps, after the door had closed behind them, Eliza said, "Danny, dear, please don't let Barbara wear that necklace to dinner. I—well, I don't want your father to see it."

Danny said nothing. Then, very quietly, "You mean, you don't like it?"

"I think it's beautiful, but I think it's much too expensive for a bride of twenty-three."

Danny clenched his fist. Eliza reached out her hand, but he brushed it away. "Look, Mamma," he said finally, "the trouble with you and Father is that you have never seen Barbara as she really is. You just don't understand her at all."

"I think I do," Eliza said.

"And Mr. Sherwin said the diamonds were especially fine."

"I'm sure he did. Did he also say they were suitable for a young girl?"

Danny bit his lip. "Barbara refused—" he started but stopped and turned away.

"Danny, oh, Danny, I'm sorry." Eliza was almost in tears. "Please, darling, understand. It's just that I so desperately want your father to approve of Barbara. That's why I hope you can persuade her not to wear that expensive necklace in Clarkston and when he's around. I know what his reaction will be."

"I'm sorry, too, Mamma," Danny mumbled. "I'll see what I can do." He started back toward the house and Eliza walked slowly down the driveway.

Barbara was sitting quietly in the living room working at some needlepoint. She looked very beautiful, the light shining on her yellow hair. Danny studied her for a long moment before she saw him. I can't ever ask her not to wear it, he thought. Damned stuffy of my mother—I bet she was no shrinking violet when she was Barbara's age.

Eliza went to the door to greet them. If, as she feared, Barbara was wearing the necklace, it would be better to be braced for Fred's reaction. Barbara stepped inside the hall. Danny, looking defensive, followed. Eliza glanced at him and was sure the necklace was around his wife's neck.

"I'm so glad to have you both here," Eliza said, kissing Barbara on the cheek and stepping beyond her to give Danny a hug. "Come on in." She started towards the living room. "Your father can't wait to see you."

Fred was on his feet, managing a smile, Eliza saw, that wavered between cordiality and wistfulness. "Hello, Barbara," he said, coming forward. Eliza's attention was riveted on her husband. With relief, she saw that he faltered only for a second when he caught sight of the diamonds. "Nice to have you with us, Barbara." He bent forward and kissed her gingerly on the brow. "Hello, Dan, old top. Glad to see you."

Somehow they got through the evening. Eliza gave Fred credit for behaving superbly. She found herself chattering like a magpie and she noticed Danny laughed excessively. Everyone had more than their quota of claret, and though it was possible to question Barbara's expensive taste, no one could fault her manners. She treated Fred with exactly the right blend of deference and coyness.

For the next seven months, it seemed to Eliza, they all lived their lives in submerged hostility. Eliza had known from the beginning that she and Fred would have to suspend judgment about Barbara if they wanted to keep their relationship with their son, but Fred could not seem to temper his feelings about Danny's wife. Then abruptly Fred's unhappiness was overshadowed by a new anxiety: Dexter had suddenly become critically ill with pneumonia.

CHAPTER 13

Clarkston
May 1895

"HE'S AWAKE NOW, Mrs. Clark," the nurse said, coming into the parlor. Jessie was seated in her favorite chair next to the fireplace trying to concentrate on a volume of Wordsworth. She jumped to her feet at the sound of the nurse's voice.

"I'll come right up," Jessie said, dropping her book on the chair. It was four in the afternoon. Ever since yesterday evening when the doctor told her that Dexter's life was in danger, she had been conscious of a pounding in her ears and a feeling of helplessness. Dexter's shallow breathing and flushed face terrified her. She yearned to do something for him—anything to restore him to his former rugged self.

He smiled at her feebly as she came into the bedroom. "Jessie."

She walked to the bedside, took his hand, and flinched; it was clammy and had no strength. His face was splotchy, his eyes bright and watery. If anything, he looked worse than he had at noon.

"Don't worry, Jessie. You've always been so brave." He said it in a hoarse whisper, and she realized illness had somehow heightened his perception. She must try harder to keep her fear hidden.

"It's all right." She turned her head and then looked directly at him. "It's just that—I hate seeing you sick, Dex." She forced a smile. "But you'll be better soon, I'm sure."

"Don't know, Jess," he said as if it was a matter of indifference. Then he looked at her intently. Jessie trembled. The expression in his eyes was peculiarly close to the one she had seen there so many years before when they were first married. For some reason this frightened her as much now as it had then.

She felt a faint pressure on the hand that was still in his. "Despite—" he released her hand as he began to cough and gasp for breath.

"Dex, don't try to talk until you feel better." As she said it, she started to pray.

He turned his head, ignoring her plea. "Despite," he began again, "everything, I love you. Always have. Know that."

"I do." Jessie barely breathed the words. It must be his way of telling her he was aware she knew about Gertrude and he was asking forgiveness for something that had been forgiven long ago. "It was my fault, too." If only she could make him understand that. And that it had been too late when she finally recognized his need. Now, if he was going to die, she must make it possible for him to die in peace.

"Dexter, our life together was—is wonderful. I thank the Lord for what He has given us, and our happiness, every day. I'm afraid I've never thanked you for all that you've meant to me. But I do now and with all my heart."

The sunlight was coming through the west bedroom windows and touched the rug with golden dapples. After she spoke, Jessie, unable to look at her husband for a moment, gazed at the streams of yellow light, and it seemed to her that the shimmering beams represented a continuation of life. She had never felt closer to her God.

She turned timidly back toward Dexter and took the hands lying on the counterpane in hers. "I wish," she was still whispering, "I could have given you all you wanted because you have given me so much. It's my only regret."

He spoke, and to her astonishment his voice was strong. "Regret nothing, Jessie." Then his voice thickened, and she could barely distinguish the words. "You, Fred, Dan—"

He stopped and coughed, and without warning the pillow was covered with blackened blood.

"I came as soon as I heard," Katie said to Mary in the kitchen. "How is she?"

Mary wiped her eyes; they were red from weeping. "Wonderful. Not, not a tear." Mary tried to stifle a sob. "She's doing her best to cheer everybody up, busy arranging the funeral, the music . . . Oh, I don't know, Katie, go on in and see her. She's always glad to see ye."

"I will. Is she upstairs or in the parlor?"

"In the parlor, I think. There's been a steady stream of visitors, but no one is there now."

Katie started toward the door.

"Wait, Katie, I want to tell you something before you go. She doesn't know it, but the nurse was there all the time they was talking—at the last, I mean."

"Talking?"

"Aye. You wouldn't believe it, but well, you remember once I asked you whatever did he see in her?"

Katie nodded.

"He—he—" Mary was momentarily overcome. She buried her head in her arms and sobbed convulsively. Finally, she looked up and, tears streaming down her face, said, "He told her he loved—her—always had." Mary put her head down on the kitchen table, surrendering herself totally to the comfort of sorrow.

Katie went to her and patted her on the back. "Now, don't take on so," she said, barely able to hold back her own tears. "I'm not surprised, but I'm glad for her—to know it. That's no doubt what's keeping her going now," she added philosophically.

When Mary quieted down, Katie gave the still shaking shoulders another pat and went in search of Jessie. She found her at her desk in the parlor, writing.

"Mrs. Clark," Katie said softly, hating to disturb her and dreading to face her.

Jessie looked up and smiled. "Katie, how good of you to come."

There was an inner radiance about Jessie that Katie didn't remember in the past. Her face was drawn and there were shadows under the lovely eyes, but serenity was in them, too.

"I'm sorry," Katie said numbly. What else was there to say?

"I know. Mr. Clark was so fond of you, Katie. The funeral is tomorrow at four." Jessie gestured toward the desk. "I'm just writing out instructions about the music—all the arrangements."

She glanced at Katie affectionately. "There's a special pew for you, and your family, and Mary."

"Thank you, Mrs. Clark. I'll look forward to coming," Katie said and cursed herself for her awkwardness. "That is—I'll be there."

"Yes."

"Mrs. Clark, I—" There seemed to be so little to say, Katie thought. She had never been quite this much at a loss. "Is there anything I can do for ye—for you?"

"Not now, Katie. Later—when I have time to plan. I have a lot I want to think about doing, and you can help me then. You know the needs of the miners and their families, Katie, and I want to carry on as Mr. Clark would have wished me to."

Katie saw it then. That was what was holding her up. She doubted very much that Mr. Clark had ever cared that much about his wife's acts of charity, but his death had stirred up Jessie's natural zeal for doing good. If only she didn't sound so high and mighty about it.

"Well, I'll be going now," Katie said. "I'm glad you're bearing up and I'll see you tomorrow."

"Good-bye, Katie, and bless you for coming."

"Thank you, ma'am."

Mary had recovered by the time Katie got back to the kitchen. She was, in fact, sweeping the kitchen floor. She put down the broom as Katie came in. "How is she?"

"Fine," said Katie. "I wouldn't worry about her if I were you."

The news of Dexter's death reached Gertrude in New York the day after he died. She opened the New York *Herald* to the obituary page and there it was. "Head of Clark Brothers dead in Clarkston." No man as vital as Dexter could possibly be dead. She had not written him about herself and John. It had all happened so fast she hadn't yet been able to make herself do it. Only a week before she had given up her job at the library and she had a million errands to do. It was impossible to contemplate doing any of them now. She picked up the newspaper she had put down in shock. It was there; it must be true, the funeral was scheduled for two days from now.

I must take the silk shoes to be dyed today, she thought wildly—that can't wait. And I have to find a hat but not today. What on earth can I put off doing, but why would tomorrow, or the day of the funeral be any better? It would no doubt be worse. I'm no longer in love with him but . . .

She got through the day somehow. John was scheduled to pick her up at six thirty for an early dinner, and then they were to go to the opera. She had telephoned him at his office and told him she wasn't up to it. He understood immediately. He, too, had read the papers. They decided on dinner at home, at Gertrude's.

John came directly from the office, abandoning his usual habit of stopping off to change.

"You're early, my darling," Gertrude said, smiling at him. It would be typical of him, she realized, to come as quickly as he could out of concern for her.

"Are you all right?" he asked.

"Oh, yes," Gertrude said. "It's a frightful shock. I guess my first reaction was to be relieved I hadn't written him about us. But now, I'm not sure. I think he might have been glad to know how happy I am and glad to know that after all these years I'm going to be married again."

"Perhaps, but I doubt that any man could ever get over loving you, and I've wondered about Dexter, although I think from what you've told me, he and Jessie were pretty well suited to each other."

"They were—there was just one thing lacking, really."

"You may have made even that better," John said thoughtfully. "In any event, had you been able to marry him, I don't think you would have been happy for long."

"I don't either," Gertrude said. "I knew that instinctively all the time, I think. Beyond the horror of living in that tiny, closed-in town there was Dexter himself. He didn't really understand, or rather he put men and women in completely separate categories. I remember I quoted Lucretia Mott once, 'Mind has no sex.' He didn't have the faintest idea what I was talking about."

John laughed. "What a thing to say to such a man!"

"Poor Jessie. What on earth will become of her now? Her whole life was Dexter."

"Was it? I rather thought it was Clarkston. I haven't seen her in years, but I would say she was a pretty self-reliant kind with enough discipline to come out of this all right. She'll probably busy herself with the town and good deeds—and even take over some of her husband's prerogatives."

"You're probably right," Gertrude said and was struck with this man's vision. John Sterling was a widower to whom Gertrude had been instantly attracted. Soon after they met, they both realized they were in love. Gertrude, feeling a relationship like theirs demanded total honesty, told John about Dexter the night he proposed to her.

He had taken her chin in his palm and tilted her face up toward his. "You can't be telling me this out of a sense of guilt, can you?" he asked. "Do you think it could make any difference to me?"

"I wasn't sure," Gertrude said, aware that to most men it would.

"My darling, I think you've carried around a burden of guilt for longer than you realize. I wouldn't expect a woman like you to live like a nun. Anyway, it doesn't make any difference to me. How could it?"

"Thank you," Gertrude whispered and began to cry. She buried her face in his chest and realized how wonderfully safe she felt with him.

"I can't imagine what I've done to deserve you," Gertrude said now, struggling with two conflicting emotions. She was overwhelmed by infinite sadness at Dexter's death and deeply conscious of the man by her side whom she would marry in a week.

Danny, trembling with fatigue, sat down in the second pew, beside Barbara. He should not have insisted on walking behind the cortege all the way to the church, he supposed, but it was something he had wanted to do for his uncle. The road to the church was lined with men, women, and children dressed in their Sunday best, their work-worn faces inscrutable in the May sunshine. Danny, Barbara, Fred, Eliza, and all the cousins followed the coffin; of the family, only Jessie rode in a closed and curtained carriage.

In the two days after Dexter's death Danny had seen Jessie

break down only once, the first time he and his father came to call. It had been terrible to witness; right after they came in, silent, uncontrollable tears began rolling down Jessie's face, and it was then that the full realization of Dexter's death reached Fred. In those seconds Danny watched his father grow old and gray. Looking across the pew at him now, he saw that he was staring straight ahead with blank eyes. He either couldn't or wouldn't acknowledge the coffin in front of him. Danny looked at him with compassion. At times he had hated his father for his unrelenting coldness toward Barbara, but now a return of the love he had always borne for the man swept over him; it was impossible to hate someone who looked so old and broken.

As the minister began the eulogy, Fred's mind wandered. Only a few days before he had been in Dexter's office discussing the state of the business. He remembered feeling smug; he had even said to Dexter that he guessed they had become middle-aged and successful, able to take a few weeks off now and then. Dexter had agreed but added, "That is, things should be all right if the labor situation doesn't blow up in our faces. And I wish that just one of James's boys would show some interest in the business. There's no one left to carry on except Danny."

Fred said hesitantly, feeling a comforting euphoria settle over him, "Oh, I don't know. I have a lot of faith in Freck, little as he is."

Dexter laughed. "Good God, he's only five! Still, he's just like Danny or just like Danny was at his age."

"Danny's great with him. He took him for a ride in the cab of Number Seventeen yesterday. Anna said she'd never seen Freck so excited."

"Danny's an extraordinary fellow, Fred. He's a genius but unlike most geniuses, genuinely loved."

"I know. If only he hadn't married that—"

"Fred," Dexter said sharply. "I thought you'd forgiven them. Damn it, you must. Forget it. There's nothing you can do about it, and as far as I can see, Danny's very happy."

"That's what Eliza keeps telling me. And in front of her I pretend I have forgiven Danny, but I can't. Nothing good can ever come of the marriage. She's a common gold digger like her mother. I suppose you've seen the diamond necklace?"

"Yes. They came to dinner. I gather she never takes it off. But what does it matter, Fred? Danny's pleased he's made her happy."

"You wouldn't be so damned tolerant if it were your son, Dex." With that Fred got up and stalked out of the office.

Fred forced himself back into the present as the minister concluded his eulogy; then he wished he hadn't. Unbidden, the thought came to him that what he had never wanted in the first place was all his now. He had borne the strain, the turmoil of administering the business, and the loneliness of living in Clarkston because of Dexter. It was bearable when Dex was alive. Now he wondered how he would be able to endure it. It seemed intolerable. He wanted to cry aloud.

Eliza, clinging tightly to his hand, was miserably aware of her husband's suffering and of how little she could do about it. The congregation rose to the strains of "Nearer My God to Thee." As she stood, she was conscious again of the prominence of the people who filled the church. It might comfort Fred if he realized the extent to which Dexter was being honored; the governor of the state, delegations from the State Senate and House of Representatives, from the American Institute of Mining Engineers, the American Society of Mechanical Engineers, and the American Society of Civil Engineers. Members of the Board of Trustees of Lehigh University, officials of the Lehigh Valley Railroad, the trustees of the state hospital, and directors of the Middle Coal Field Poor District. Eliza had recognized many of them as she walked up the aisle. She knew Danny had arranged for special trains to bring them from New York, Philadelphia, Harrisburg, Bethlehem, and Wilkes-Barre.

Eliza stole a glance at Fred. He remained staring straight ahead, apparently seeing and feeling nothing.

The final moment was near. The pallbearers came forward to hoist the coffin to their shoulders and carry it out to the grave in the churchyard. Katie and Stephen, in a pew in the middle of the church, watched somberly as Jessie, on her brother Josiah

Tucker's arm, trudged valiantly after the casket, leading the rest of the family down the aisle. Jessie looked tiny under the weight of a heavy crepe veil that covered her widow's bonnet and shoulders and reached to the hem of her skirt. Fred and Eliza followed her; Katie noticed that Eliza's face, unlike Jessie's, visible through her thin veil, was wracked with concern. And no wonder, Katie thought, her own husband looks like living death.

Finally, the Malloys' turn came to shuffle down the aisle and take their places in the graveyard to watch the committal. As they stepped outside into the sunshine, Katie was aware that far into the distance the road was thronged with onlookers. The church and churchyard had been roped off when it became clear that not another mortal could squeeze in. Beyond the ropes, Katie spotted John Murray, looking arrogant. As they came out of the church she saw him recognize Stephen and herself and turn away. Then he turned back and his eyes focused directly on Stephen; with a gesture of contempt, he spat. Mother of God, she thought, what is that terrible man planning next? She glanced at Stephen, but he seemed oblivious, his eyes carefully following the coffin ahead. She doubted if Murray would forgive him for paying homage to the dead man.

At the graveside Danny leaned heavily on his crutches and tried to imagine what it would be like without his uncle. It would be impossible, he thought. He watched in numb despair as the pallbearers lowered the casket into the open grave lined with green hemlock and branches of purple and lavender lilac. He reached for Barbara's hand; at least I have Barbara, but Jessie, poor Jessie, has nobody.

Then it was over. The minister had said the final words. Danny, watching her with a new-found compassion, saw Jessie speak to the clergyman briefly, thanking him. Next she said something to Fred. Then she turned quickly toward her carriage.

Fred joined Danny. "Jessie wants to see us first thing tomorrow, after the people from out of town have left. She wants to start planning things. She said she was sorry, but she'll be busy with out-of-towners all day today." Fred looked bewildered. "How does she do it?"

Danny shook his head. Perhaps his sympathy had been misplaced. "Damned if I know," he said.

"The truth is, Jessie hasn't the faintest idea what Dexter's death means," Fred forced himself to say out loud. "I don't know how we'll manage, Dan. I don't think I have the strength."

"Father," Danny's tone was sharp. "Of course, you'll manage. So will I. Let's go home. We both need a drink and a good night's sleep."

Fred nodded as they walked to the carriage, where Eliza and Barbara were waiting for them.

CHAPTER 14

Clarkston 1895

A WEEK AFTER THE FUNERAL Jessie appeared without warning at Fred's office.

"I'm sorry to interrupt you," she said, sounding out of breath. She drew a letter from her pocket. "This just arrived, and I thought it would please you so much that I came right away."

Fred, astonished by the visit, was also amazed to see that Jessie was smiling. She looked almost happy. She thrust the letter at him, and he noted that it came from the Ministry of Public Works, École Nationale Superieure des Mines, Paris, and was signed by Haton, the inspector-general of mines.

Translating slowly aloud, Fred read

. . . to inform you that on the 27th of April I addressed to the Minister of Public Works a letter requesting him to recommend to his colleague, the Minister of Foreign Affairs, a decree, conferring upon Mr. Clark the decoration of Chevalier of the National Order of the Legion of Honor.

"I suppose that's quite an honor, Jessie." Fred glanced through the rest of the letter and handed it back to her. "A lot of good it'll do Dex now. I'm glad you get satisfaction from these things. I can't. There's too much else to think about."

Fred saw by her injured expression that he had hurt her. Nonetheless, the fact that she couldn't seem to understand what he was up against maddened him. "Look, Jessie," he said patiently, "I realize how proud you are of all the accolades you've had since Dex's death, but I have to continue his work—the future of Clark Brothers is in my hands—your financial future and that of all the women and children in the family—I have all that." Immediately, he wished he hadn't said it. He knew he sounded sorry for himself.

"You have Danny to help you." Jessie was irritatingly reasonable.

"Yes, Jessie, but I don't have to tell you Danny's never really been strong. If anything should happen to him, God knows where we'd be! Do you realize I'm fifty-seven years old? I haven't much more time, and the future—I don't know what it holds."

Apparently that had struck a chord. Her lower lip was trembling.

"I'm sorry," she said. "I guess I shouldn't really interrupt you at the office."

As usual she had missed the point and Fred said nothing. Then, as she got up to leave, he thought she seemed less certain of herself and he was about to apologize for his behavior when Emerson Untermeyer knocked and came in.

"Mrs. Clark, I just wanted to ask if it would be all right if I came at three this afternoon rather than at two? Some new schedules must be posted and I should stay here to do it."

It seemed to Fred that the minute Dexter died, Jessie appropriated Untermeyer. Immediately after the funeral she took over Dexter's study and Untermeyer along with it.

"Jessie," Fred said, "just when are you going to get your own personal secretary? The demands on Emerson's time are getting out of hand."

"I've been extremely careful," Jessie said stiffly, "not to make demands on more than half of Emerson's time—often less than that. Right now he is the only person who can help me with all the letters and the requests for grants because he's familiar with the background. You know that, Fred."

"That's true, Mr. Fred," Untermeyer said timidly. "Why, just today we received a letter from Lehigh University. The president is suggesting that Mrs. Clark endow a laboratory there in honor of Mr. Clark."

"Oh, yes," Jessie said, her composure apparently restored. "He spoke to me about that right after the funeral, and I told him I thought it was a marvelous idea."

"And Mrs. Clark, there have been five requests in the past three days from churches in the region. The Reformed Church in Oneida came in this morning, but as you know, there's been a terrible battle for position going on between them and the Methodists."

"We'll have to persuade them to come together and make it very clear to them we can't help warring Christians."

"For the—!" Fred began and subsided.

Jessie turned to Fred. "Fred, I'm sorry. Of course, you may have Emerson for posting the schedules. I wouldn't dream of taking him away from anything that is vital here. Just walk with me to the door, Emerson. Good-bye, Fred, and thanks so much."

As they walked out of the room, Fred buried his head in his arms. Perhaps he'd better give up and let Jessie have Untermeyer altogether. After all, they appeared to be two of a kind.

"How are you, Aunt Jessie?" Danny asked as he leaned over to kiss her. He looked at her with admiration. Not for a moment had Jessie adopted the role of the sorrowing widow. The blue eyes sparkled with intelligence; the frilly white cap and white hair showed off a radiant pink and white complexion. Even the black silk dress, its high neck topped with a white fichu, emphasized Jessie's vitality.

Jessie loved Danny dearly and often wondered if Eliza was worthy to be his mother. She knew her sister-in-law cared about his health and physical well-being. But did she understand or appreciate his extraordinary creative talent as an engineer, his sympathy for the men, even his love of poetry? Jessie flattered herself she was closer to Danny in many ways than his own mother.

"It always makes me feel better when I see you, Danny."

"Thanks. But this time I'm afraid I've come to you for help. It's about a boy from Hanley who used to play on my baseball team. Reminds me of Tommy Malloy when he was that age. Six months ago he slipped on a muddy bank going home and fell under a loci and had to have an arm and a leg amputated at the state hospital."

Jessie nodded; then she pressed the bell under her desk. "I'm just sending for Emerson. I think probably the best place for the boy temporarily would be the Hospital for Crippled Children in Philadelphia."

Emerson Untermeyer scuttled in, bearing an unassorted array of papers.

"Oh, is that today's correspondence, Emerson? It'll have to wait until later. Right now I'd like you to go with Danny to the state hospital in Hazleton to see a young boy there. He's been badly injured and, depending on what you think, I'd like you to go to Philadelphia tomorrow to see if they have room for him at the Hospital for Crippled Children."

"You do more than any other five people put together. Thanks, Aunt Jessie," Danny said, starting out, with Emerson trailing after him. "I'll see you, soon."

"Uh, Emerson," Danny said, as they climbed into Danny's brougham, "I understand you were with Mrs. Clark when she spotted that ailing tree?"

"What's that, now?" Emerson sounded preoccupied.

"Oh, never mind," Danny said, "it's not important."

Yesterday afternoon Fred had come into Danny's office in a rage and said explosively, "That woman is making it impossible for me to run Clark Brothers!"

Danny looked up and said mildly, "Aunt Jessie?"

"Who else. She's constantly sticking her nose in where it doesn't belong. The other day she was out driving with Emerson and she saw some men deepening the ditches along the highway. Then apparently she had a fit of hysterics about a tree that seemed to be listing slightly, so she orders Emerson to requisition three men from our outside department to go and build a retaining wall around the tree. The head of the department is furious and so am I."

It was impossible not to laugh. "I'm surprised that Emerson had the getup and go to requisition anybody," Danny said.

Fred threw his cigar into a wastebasket. It had long since gone out. "The poor fool's a slave to her. The sight of Emerson in church last Sunday taking Dex's place, his quavering tenor warbling along with her contralto was unbearable."

"Come, Father, Aunt Jessie knows her music."

Fred grunted. "It's not her voice—it's her manner. She seems to think she's on the front seat of a train going straight to Heaven—and she's the only passenger."

"Maybe. But whether you like it or not, she accomplishes a lot of good."

"Oh, sure, and at my expense." Fred fished a fresh cigar out of his vest pocket. "Damn it, she's enjoying my brother's death, and she's been reveling in her increased importance ever since he died." He punctuated the remark with a jab of the cigar. "I'll never forgive her for capitalizing on his brains, his work, and his talent. There's no end to what Jessie sees as her right to interfere with or give away. My God, she's giving free milk to every family with children in Clarkston."

"They can use it well enough," Danny said, feeling futile. It was hopeless trying to argue with his father when he was in this kind of mood.

"We're a mining concern—not a goddamned milk dispensary." Fred threw the second Corona at the wastebasket and stalked out of the room.

CHAPTER 15

Freetown, Lattimer, and Clarkston
September 1897

STEPHEN WALKED INTO MULLIGAN'S SALOON, the first one in Freetown on the road from Clarkston. Stooped over, his limp showing more than usual because he had stood an extra watch the day before at the mines, he wished he was at home in bed. But Murray had insisted on meeting him tonight, and had made it sound urgent. It was bound to mean trouble and Stephen had tried hard to refuse.

Murray was sitting at a small table toward the end of the room. That was ominous, since his habit was to stand at the bar surrounded by companions. This time he must feel the need for privacy.

He raised a hand in greeting as Stephen came in. Stephen limped toward the corner, cursing himself for not having more backbone.

Murray waved his jar of bitter in greeting. "What'll ye have, man?"

"The same." Stephen sat down, watching Murray anxiously. "How's the family?"

"Fine." A smile crossed Stephen's face. "I told you once Tommy would be an educated man. This year he'll be through college. College. I never dreamed it."

"I know. Tommy's a credit to you, Stephen." He caught the bartender's eye and made a circling motion. "Now you won't mind me saying so, but Tommy would be a breaker boy yet—oh, perhaps a miner by now, crawling around down there under the earth, if he hadn't the good fortune to break his wrists. That's true enough, is it not?"

Stephen shrugged. "Maybe. Maybe not. He's going to be an engineer."

"I always said Tommy had the brains in the family."

Stephen could remember no instance of Murray's having said anything of the kind, but he let it pass. Murray's conciliatory, flattering attitude certainly meant he was after something.

"Brains or not, he wouldn't have got to college without the support of the Clarks, now, would he? But then it was the Clarks who was responsible for the accident, and for once they made up for something they was responsible for. I certainly am glad me own godson Tommy got the benefit."

"Always the Clarks. Can't you leave them alone, John, and let us have our beer in peace? They done all right by Katie and me."

"That they have, man, and I have no wish in the world to say anything against the Clarks." Murray was solemn in his sincerity. "But the Clarks, along with the rest of the owners, are going to be in trouble shortly. Bad trouble." Murray sat back and looked thoughtful.

There it was, thought Stephen. He was damned if he'd ask why because one way or another Murray would tell him. But this time he was not going to have any part in Murray's schemes.

"Ah, there they are," Murray said unexpectedly.

Stephen looked up to see the O'Neill brothers heading toward their table. The fire setters. That was what he had been calling them to himself ever since he learned they had been responsible for the burning of Black Creek Hall. They didn't look very violent now. They were, like himself, bent from their years in the mines, with patches of white in their hair and wrinkles seaming their faces. Tim, the younger brother, was leading and Stephen noticed that his left arm hung limply by his side. He had broken his elbow on the elevator coming up from the mines a couple of years before, Stephen remembered, and had made quite a fuss about getting compensation.

The brothers grunted in response to Murray's greeting and sat down. The O'Neills were men of business and of dour persuasion.

Jamie, the elder, was the first to speak. "What is it ye're after this time, Murray?" he asked.

Tim, embarrassed by his brother's bluntness and in considerable awe of Murray, said, "Don't ye take on so, Jamie. He didn't mean nothing, John."

"That's all right, Tim," Murray said. "Ye're perfectly right, Jamie. It's true I asked ye to come for a purpose. Now all of ye, do ye know about them mule drivers?"

Stephen guessed Murray had decided to take the part of the mule drivers and was horrified. "Good God, man, they're Polacks."

Murray stared at him. "That's right, Stephen, and they have as much right to be paid as we do."

Jamie looked at Murray with contempt. "But that bunch of Dagos, Polacks, Hunkies, those damned immigrants, they're what's been holding our wages down all these years. Ye said so yerself, John Murray, and not so very long ago."

"Jamie, ye'll never understand the principle of unionism. It's the same as democracy. 'We must all hang together, or assuredly we shall all hang separately.'"

It was Murray's voice, Stephen thought, that got him where he was. It was spellbinding. Even Jamie's attention was riveted on Murray.

"Those mule drivers were discharged because they protested at not being paid the overtime wages they was entitled to."

"There's not one of us here wouldn't have done the same." Tim nodded his head in agreement with Murray.

Warming to his subject, Murray asked, "And is there a man here who does not realize his future is in danger if the filthy mine owners get away with this?"

All the occupants of the bar had by this time gathered around Murray, Stephen, and the O'Neills.

"And now these same thieving mine owners won't even see or talk to the men who were dismissed only because they asked for wages they was entitled to. They won't even discuss it." There was a chorus of "Shame, damn bullies."

"And we miners have no union. Remember that. No more than the mule drivers had. The soft coal workers have a union, but we don't. The men working the bituminous mines have a chance; they're joined together. I tell you, men, our time has come. It's here. Now."

"Have you talked to the Hunkies, John?" Stephen asked uneasily.

"How can he? They don't speak English," Jamie said.

"It's true enough not many do, not having had a chance to learn. But their leader Vosher does, and it's him I've talked to. It doesn't matter what they speak, Jamie. They have numbers and numbers is what we need." Murray clenched his fist for emphasis. "The more men joined together, the more power they have. That's the only thing that will scare the bejasus out of the owners."

"Just what are you proposing, Murray? Come to the point, man." It was Jamie again.

"We are going to march on Lattimer to start with, and we're going to demand our rights. There is going to be a strike all through the mines and terror in the land."

"For God's sake, Murray." Jamie stood up. "Count me out. Ye've tried marches before, remember? And what good did they do? All they ever meant was that we was out of work and out of pocket. And now ye're proposing we go along with a bunch of Hunkies. No thanks." He put his mug down on the table hard. "Thanks for the drink," he said and turned on his heel and went out.

"Me, too," Stephen said quickly. "I'm sorry, John. Make Tim here your deputy."

Murray looked stunned. "But ye must join us, Stephen. Don't you understand? This is the chance of a lifetime."

Stephen shook his head. "I'm too old and too tired. I just want peace in me old age. Good luck to ye both." He rose and started limping toward the door. Halfway there he stopped and said, "And thanks for the beer. I mean it about the luck. The best to ye."

The first meeting of the strikers John Murray called was a shambles. He decided to have it after a week of trekking from village to village with Vosher and O'Neill. They were out to recruit miners to join the union. Murray was not sure any of them spoke English, so Vosher had to be depended on to translate his ideas. During the week of recruiting the entire region lived in terror. Murray had not reckoned on the volatile nature of the Italians, Poles, and Hungarians. He had only to hint of insurrection and the men went wild; there were marauders on the highways, women were molested, houses broken into and robbed.

Clarkston, Hanley, Sheppton, and Oneida were under curfew. Shutters were closed and doors barricaded. Even in Hazleton women and children were kept indoors, only emerging in pairs to make a quick trip to the grocery store. In the villages chickens and dogs were brought into the kitchens for safekeeping. Mistrust and suspicion were rampant among the miners themselves. A man was reluctant to leave his family to spend twelve hours underground for fear of what he might find when he returned. Irishman mistrusted Hungarian, Hungarian mistrusted Pole, Pole despised Italian, and all found only one reason to unite and that was a burning hatred of the owners and operators.

The meeting of miners and laborers, three hundred strong, was called in Harwood at ten in the morning. Murray tried to run it by addressing the men in English and having Vosher translate. He explained his plan was first to march on Lattimer, leaving Clarkston and Hanley until later. The men were in a savage mood. They knew that Sheriff James Martin had been summoned back from Atlantic City by the mayor of Hazleton, and there was talk of calling out the militia. Even though Murray and Vosher had convinced the miners they were strong enough to defy authority, they were uneasy when they learned the sheriff had posted signs in all public places forbidding any crowds to assemble. Every time Murray spoke, there was a roar from the mob, and Vosher was barely able to make himself heard. Murray began to realize these men were twenty times more violent than the Irish. They wanted action and they wanted it immediately. They could be no poorer or hungrier than they were now, so they had not the same fear of the future that sometimes made the Irish timid.

"We march today," Murray cried finally and jumped down from the hastily built platform, directing Vosher to pick up the American flag. It was ten miles to Lattimer and the sun was hot. The marchers, their fury temporarily diverted by marching, sang their native songs as they walked. They were dressed in the fashion of the old country, wearing alpine slouch hats, peg-top trousers, a variety of galluses, and impressive handlebar moustaches. Colorful and carefree, they could have been going to a picnic.

By the time they walked through Crystal Ridge and Cranberry, their ranks had swollen to four hundred and nobody had tried to interfere with them. But as they approached West Hazleton, Sheriff Martin and his deputies suddenly materialized. The sheriff and his men sprang out of a trolley car, hidden behind a culm bank, shouting, "Stop. This is against the law."

"I don't care, I'm going to Lattimer," Steve Yusko, a Polish miner, shook his fist at the sheriff and continued to walk. Two deputies pulled him to one side and one of them, in an unexpected act of brute force, swung the butt end of his rifle down on Yusko's arm and broke it.

John Murray, enraged, bellowed at the sheriff, "Tell me that man's name. I'll swear out a warrant for his arrest for injuring an innocent citizen."

Instead of answering, the sheriff tried to cram a piece of paper into Murray's hand. "This is my proclamation. It is against the law to go farther." Murray refused the proclamation and the sheriff stuffed it back into his pocket.

Edward Jones, Hazleton's police chief, who had been standing on the sidelines, stepped over to the sheriff and told him that the strikers had a perfect right to walk on the public highways.

Meanwhile the marchers had come to a halt, and some of them used the pause to fill their pipes. One of them, Anthony Kislaviez, picked up a stone to strike a light. The moment he did so, one of the sheriff's men shouted, "Arrest that man" and immediately two deputies seized him.

"We are not disobeying the law," Murray called defiantly.

His words were ignored. The sheriff turned to follow the deputies, who were leading Kislaviez and Yusko away. Later they would be put in the county jail without a hearing.

As the sheriff and his men disappeared, Murray called to his strikers to resume their march. He ordered them to take a roundabout route to Lattimer because he had been advised by the police chief not to go directly through Hazleton. Neither Jones nor Murray realized that the sheriff meanwhile had loaded his deputies into a waiting trolley that could take them to Harleigh, a hamlet between Hazleton and Lattimer. There the sheriff intended once more to confront the strikers.

It was a little after three o'clock when Murray led his bohemian band over a small hill. They were in sight of Lattimer and had planned to walk peacefully through Harleigh and its cluster of miners' shacks. As they rounded a bend in the road, Sheriff Martin, surrounded by deputies, walked forward to meet them.

"Halt," the sheriff waved his proclamation. "Where are you going?"

"We go to Lattimer mines," someone in front shouted.

"Stop," the sheriff ordered. "You are disobeying the law."

"Come on," John Murray said and continued to walk forward.

"Who said 'Come on'?" With his left hand, the sheriff clutched the coat collar of the miner nearest him and, with his right, drew his revolver.

Murray started toward the sheriff. "I tell you again we are not disobeying the law. We have no arms of any kind. We are not going to kill or murder. We want to go on through the town and you have no right to interfere with us."

The men behind Murray pushed forward as the sheriff pulled his captive to one side, shoving him to his knees. In seconds the crowd had started an uncontrollable stampede. Then a rifle went off, then another and another. The mob retreated as more and more shots rang out. Men scattered to the right and to the left in helpless confusion. Some dragged themselves across the trolley tracks and into the underbrush. Those in front dropped like wheat stalks before a scythe.

Most of the victims were shot in the back. Those who tried to reach a thin row of trees beyond the trolley track were shot down by deputies, who broke rank and followed them as they fled.

It would be days before the full toll of the massacre was known.

Danny, who had been up all night, heard them first and went to the front door. It was six o'clock Saturday morning, September eleventh, the day after the Lattimer massacre. There was a family at the door; one man, one woman, and six children, all of whom were talking excitedly in Italian. The woman had been crying; she was terrified and her husband was trying to comfort her.

Barbara came downstairs in her wrapper, looked questioningly at the group and then at Danny.

"From Lattimer, I think," Danny said.

"The strikers come back, come kill us like their friends get killed," the man said breathlessly. He wiped the sweat off his forehead with a dirty, gray rag.

"The strikers are coming back to Lattimer?"

The man nodded his head vigorously. "They come back to kill us. Why? We no kill no one."

"Come in. We'll get you something to eat." Danny led the way as Barbara started turning on the gaslight. The shutters were closed tight, and although the sun was up, the house was pitch dark. Ever since yesterday afternoon, when the news had come from Lattimer, all of Clarkston had been living as if under siege. No one seemed to know exactly what had happened, but twenty Coal and Iron Police were stationed at the Clarkston colliery, there were three guards in front of each of the Clark houses, and every window on every house was shuttered.

The women and children were led into the kitchen, and Barbara, still sleepy herself, roused the maids and asked them to get the frightened stragglers something to eat. Danny beckoned the man to follow him and led the way into the living room. "Sit down," Danny said. "As soon as the rest of your family has been fed, we'll get something for you. Tell me your name and who you work for. Where do you live?"

"In Harleigh. I Bruno Gaccione," the man said. "You no know me, Mr. Clark, but I know you. I see you on engine when you go round mines. I work at Pardee in Lattimer."

"How long have you worked there, Bruno?"

"'Leven years, *signor*."

"Can you tell me what happened yesterday? Were you there when the sheriff and his men met the strikers?"

"*Si, signor*." Again the man nodded vigorously. "On my way home from the mines I see lotta men in front of master mechanic Taylor house. Our house next Signor Taylor. Is a nice house."

"Weren't you home very early?"

"*Si, signor*. Hurt my foot with pick and foreman send me to doctor but no see him. Sheriff and men standing near my house, a big crowd come around bend. Sheriff tell them stop."

"Did they?"

"*Si, signor*. They stop. Sheriff show them paper and tell them to obey him. They no understand. Big Irishman tell sheriff they go to Lattimer, leave them alone. But sheriff grabs striker, pulls out gun. I see him pull out gun."

"Did you see any other guns?"

"No. I no see, but after sheriff pull out gun I hear plenty shots. I run, hide."

"What happened to the big Irishman?"

"I dunno. Maybe he get killed. Lotta shots, everybody run,

scream, fall down. Everything happen very fast. Sheriff's men yell. Everybody run. He run, too."

"You mean the strikers ran away?"

"*Si, si*. They no got guns. Some go across trolley tracks. Some lie on faces in dust. Doctor heard shots and come fast. Other men, too."

"Do you have any idea of how many men were killed?"

"Twenty maybe. Maybe more. One man I pick up after shots stop. He dead already. Blood come out all over his head. I go home, see my wife, children. She bad scared. See things out window. She say lotta men die. I get her quiet, go back. Many men hurt. We take them to school, put some on trolley. They go Hazleton Hospital, on mule cart."

"Why were the men there? Were they coming to Pardee's mine to get his men to quit work?"

The Italian frowned as if he didn't quite understand.

"Did the men want Pardee's men to strike. To join the union?"

"*Si*. We all know there's gotta be union."

"Do you belong to the union?"

"Not yet."

"And the men on the march, the strikers, they never did get to Lattimer, did they? Or to Pardee's men?"

"No, that's the trouble. A lotta men killed on Harleigh Road. Now they come back. At one o'clock in the morning a man told nightman at Pardee all the men were gonna come back for vendetta. Gonna kill everybody, so we got up to take women and children to Freetown."

"Jesus." Danny picked up a crutch. "I want to call the chief of police in Hazleton, although I suppose he must already know this?"

The Italian shrugged. Danny got up and walked into the hall, where the telephone was. He reached up and turned the handle twice The ring echoed harshly through the house. Danny took the receiver off the hook. "Edward Jones, in Hazleton, please, Bertha." He waited for two minutes, leaning on his crutch, for the operator to make the connection. There was a series of uneven rings and finally Danny shouted into the mouthpiece, "Ed, Ed, are you there?"

In the living room, the Italian waited, sitting on the edge of his chair, turning his cap in his hands. A faint voice came from inside the instrument Danny was grappling with.

"Ed, is that you? Can't hear you very well. There, that's better. Dan Clark here."

"Dan. Glad you called. You all right in Clarkston?"

"Yes, but Ed, a family from Lattimer is here. They stopped on their way to Freetown."

"I'm not surprised. Lattimer is just about evacuated. Hazleton's no bed of roses either. My God, mobs of people streaming through the hospital trying to identify their relatives. Bodies piled up all over the place."

"Christ." Danny shifted his crutch. "You petitioned the governor for troops?"

"Yeah. So's the sheriff."

"Want me to send a wire for Clark Brothers and"—he turned slightly and caught a glimpse of the Italian, twisting his cap— "for just plain citizens?"

"You bet. God, Dan, this is a hell of a tragedy. Nineteen known dead and God knows how many wounded and dying."

"What mine were they from mostly, Ed."

"Harwood. At least those were the men who started the march. But they picked up quite a lot when they went through Crystal Ridge and Cranberry."

"What exactly happened, Ed? I've had some pretty garbled reports."

"Myself, I think that goddamned fool Sheriff Martin lost his head. I warned him when he tried to stop them in West Hazleton that they had a perfect right to march on the public highways, poster or no posters, and they were still on a public highway when he slaughtered them."

"Harwood has more green and inexperienced Poles and Lithuanians than any of our collieries, doesn't it? My God, practically none of those men could have understood English, much less speak it."

"That's right."

"I've been telling them for years they'd get in trouble importing cheap labor."

The chief grunted. "Yup. They've been spoiling for trouble all summer, and Murray—I think he may be dead—that fellow from your place has been stirring them up for weeks."

"Murray! Good God, 'the big Irishman.' I should have known right away. First, what's this about his being dead?"

"I was going to call about that soon as I had a chance, Dan. I think one of the bodies laid out at the stables may be John Murray, but I can't be sure, and he has no family to identify him. Think you could come down and do that?"

"I—uh, let's go back to the beginning. I didn't even know Murray was involved. I didn't think any of the Irish would work with the Hungarians."

"Yeah. Well, I guess a lot wouldn't. But Murray was a sort of leader. With Vosher. And I'm told one other Irishman was involved, but I don't know who."

"O'Neill." Danny said it quietly.

"What's that, Dan?"

"Oh, hell, I can't be sure. Just an educated guess."

"Well, there's just one dead Irishman, far as I know. At least that's all we've uncovered up to now."

"Vosher speak any English?"

"Yeah. For a Hungarian he's pretty literate."

"Anyone mention the name O'Neill among the marchers?"

"O'Neill? I think maybe—wait a minute. One of Pardee's men, a mick, said something about the O'Neill brothers. Said one of the brothers refused to go along with Murray but the other one did. I wasn't paying much mind at the time."

"That means he's left along with Vosher to lead the men—that is, if Murray's dead."

"I guess. Anyways, there's talk about their coming back on a revenge march. That's why everybody's evacuating."

"That means trouble everywhere. Our mines, too. I'll be there as soon as I can." Danny hung up the telephone and, forgetting his crutch, hurried back into the living room.

Danny decided that before he left for Hazleton he should let his father know about Murray's possible death and the men's threat to come back. He walked into his parents' house just as Fred was finishing breakfast.

"Thought I'd better tell you what I've just heard, Father," Danny said from the dining room door. "The marchers—those who weren't killed—are threatening to come back for revenge. I don't know—"

"I've already heard about that. Militia ought to be able to take care of them. Just got word they're on their way."

"Oh. I also just heard that John Murray was one of the leaders of the march."

Fred threw his napkin on the table. "Goddamned troublemaker. Evidently Murray won't stop at anything."

"Well, he's stopped now—maybe. There's a strong possibility he was killed."

Fred looked surprised. "Sorry, all I can say to that is good riddance."

"I'm not so sure, Father. God knows he's given us enough trouble over the years, but he was a strong man and a natural leader. And, I suppose, if it hadn't been John Murray, it would have been somebody else."

"No doubt. That goddamned union. They'll destroy the country before they're through. Bunch of anarchists and murderers."

"They were the ones who were killed, Father."

"For God's sake, Dan. They were ordered by the sheriff not to congregate in public places, an order they deliberately disobeyed, and on top of that they threatened the sheriff and his men. What in hell did you expect the sheriff to do? Stand there and get shot?"

"According to Ed Jones, the sheriff lost his head," Danny said mildly, "and legally you can't order anyone not to congregate on a public highway. I imagine John Murray was smart enough to know that. Besides, they weren't armed, but I don't want to argue with you about it now. I've got to get to Hazleton and see if I can identify Murray."

"You? Doesn't he have any family?"

"No. Don't you remember? Katie Malloy always told Aunt Jessie that was why he caused so much trouble."

"Oh, Jessie. She's almost as much trouble as the union. God, I wish Dexter were alive to keep her in line."

Danny shook his head. This was one of the times when it was useless to try to argue with his father. "Well, I'll be back as soon as I can and come direct to your office. I think we're going to have trouble in Clarkston and Hanley even if there are troops in the region. But for God's sake, let's do everything we can to avoid more bloodshed."

"I agree with you there, Dan. Get back as soon as you can."

Danny borrowed Jessie's buckboard with Eroh to take him to Hazleton. He told Eroh his mission was to try to find John Murray and suggested the deserted stables behind the hospital as the first place to go.

"Katie came by early this morning to see Mrs. Dexter," Eroh said. "If Murray was one of the first men killed and that's what everybody's saying, Katie said the men who were killed first were taken to Boyle's Funeral home. Later they had so many, one place couldn't accommodate all of them."

The road from Clarkston to Hazleton ran through Harleigh and curved around the shoulder of the mountain less than a mile from Lattimer. The village of Harleigh lay like a ghost town in the soft September sunshine. Doors were locked and windows were shuttered. Not a human being was to be seen on the main street or in the back yards.

"I never saw it so quiet on a workday morning," Eroh said. Danny nodded. It was as if the town, having witnessed death, had retreated into hiding.

Father Aust, the rector of Saint Stanislaus Polish Catholic Church, was standing in front of Boyle's Funeral Home as they drove up. The priest recognized Danny and came over to the carriage.

"I'm sorry, Father." Danny held out his hand. "It's a terrible tragedy." There were deep shadows under the cleric's eyes. "You look as though you'd been up all night," Danny said.

"I have, but you look about the same as I do, Dan." The priest shot him an admiring glance. Something noble and aristocratic about the young man's head, he thought.

"I guess I haven't been near a razor in twenty-four hours, at that," Danny said, passing a hand over the faint stubble on his chin. "Father, I've come to see if it's true John Murray is one of the dead. The police chief thinks he is and John hasn't any family. He—"

Father Aust stopped him. "He is one of the dead, Dan."

"I was sure of it. He was an intelligent man and a leader, but he was a firebrand, always stirring up trouble."

Danny got out of the buckboard and Father Aust touched his arm. "It's a pretty grim sight," the priest said. "I think perhaps I should go with you."

"Thanks, Father, I'd appreciate it."

Just inside the door to the left three strapping young men were laid out side by side on wooden trestles. One had auburn hair, the other two yellow. The last man in the row was an especially appalling sight. His face and neck had been riddled by bullets. Danny turned away and saw that an older man was stretched out on a trestle against the opposite wall. He was all alone. Reddish hair straggled over a high domed forehead, and his jaw was as jaggedly set in death as it had been in life.

Danny gave a start of recognition. "There he is. Poor devil." He walked across the room and looked down at Murray. A man who died for his cause.

"If this man had worked with us instead of against us, he'd have been at the top of the heap today," Danny said.

"Poor soul," Father Aust said. "I know a little about his past. He had a terrible childhood in New York and he hated the church almost as much as he hated Clark Brothers. He was in those bloody Civil War riots as a boy, and I don't think he ever got over it. He was always a bitter man."

"And a fighter. And in death he won." Danny was mumbling, as though talking to himself.

"What—?" began Father Aust.

"Oh, the operators can't see it, but unionization is bound to come," Danny said. "Just as Murray was bound to be destroyed fighting for it. Actually he was one of the few who understood the strength that comes from banding together. He was an ideal union organizer, but I think the men sensed the violence of his nature and were frightened of him. He was jealous of my family's power and he was fiercely independent. For instance, I'm sure he resented my Aunt Jessie more than all the rest of us put together."

"But why her? She is so—"

"I know. Good to the men. But Murray thought her patronizing. It's hard to get men to rebel against kindness. Murray would never thank anyone, including the "Angel of the Anthracite," for giving him something to which he thought he had a right. And he believed he and the other miners had the right to a decent living wage."

"You're not any more typical of the operators than John Murray was of the miners, are you?" the priest said slowly.

"I? Oh, there's a big difference, Father. I haven't been killed for my ideas."

Both men contemplated the dead man in silence for a moment. "Father Aust," Danny said finally, "would it be possible—well, John Murray had no family and he didn't live long enough to belong to the union, so they can't bury him. He doesn't belong to Saint Stanislaus Church either, but the fact is he didn't belong anywhere. I'd like to see him have a decent burial and even though he might hate it, Clark Brothers will take care of the casket and any other arrangement. Could you give him your blessing and include him in the mass funeral to be held on Monday in church?"

The priest nodded, closed his eyes, and knelt beside the trestle, praying in a low murmur. After a few moments, he made the sign of the cross, rose to his feet, leaned down, and kissed Murray on the forehead, once more making the sign of the cross above him.

"It may not be the will of the church," he said, "but I believe it is God's will."

"Thank you, Father," Danny said and held out his hand. "I'll be at the church Monday morning and stand in for John's family."

It had taken John Fahy eight hours to make his way from the bituminous mines in the western part of the state. He got off the train at Hazleton the day after the massacre and went straight to Boyle's Funeral Home.

Philip Boyle let Fahy in. The union organizer was small, almost diminutive, with bristling dark hair and a tense manner that belied the dreamer in the light, gray eyes.

"I'm John Fahy," he said in clipped tones. He stuck out his hand and smiled, showing a brilliant array of teeth. "You don't know me. Mr. Boyle, is it? I'm a stranger in town. Here from Pittsburgh. I'm a union organizer. Had a terrible time here, haven't you?" Fahy bowed his head. "I'm deeply sorry. Tragic times, these. I'm here to do what I can to help."

In ten minutes Fahy had extracted all the information he wanted from Boyle, especially the fact that the O'Neill brothers seemed to have taken over Murray's leadership role. After viewing the dead and making appropriate remarks, he hired a trap and made his way as quickly as he could to Clarkston. Once there, he asked the first miner he saw the way to the O'Neills'.

Introducing himself, Fahy told Jamie and Tim he had come from the organized mines to help. The union was the "potential savior of mankind," he said. Joining the union was the only way to "exact justice and a living wage from those now living on the fat of the land and the sweat of the laborer's brow. Strength lies in numbers, my friends, and only when we join together under strong leadership can we bring the operators to their knees." As he talked, Fahy could see a glimmer of intelligence in Jamie's expression, even though his responses were limited to an occasional grunt. Tim was even less encouraging; from time to time he would ask a timid question that indicated his inability to comprehend the whole of Fahy's grand design.

"The time is now," Fahy declared. "And you," turning to Jamie, "and your brother are the designated leaders of the miners in this county, now that John Murray, God rest his soul," Fahy made the sign of the cross, "has gone to his just reward. The funeral of those poor souls who have died so that the rest of us may go forward is on Monday. Monday night, then, is when you must call a meeting of all the men to join the union and stand together as one. Then and only then will a strike bring results. Organize and fight—it's the only way."

"Don't count on me to lead no meeting." It was the first full sentence Jamie had spoken.

Fahy reeled back as if he had received a physical blow. He looked at the floor for a moment, then raised his eyes and stared into Jamie's as though prying into the inner regions of Jamie's soul. "You would be betraying our cause if you would not help lead these men into battle," he said.

"My brother Tim can do the leading if he's so inclined, or, better yet, do it yourself." Jamie stretched his shoulders and stifled a yawn.

Fahy shook his head. "Not I. The men must see a face they're accustomed to, the face of a man they can trust. Tim understands that, now don't you?"

Tim looked anxiously at his brother.

"It's up to you, Tim," Jamie said.

"But what about—"

"Surely your brother will be at your side, Tim," Fahy said. "With him there you cannot falter. And, don't worry now. I'm well used to these meetings and I'll spend every waking minute with you from now until Monday. You'll know exactly what to say and how to bring the men around."

"Should I do it, Jamie?" There was a quaver in Tim's voice.

"You may as well, Tim, there's no one else. And now, if you'll excuse me, I'm going out for a bit of air."

All day Monday Clarkston and the neighboring villages lay under a pall. The threat of the returning strikers, the deaths, the mourning families, the uncertainty about what would happen next, all contributed to the unbearable tension in the air. Twenty-seven hundred troops had been sent by the Governor and were deployed in five camps surrounding Hazleton. Within telephone communication of General Gobin and equidistant from his headquarters in Hazleton, they were a constant reminder of the probability of violence. The funeral Monday morning, the mass array of caskets, the widows and children, some sobbing pathetically, the look of hopelessness on the workers' faces, hung like a black cloud over the region.

After the funeral, Danny went back to Clarkston and directly to his father's office. He was exhausted and showed it. Barely greeting Fred, he sat down heavily in the armchair.

"You all right, Dan?" His father was seated at his desk, a cigar smoldering in the ashtray beside him.

"As much as anyone can be. I gather you gave permission for our men to hold their meeting at Black Creek Hall?"

"That's right. And it's pretty damned broadminded of me considering they burned it to the ground seven years ago. Anyway, I've put on ten extra men."

Danny sat bolt upright. "Good God, Father, you can't do that."

"What do you mean, I can't? I'm certainly not going to take any chances. Those men get out of line, and they're going to be put down."

"And murdered? Like the ones the sheriff shot down?"

"Danny—" Fred got up and reached for what was left of his cigar. Despite his anxiety, Danny could see that his father was making a monumental effort to control his temper.

"Danny," Fred said, "I haven't wanted to tell you this. Now I see I have to. While you were at the funeral, I got word that the D. S. & S. depot at Hazleton Junction was broken into last night. The doors were battered down, the telegraph instruments smashed to pieces—the place is a shambles. Now, do you see why it's necessary to guard the hall?"

"Damn." Danny felt an aching disappointment. He loved the D. S. & S. and he'd supposed his men did too. The pain was as sharp as a physical blow, but he made a supreme effort to be objective. "It's still not murder," he said.

"No, I suppose not. But don't you see that these men are completely irresponsible. Basically, they haven't got the sense to manage their own affairs. That's why they're laborers in the first place, and on top of that they're now out of control, and unless we take every precaution, there is bound to be more killing. That's exactly why I'm surrounding the hall with—"

There was a knock at the door.

"Goddamn it," Fred squashed out the cigar and went to the door. It was Jessie.

"Oh, Jessie. What brings you here?" Fred stood squarely in the doorway doing his best not to let her come in.

Jessie peered around him and spotted Danny. "Fred, Danny." She tried in vain to inch forward. "I have some vital news I want to tell you both."

"I'm sure it can wait, Jessie. We're very busy just now."

"No, it can't, Fred."

Danny was intrigued to see that she managed to press by his father. Once inside his room, she walked over to a stool opposite Danny's chair and sat down. Fred turned to face them both and Danny could see two bright red spots appear high on his cheeks.

"I'm sorry to intrude, Fred," Jessie said politely, "but I've just had a visit from Katie Malloy, and for the first time in my life

I'm terrified. Katie said the men are planning to meet tonight at Black Creek Hall to discuss the strike and joining the union, but I'm sure you both know that. What is so terrible is that some of them are spreading the rumor that the Coal and Iron Police have been called out and will be there brandishing their guns the entire time the men are in the meeting."

"I don't know about 'brandishing their guns,'" Fred said, "but it is not a rumor about the Coal and Iron Police being there. They most certainly will." He walked back to his desk and sat down. "And that's final." He looked at Jessie coldly. "And now that you've brought us your piece of 'vital news,' Jessie, I'd appreciate it if you'd let us get on with our business."

Jessie drew herself up very straight. "Fred, you and I have often disagreed, but right now we must manage to forget our differences and you must listen to me. You see, I know these men in a way that you and Dexter never have."

"Oh, for the love of God, I just happen to work with the men, that's all. That seems to be something you overlook."

Danny looked at Jessie imploringly. It was true she had a much better grasp of the men's rights and needs than his father or his uncle but she was only stiffening his father's resolve and her timing was disastrous.

Jessie turned to Danny.

"Danny, you remember the march when you and Fred and Dexter were all in Philadelphia and Schlenker called out the Coal and Iron Police?"

"Yes, of course, Aunt Jessie. "You—" Danny stopped. If, in his father's mind, he was allied with his aunt, it would be fatal. Somehow, without hurting her feelings, he must get her out of here. "Aunt Jessie," he said gently, "we have all been under a terrible strain and terrible things have happened. You are quite right to report anything you know to us, and Father and I realize how dangerous the situation is." Danny pushed himself to his feet. "The minute we know anything more I'll come and report it to you."

"But, Danny," Jessie looked as though she was about to cry, "please promise me you won't let the Coal and Iron Police anywhere near Black Creek Hall tonight."

"All right, Aunt Jessie, I'll be in touch later."

"What do you mean, 'all right,' Dan?" Fred stood up. The splotches of red on his face had grown and he was shaking. You'll promise no such thing, goddamn it. I'm running this company and I will not brook this kind of interference." He stalked to the door and flung it open. "Good day to you, madam." He walked out, slamming the door shut after him.

Danny sat down. He knew that his uncle's death had greatly increased his father's resentment at the burdens of Clarkston and that his father was sometimes the victim of terrible rages, but this was the first he had personally witnessed.

"What will we do, Danny?" Jessie's voice was a whisper.

Danny was beyond being able to console her. "I just don't know, Aunt Jessie. I just don't know."

Barbara helped him make up his mind. He came home directly from Fred's office thinking that he would give his father time to simmer down. In the meantime he knew he must find some way to be in contact with the men themselves. Even the suggestion that the Clarks were putting on police would lead to an ugly and probably violent situation.

"Of course, you're right, Dan," Barbara said. "Go to your mother. She's the only person who has a chance of making him see reason."

"I still don't know," Danny said. He felt raw. "He's always been reasonable with me before this, but I never have been able to make him or Uncle Dex understand how the men feel. Aunt Jessie's arrival this afternoon was a disaster, but she was right about one thing. Neither Uncle Dex nor my father has ever known the men as human beings. Aunt Jessie doesn't understand them thoroughly herself. She feels doling out charity is a sure cure for everything, and it isn't. But at least she recognizes the danger of inflaming them further."

Barbara came over and took his hand. "You've had a bad time, Dan. Go see your mother right now. I'll be here when you come back."

He looked at her gratefully. "I know. You'll always be there. And maybe you're right. At any rate, I'll have to give it a try."

Tommy Malloy was in the living room when Dan came back

from seeing his mother. Barbara, who had been sitting with him, hurried to the front door when she heard Dan coming in.

"How did it go?" she whispered.

Danny shrugged. "She'll try. I don't even know where he went after he slammed out of the office. She says he sometimes goes for a long walk after an explosion like that. Anyway, she'll do her best. She says he may feel ashamed of himself and that may help."

"I'm sure it will, Dan. Tommy Malloy's in the living room and anxious to see you."

"Tommy? Good," Danny smiled. "Hey, there, Tommy," he called as he started toward the living room. "Boy, am I glad to see you! I caught a glimpse of you this morning—on the other side of the church."

"Yeah, I saw you, too," Tommy said, coming forward. "How are you?" He put an arm around Dan's shoulders. "Great to see you, but I wish, well, poor old Uncle John. I came up from college soon as I heard. Thanks, thanks a lot, Dan, for doing what you did about the funeral. Father just told me."

"Oh, that's the least we could do."

"I'm not so sure about that. John Murray wasn't exactly friendly to Clark Brothers, and when word got around about what you'd done, I can tell you everybody was pretty impressed."

"For God's sake, nobody was supposed to know. Oh, hell, let's just skip it."

"All right, Dan, if that's the way you want it. Anyway that's not what I came to talk about. The men are saying that Clark Brothers have called out the Coal and Iron Police for tonight. I've never seen them so angry." Tommy stopped and looked at Danny anxiously.

"Go on, Tommy," Danny said.

"They're saying they'll burn down every breaker along with Black Creek Hall, and they're talking about getting arms. It's bad enough that the governor's called out the militia."

"Tommy, that's a lot of talk. They can't very well burn down anything with a whole army surrounding them and they must know it."

"I know. But there'll be deaths."

"Not if I can help it. Look, Tommy, if I guarantee there will not be one single Coal and Iron Policeman present, will they let me speak to them?"

"You, Danny? You're a—but you're different. Let me think. They're afraid of informers and"—he looked apologetic—"Clark Brother's spies, but after this morning with everybody knowing what you did for Uncle John. They trust you, I think, which is more than they do for the rest of the family, except maybe Mrs. Dexter. I think maybe they'd let you speak to them."

"Tommy, can you get word to them that I'll guarantee them a free meeting and no Coal and Iron Police if they'll let me speak to them?"

"I don't know, Dan. I can try. I guess I'll talk to my father, first. Are you sure you can guarantee the police won't be there? Way I hear it, your father is determined."

"I give you my word," Dan said and wondered what kind of miracle he was expecting.

"That's enough for me," Tommy said as he got up to leave.

The moment the door closed on Tommy, Danny turned to Barbara. I'll have to go back to see my mother. I don't think I put it strongly enough."

"Poor darling. You're exhausted. I wish I could do it for you."

But Danny was already partway down the drive. In ten minutes he was back. Barbara took his hand and led him upstairs. "You have two hours to rest," she said. "What happened?"

"I told Mother this was a case of life and death—*my* life and *my* death—that I was going to the meeting and had given my word. I said if Father persisted, it might be the end of me."

"Oh, darling, what did she say?"

She looked at me. Her eyes filled with tears and her mouth went very hard. Then she said in a kind of whisper, "I'll make him understand."

"She didn't try to stop you?"

"I guess she knew it was no use." Danny threw himself across the bed.

"I'm not even going, Tommy," Stephen said. "I just haven't got the strength, and God knows I don't want to see a strike."

"I understand, Dad," Tommy said. "But I promised Danny. Who'll I go to?"

"Tim O'Neill," Stephen said wearily. "Now that John's gone, he'll take over. He's no man for it, either, but that's what they're saying. He's leading the meeting tonight, I've heard."

The O'Neills' house was two blocks from the Malloys. Tommy was lucky enough to find Tim alone.

"I've just been to see Dan Clark," Tommy said.

Tim eyed him sharply. "So?" Tim's voice was hoarse, his eyes sunk in his face. He looked as though he hadn't slept for a week. "He have anything to say about the killings?"

"He feels the way you do, Tim," Tommy said quietly. "You saw him at the funeral this morning and you know what he did for John Murray."

"Neither he or any of the other lousy Clarks did anything to stop that bastard sheriff, now did they?"

"God knows Danny would have if he could. He didn't know anything about it until it was all over."

"No? Oh, what the hell do you know, lad? Them Goddamned mine owners are planning to surround the Hall tonight with the bloody Coal and Iron Police. Did you know that? And do you know what it means? More bloodshed, as sure as I'm sitting here."

"That's why I'm here, Tim. Dan Clark will guarantee there will be no police if he is allowed to talk to the men at tonight's meeting."

"Him? A Clark? Are you off your rocker, lad? Or do you just want to see him killed?"

"No," Tommy said and felt a thrust of fear. "But nobody—I don't think any of the men hate Danny. And—"

"For God's sake, lad. He's a Clark. Get that through your head. And how do you think the men are feeling anyways, after the killings and John Murray dead?"

"But Tim, if you tell them he's the one who kept the police away? Dan is on the men's side. I know he is."

Tim put a hand to the back of his head. "You say he'll guarantee no police?"

"Yes."

"I dunno, lad. Mayhap he's got the courage to show his face

in that hall and the men might lay off outta respect for him being so foolhardy. But I wouldn't want to guarantee it. Ask me, he's laying his neck in a noose."

"Dad said you'd be leading the meeting with Murray gone?"

"Aye."

"Well, then would you tell them that Dan made the Clarks hold off the police. And that he has something to say to them. Could you do that?"

"I could."

"Then, can I tell Dan you'll do it?"

"You'd also better tell him it's not likely he'll come back from the meeting alive."

For the past day and a half, Fahy had coached his pupil. Tim was a slow learner, but eventually he began to get the knack of delivering ringing phrases. Fahy was a chameleon; his manner was brisk and to the point in ordinary conversation, but at the thought of addressing an audience he became an orator promising to deliver Valhalla to anyone who would work for it.

Monday afternoon, shortly after Tommy's visit, Fahy returned from a survey of Clarkston to continue his coaching. When Tim told him of Tommy's proposal, Fahy's eyes lit up. If only Tim didn't ruin it, this would give them the chance they were waiting for.

The meeting was called for seven upstairs in the Assembly Room of Black Creek Hall. Tommy was standing in the back, partly hidden behind one of the open double doors, feeling sick. Immediately after he had left Tim O'Neill, he had begun cursing himself for his part in the arrangements. He should have had the wit to lie to Danny and tell him the men wouldn't let him in. But that probably wouldn't have worked either. Danny was bent on coming. If he were killed tonight, Tommy would never, never forgive himself.

Danny was to arrive at the hall at seven thirty and wait quietly outside for Tommy to come down and get him. Tommy would do this as soon as O'Neill told the men Danny was coming to talk to them. Tommy wondered if Dan would make it to the front of the room without being hurt.

The men started shuffling in a few minutes before seven. Sullen and despairing, they walked in silence to their chairs and sat down. They could have been attending another funeral, but underneath their glum exteriors Tommy sensed a terrible hostility. He shivered and started to pray. Soon all the seats in the hall were taken, and men were standing against the walls.

Tim O'Neill and Ferenc Vosher came in and seated themselves at a table on the platform. A couple of minutes later, to Tommy's surprise, Jamie O'Neill walked up the aisle and took a seat beside them. That might be a hopeful sign, Tommy thought. Jamie had more sense than his brother, and he had never been as violent as John Murray.

The hall was packed when Tim got to his feet. He cleared his throat and picked up a piece of paper. Tommy frowned. He was pretty sure Tim could hardly read.

Tim began to speak. "Nineteen men died the day before yesterday. They were murdered, killed in cold blood, killed by a law officer who had no right to do what he did." A roar of outrage filled the hall.

Tommy sat back, puzzled. There was something funny here. Tim had said that as though he'd practiced it a hundred times. Even his voice was different.

"And among them—the—those—killed was our leader." Tim put a hand over his heart. Unfortunately it was the one holding the paper. "John Murray." The crowd got to its feet. Men were clenching their fists and waving them in the air.

"Men—" Tim had to shout to make himself heard, "Men— are we going to let the bloody owners get away with this?"

Tim waited and Tommy saw him talk briefly with Vosher. He wondered again why Jamie was there. He seemed to be just a bystander. Then he noticed a movement in the curtains at the side of the stage. Someone must be back of that curtain. Tommy crept over to the opposite side of the hall. He could make out a man standing behind the curtain gesturing with his arms and cupping his hands from time to time apparently to issue instructions. Tommy edged back to his place. He was sure now that the man backstage had a lot to do with what was going on.

"Quiet! Quiet, men!" Tim was still shouting. Slowly the men began to sit down. Before Tim could speak, a voice from the back called, "I say strike and this time if they try and stop us, we'll kill them—just like they killed us."

"That's right, men," Tim called out. "But first we got to organize—" Tim's voice trailed off, and he looked confused. Tommy realized the significance of the man behind the curtain. He must be a union organizer. But he had picked on poor material when he asked Tim to lead the men. No amount of coaching could make Tim a leader; he had nowhere near the strength or intelligence of Murray. "The union," Tim was saying. Momentarily he regained his poise. "Men, say aye or nay—will you join the union?"

A foreman in one of the front rows stood up. "And who's the leader of this here union, Tim? You?"

"Aye. Now that John Murray's dead—" He stopped and leaned toward the curtain.

Tommy saw Jamie turn his head and spit on the floor. Unexpectedly Vosher got to his feet.

"Ve must vote," Vosher said.

"Aye, we'll vote now," Tim said. "All them—awk—all of you wanting to belong to the union raise your hands and say aye."

There was a wave of bewildered murmuring. Tommy thanked God Tim was making a mess of it. He'd a lot rather have the men confused than angry and determined. Tim had asked them to vote for something without explaining the purpose. Tommy looked at his watch. Seven thirty-two. Oh God, Danny was outside, waiting.

"Fer God's sake"—it was the same foreman—"when do we strike?"

Tim was making a desperate attempt to pull himself together. Tommy almost wanted to laugh as he saw the curtain do a dance.

Tim's voice had regained some of its strength. "First, we vote to join the union, then we vote to strike, and then I have something very interesting to tell you."

Tommy reached for the handle of the door, knowing that last must refer to Danny. Now he was sure Tim had been coached first to inflame the men and then let Danny in.

"All right now. Do you want to join the union? Raise your hands and say aye."

A roar of ayes went up with the men's hands. Half the hall was on its feet.

"And the strike? Do you vote to strike?" Tim asked.

Another roar of ayes as all the men got to their feet. Chairs were overturned, men were thumping each other on the back and yelling. Tommy was about to slide out downstairs and physically carry Danny away when he saw Jamie waving his hands trying to make himself heard. Slowly the hall began to quiet down, chairs were righted, and men's shouts dwindled to murmurs.

"Quiet. Quiet," Jamie O'Neill's voice boomed out. "Didn't you hear Tim say he had something very interesting to tell you?'

Tommy's hand tightened on the doorknob.

Suddenly the men were quiet and Tim started to speak. "We have a little surprise for you this evening. How would you like to hear what the Clarks have to say for themselves?"

The abrupt silence was followed by an ugly roar. Jamie got to his feet and pounded the speaker's table. The roar continued. To get attention he was finally forced to come around the table to the front of the platform, both arms raised.

Tommy clenched the doorknob, torn between wanting to get Danny away before he was hurt and anxiety to hear what Jamie would say. He couldn't be sure what side Jamie was on, but a couple of times he had glowered at his brother and when he spat on the floor, his expression had been filled with contempt.

"Hold on, men," Jamie bellowed. "For God's sake, be quiet so as you can listen."

"To a Clark? You be our leader now, Jamie, in place of your brother?" It was a miner, an old-timer, leaning against the wall.

"No, but never mind about who's leading. I just want to point out something to you. You've voted to strike. You may be outta work for months. Now the member of the Clark—" Once again the hall erupted, but this time not for long. "Shut up, will you, and listen." Exasperated, Jamie shook his fist. "The Clark who wants to speak to you is Dan Clark." There was a low rumble. "The least you can do is to listen to what he's got to say before you kill him."

Shaking, Tommy slid out the door, prepared to bolt, carrying

Danny with him. Before Tommy could grab him or speak to him, Danny had passed him, swinging through the hall toward the platform. He was on crutches and going too fast for Tommy to stop him. He must have, Tommy realized, used the crutches for the stairs. Tommy started after him, wishing he had some sort of weapon to defend them both.

The men were muttering, staring at Danny with frank curiosity. Tommy, trying to take in everything at once, wondered whether the sight of the misshapen figure on the crutches might overcome some of their hostility. But there was nothing pathetic about Danny. Tommy noticed for the hundredth time what a proud look he had: something about his head and the way he held it and his wonderful, warm smile. He caught up to him at the front of the hall.

With Tommy's help, Danny got up onto the platform. Jamie hesitated a minute, then walked over and put out his hand. Danny took it and smiled at him. The hall was still, the men watching the stage intently, suspicion on every face. Tommy held his breath and tried to look around without turning. Not a man there, it seemed to him, had moved a muscle.

Danny walked forward to the table, placed his crutches against it, and leaned on his elbows for support. "I—" he began and got no further.

"You and your family pleased with the work the police did on Friday?" someone yelled.

Danny started to raise a hand.

"The murderin' Clarks—that's what yer names is now," came from someone halfway back.

Danny grabbed the edge of the table to steady himself and nodded to the three men on the platform to sit down. His eyes were flashing behind the thick glasses, his warm smiled vanished. "Now shut up," he roared in a voice that penetrated the rafters. "Shut up, you goddamned sons of bitches. You shut up and listen to me."

Silence.

"The first thing I want you to understand is that Clark Brothers didn't have one damned single thing to do with the sheriff and his deputies. Clark Brothers, in fact, will do their best to see that they are prosecuted for murder.

"Second, Clark Brothers has and will protect its women and children, its workmen and property, with police guards against anyone who tries to injure people or destroy property.

"Third, I refused to allow any police or guards to come anywhere near Black Creek Hall while you were meeting. It was pointed out to me that you'd burned it down before and that I was a fool. And that I was an even bigger fool to come here myself."

Danny paused for breath. Tommy, who had been holding his, let it out. It looked as though Danny might come out of this alive. The attention of every man in the place was riveted on him.

"Now let me say that I know your hours are too long and your wages are too short. But, despite that, I don't want you to strike now."

The men began to stir.

"I know," Danny said, "that you think I'm saying that because I'm a lousy Clark."

Tommy wanted to applaud. He had taken the words out of their mouths.

"That's true in its way," Danny went on, "but it isn't the whole truth. Let's look at the facts for a minute. We have lived through the worst three days this region has ever known, and your greatest tragedy is that you lost John Murray. If you strike now, you'll be pitted against every mine owner in the country and you'll be out in the cold without any organization and without a shred of support either within or without. I don't want to see that and I certainly don't want to see any more bloodshed.

"I promise that Clark Brothers will do what they can to better conditions for you. We can't, however, meet your demands just like that. There are too many things beyond our control—the railroads, a thousand complications in marketing and adjusting the price of coal—I could give you a hundred reasons why we can't automatically just say yes to the things you think you deserve. But that's not your concern.

"What does concern you is leadership. You've made a start tonight by getting together. That means you know the importance of acting together. But you'll need a month or more to find a leader to take Murray's place. He was a strong man and he hated Clark Brothers, but, whether you believe me or not, I'll miss him. When you get a new leader, go ahead and organize. I'm not going to stop you. I know the day will come when I couldn't if I wanted to."

Danny picked up his crutches and turned away from the table. He began walking toward the platform steps. He was halfway down them when the applause began.

Danny's moral triumph left him a physical wreck. Barbara kept him in bed for a week and struggled valiantly to boost his spirits. Once in a bitter mood, he burst out, "The truth is, if I can't stand up to the kind of test the men put me through the other night, there's not much hope for Clark Brothers. But worst of all, I don't think I'm much of a husband for you."

"Nonsense. Now stop it, Dan. Neither of us was exactly perfect when we married, and so far it's been wonderful and you know it."

"You're right," Danny said, smiling.

CHAPTER 16

Atlantic City and Clarkston
September 1897

THE MOMENT THEY STEPPED INSIDE THE BRIGHTON HOTEL, the manager was at their side.

"Mr. Clark?" He sounded anxious. "Could I see you alone for a moment, sir?"

Fred disengaged his arm from Eliza's and followed the manager to a corner of the lobby under a potted palm. Fred eyed the man curiously. "What is it?"

"I've had three telephone calls, sir."

"So? Come to the point."

"There's been an accident, sir. They didn't want me to leave the hotel to meet you because they're arranging a special train to take you back from Philadelphia to Clarkston. I had to wait here for them to telephone me again about the time. They just called and your special train will leave Philadelphia at ten so you can catch it if you leave here at five."

"Accident?"

The manager blinked. "Yes, sir. To Mr. Daniel Clark."

"Oh, God. How badly is he hurt?"

"He's dead, sir."

The floor beneath him began to recede. Fred shook his head hard and tried to focus on Eliza, standing still as a stone where he had left her, her face white and immobile. She must have sensed . . .

"I have a few details, sir, if you—" the manager was saying.

"No. What difference?—Never mind—" His knees seemed to have become useless. He dug his nails into his palms until they hurt; then he turned and walked unsteadily toward Eliza. He noticed abstractedly that she was swaying slightly. He'd better get something to help her. "Brandy."

"Yes, of course, sir. Right away, sir."

Fred reached her and put his arms around her, wondering if he could hold them both up. She looked up at him as if begging for her life. "Is it Danny?"

He could only nod.

Dr. Herbert and Dr. Penwood were in the living room of Danny's house when they arrived. Dr. Herbert was the first to speak. "Danny's upstairs in his bedroom," he said. "Barbara's in the room next to him, asleep. I've given her a sleeping draught. She's had a very bad time of it."

Dr. Penwood came across to Eliza. "It was all over by the time I got here, my dear. Go up and see him. He died quietly with his wife standing by his side, holding his hand, and he is at peace now. His wife, poor young thing—she is the one to be pitied."

Eliza turned toward the door. "Fred?"

"No. You go, Hodie, if you want. I must find out what happened."

"I'll go with you," Dr. Penwood said, taking Eliza's arm.

"Bentz is with him," Dr. Herbert said. "He hasn't left his side since it happened."

"I'd better talk to him," Fred said.

Dr. Herbert nodded. "Send him down to us, would you, doctor?"

Fred motioned him to a chair.

"It was about four in the afternoon," Bentz said in answer to Fred's question. "Dan told me he wanted to try out some new brakes he'd installed. He was alone and drove the engine from the meadow back of the house, out the drive, and up to the turnaround. I was working in the shop at the time, and he called to me to come out and take a look. You see, Mr. Clark, I'd helped install the brakes."

"You've helped on just about all of Danny's projects, Bentz." The ghost of a smile crossed Fred's face.

"That's right, sir. Anyway, after we were both sure everything was working all right, he waved at me, rang his bell, and started off down the hill. He wasn't going fast but, of course, he gathered some momentum from the downgrade, and just as he took the curve to cross the road into your drive, there was a fearful crash and the engine toppled over on its side."

"What in God's name had he hit?"

"Some stones. We figured afterward that a couple of mule carts must have crossed the track between his trip up and his trip down. They must have dropped some stones, which the engine hit when it was derailed."

"Was Danny thrown?"

"Yes, sir. He landed about six feet from the tracks in a ditch. He was cursing and laughing. There were five of us in the shop at the time. The moment we heard the crash, we ran like hell to get to him. He swore he wasn't hurt, said just his bad leg was twisted and for Christ's sake to leave him alone, he'd be all right." Bentz took out a handkerchief and wiped his brow. "Excuse me, sir. 'For God's sake, get to work,' is what he said, 'and get my engine off her side. She's spilled live coals all over the ditch, and I'm afraid her boiler's cracked.'"

"Did you try to pick him up?"

"No, sir, we didn't dare. You know how Danny is. He was swearing and shouting orders like a general. But one of the men sneaked off to get Dr. Herbert."

"When I got there, I didn't think he was badly hurt," Dr. Herbert said, "but he wouldn't really allow me to examine him thoroughly then. Anyway, I managed to take his pulse. It was a little fast but not alarmingly so. When I asked him how he felt, he said he'd feel a goddamned sight better after the men got his engine righted." The doctor's involuntary smile vanished at Fred's expression.

"It took a couple of hours and a lot more men to get that engine right side up," Bentz continued. "I was standing beside Dan just as we did, and I saw a funny look come over his face. He said he had an awful pain in his side and asked us to get him back to the house." Bentz turned away. "He shuddered when we picked him up. Guess you'd better tell the rest, Doctor."

"Yes. I was able to give him a pretty thorough examination once we got him upstairs on his bed. I couldn't find much wrong, but I wasn't satisfied with the way his heart was behaving. I called Dr. Penwood in Philadelphia, who said he would come as fast as he could. He did, too, but—well, when we discussed it afterward, Mr. Clark, we agreed that your son has been living for years on sheer courage. The truth is that his heart has never been any good, and this time it failed him. He died two hours after we brought him home, quite peacefully, with his wife standing by his bed holding his hand. I—" The doctor reached out and put a gentle hand on Fred's knee.

Fred said nothing for a moment, and both men, watching his agony, were afraid to speak. Finally, with a heroic effort, Fred stood up and said, "Thank you, gentlemen, for all you've done. It's more than I can think about right now." His shoulders shook. "I don't see how we can get along without him, his mother and I."

"Danny got his strength from his family," Dr. Herbert said, "and the Clarks are strong people. You will find the strength you need. But now you and Mrs. Clark must rest and I want to give you both a small dose of laudanum so you can get some sleep. Unfortunately, there will be much to be done tomorrow and the next day."

"Thank you, doctor." Fred turned to Bentz. "My God, you've been through a terrible ordeal. You go home, too, and get some rest. I'm going to take Mrs. Clark home now."

At that moment Eliza and Dr. Penwood came into the room "He looks very peaceful, Fred," Eliza said. "Do you want to—?"

"No." Fred almost shouted the word. He looked at Dr. Penwood frantically. "Could you take us home, doctor? Dr. Herbert has suggested a dose of laudanum, and I guess we both could use it."

"Of course. Then perhaps Dr. Herbert could stay here and see to Danny's wife when she wakes up—and the servants. They'll be in a bad state of shock, too."

"Then—all right. Let's go, Eliza." Fred walked to the door with Eliza. Dr. Penwood followed.

Jessie squared her shoulders and rapped the knocker three times. Nellie opened the door. "Good morning, Nellie," Jessie said. "Would you tell Mrs. Clark I am here, please?"

"Yes, ma'am. May I take your cloak?"

As Jessie handed it to Nellie, Eliza came into the hall. "Good morning, Jessie. I thought I heard someone knock."

"Good morning, Eliza."

Eliza led the way into the living room, murmuring a platitude about the weather. She eyed her sister-in-law surreptitiously. Obviously, Jessie had something on her mind.

"How are you bearing up, Eliza? It's been two weeks."

Said with her usual tact, Eliza thought wearily. "Oh, all right, I guess, Jessie. I seem to wander through the days without thinking too much."

"'As lonely as a cloud,'" Jessie said softly. "That was one of Danny's favorites."

"Poetry? Danny?"

"Yes. He used to—" To Eliza's astonishment, Jessie looked faintly embarrassed. "Well, I guess you never knew it, but after Dexter died, he'd come over in the afternoons—for just a short while—as often as he could manage, and sometimes we'd read poetry together.

"Oh." Eliza couldn't think of anything else to say. Every day since Danny's death it seemed she learned something new about him. A few days after the funeral, Tommy Malloy stopped in. He looked desolate, making her suspect it was she who must comfort him.

"I thought he was done for that night in Black Creek Hall," Tommy told her. "Holy Mother, how he cursed them out! And it worked, too."

"What exactly did he say?" Eliza asked.

"Well, when I got him onto the platform, one of the men shouted something about the murdering Clarks, and that did it. Danny told them to shut up—I never knew he could shout so loud. And then—apologies to you, ma'am—he said, 'You goddamned sons of bitches, you shut up and listen to me!' And they did."

Eliza laughed for the first time since Danny had died. "I

think I should tell that to my husband. Oh, Tommy, I'm glad you told me." By the time Tommy left, both of them felt better.

"It must be terrible for you, Eliza," Jessie was saying. "It's hard even for me. I loved Danny very much and I miss him terribly. But I tell myself he never would have been satisfied to live anything but a turbulent and active life. He said as much to me one day and that he knew it would kill him sooner or later. Now, at least I find some consolation that he died quickly and without suffering." Jessie was silent for a moment. "Well, that's enough of that," she said briskly. "It isn't what I came for. Eliza, I am very worried about Fred and I came to see what I can do."

"Fred is—well, Fred is lost, Jessie. I can't seem to do anything."

"I'm afraid he'll break if he goes on like this," Jessie said "And I suppose you are, too."

Eliza nodded.

"Didn't the funeral, the tributes, help him at all?"

"I don't know, Jessie," Eliza swallowed. "Every time I think of the wheels and the broken axle—"

"And the telegraph poles—"

Danny's death had stirred that section of Pennsylvania as nothing ever had before. Freetown and Clarkston were draped in mourning. The road from Danny's house to the church was thronged with over a thousand men, women and children. Eliza had asked Bentz to suggest those men he knew were closest to Danny for the pallbearers. With the exception of Tommy Malloy, they were all workmen. There was not room in the church or the yard for the floral tributes that arrived from all over the state. The two most imposing and heartrending, Eliza had had placed outside at the entrance to the church, for everybody to see. On the right were two telegraph poles from the company telegraph operators. They were covered in ivy with a broken wire between them. Tiny lavender chrysanthemums had been wrapped around the dangling wire. On the left were two wheels, their spokes and rims made of dahlias with a broken axle of white chrysanthemums. These were from the trainmen.

"Freck is coming tomorrow, Jessie," Eliza said. "That may help. His grandfather is devoted to him."

"It may distract him, I suppose," Jessie said. "But Freck isn't Danny, and I have the feeling that Fred may try to make him into somebody he isn't."

"Oh, I don't know. Freck used to follow Danny around like a shadow. And he loved riding the railroad with him. In fact, Freck seems to have a tremendous interest in the mines."

"He's a little boy, Eliza, whose grandfather spoils him," Jessie said tartly. "But never mind. It won't hurt Fred for a while if he does think Freck has Danny's potential. Might even do him some good."

Jessie's words stung, but Eliza looked at her with a new respect. Jessie had been deeply grieved, too, by Danny's death, but she would bear it. Jessie, in fact, would always sail on undaunted, no matter what happened.

"What about Barbara?" Jessie said. "I never had much use for her, but she made Danny happy and that was enough for us. Everybody tells me she's prostrate with grief."

"She has been prostrate, but Dr. Penwood, bless him, has persuaded her to go to Europe. She's sailing in two weeks. And that's another thing. Fred is so bitter about her. He's never reconciled himself to the marriage, and that isn't helping him now, either."

"In that case, it's a good thing she's going to Europe. As to Fred's bitterness, Eliza—the only woman he's ever had any use for, it seems to me, is you." Jessie stood up. Eliza's hold over Fred had earned her grudging envy over the years. "I'd better run along now. Let me know if there's anything I can do to help."

Eliza got to her feet. "Thanks for coming, Jessie." She went with her to the door and stood there after Jessie left, watching the indomitable figure, bent slightly to ward off the chill of the October wind.

CHAPTER 17

Clarkston 1902

"DAMN IT, HODIE, sometimes it seems to me that nothing has gone right since Danny's death." Nellie was passing the chops. Fred signaled no to her and picked up his wine glass.

"I don't think anything's gone right since Dexter's death, Fred," Eliza said. "You've had more trouble in the past seven years than all thirty before put together."

The smell of burning leaves drifted through the open dining room windows. It was September 1902 and the strike that had paralyzed Clark Brothers had been in force since May. One hundred forty thousand men were idle in the anthracite region, holding out, in the minds of the operators, against all logic. John Mitchell, head of the United Mine Workers, refused to capitulate.

"I'm afraid the truth is that Mitchell is conducting himself like a statesman, Hodie. I can't see any end to this, but I do know that we'll never be able to run the business as we have in the past."

"But it can't go on forever. People can't live without coal. Jessie keeps reminding me that unless it's settled soon, there will be terrible suffering this winter."

"For once she's right. Anthracite supplies everywhere are dangerously low, and at the present rate none of us will have any heat this winter. These damned unions have got the country along with the operators by the throat."

"You've said that before, Fred," Eliza said gently.

"I know I have, but remember this time, besides an increase in wages and a decrease in hours, the union is demanding a more equitable system of weighing coal."

231

"Are these demands really so outrageous, Fred? *Equitable* is a pretty mild word."

"Not you, too, Eliza." Fred slammed both hands down on the arms of his chair. "I keep trying to make you understand how insidious the whole business is. The UMW is power mad, I tell you. They've got to be to insist on our bargaining with them instead of the men themselves. Our own men, for God's sake."

"Fred, I understand that, but I'm trying to get you to look at it reasonably. No, no, I don't mean that—I mean dispassionately, calmly. I don't think you do yourself any good by getting so angry. This strike has been going on for a long time, and now you're reacting to it the same way Dexter used to."

Fred snorted. "If we give in on this one, Dexter will turn in his grave."

"I suppose he would."

"Oh, hell, Hodie—if I'm going to be honest about it, I guess I don't want to face the truth. Originally, I thought President Roosevelt might be able to settle it because he's a strong man and I was naive enough to believe that the commission he set up to arbitrate the thing might get somewhere. Now I'm not so sure how much I like the idea of the President's getting into it."

"Why not?"

"For one thing he's the first president in a long time who is neither a debtor nor a creditor to Wall Street, so I don't know how much real influence he can bring to this. And I don't know how much he knows about economics. On the other hand, I'm pretty sure he's basically honest and will keep his negotiations free of politics. At least I don't think he's another Senator Hanna. Every time I think of that, I—"

"Fred, I wish you'd—"

"I know, calm down. But Hanna's such a filthy politician. The only reason he let labor triumph two years ago was strictly for his own political gain, and that settlement was the beginning of the road to disaster."

"I wasn't going to ask you to calm down again, Fred. I just wish you'd, well, as I've said before, give it all up."

"I know. You've always hated it. And, God knows, it's the same old pattern, the same financial worries, the same anxiety about everyone's safety, the same Coal and Iron Police being mobilized. Untermeyer and Philip, Jr., quivering every time they're deputized to guard the mines. By the way, last week Philip, Jr., was even made a constable."

"That must mean things are desperate."

Fred laughed. "So they are. Even the machinists are starting to make trouble. But seriously, I think the miners will beat us this time. Mitchell is too strong. My God, I wish Freck would grow up. I'm not sure I can hold out until he does."

"You can't," Eliza whispered.

"But I have to, even if it kills me, Hodie. Don't you understand? I can't let my father and Dexter down—and my grandfather too, for that matter. This is their dream, their trust. If I give up now, the whole venture will collapse. God knows why I had to be the one left with their damned dreams. But there it is. And the fact that I can sell out and make a lot of money for all our descendants wouldn't have interested them one bit. They were obsessed by their land and the coal."

Eliza knew there was nothing she could say.

"Father used to tell us all when we were boys that his great-great-grandfather, Dr. Daniel Clark of London who was physician to Charles II, bought *millions* of acres in the colonies. And his son, Colonel Daniel Clark, came to this country to add to his father's holdings." Fred pushed his chair back from the table. "Unfortunately, all that land was dissipated later, but not the Clark obsession with property. That passed straight down to my grandfather, Father, and Dexter. I never had it, but somehow, Hodie, I can't rid myself of the notion that the whole damned place has been laid upon me to preserve for Freck."

Eliza saw she was beaten.

"Has Freck recovered from his fit of love sickness?" Jessie asked, taking the sugar. Jessie and Eliza were in Eliza's living room. Ever since Danny had died seven years before, Jessie had come to call on Eliza once a week at teatime. Eliza was astonished to find she actually welcomed Jessie's visits. "She's full of surprises," Eliza told Fred and then couldn't tell him what they were when he asked. Jessie's more acute observations were ones that Fred would have found painful.

"Oh, you mean for your great-niece, Carrie Tucker? I don't honestly know. He was pretty desperate about her last summer,"

Eliza said. "I remember his anguished efforts to dance with her at one of Jemima's parties."

"The terrible trials of the young. Well, he'll get over it. How is Fred? Worried, I imagine."

"He's frantic, Jessie. At least Freck will be here for a week at Thanksgiving, and that always takes his mind off things. I'm counting the weeks. Six to go."

"He's depending on that boy much too much, Eliza. Freck's not Danny and I can never see him in the role of the head of Clark Brothers. Truth is, there's not a single young man in the family fit to take over."

Eliza shook her head. "I know it. It just shows destiny has a way sometimes of thwarting even the best laid plans for a dynasty."

Jessie was startled at this Clark blasphemy. "I suppose you're right, Eliza. I never thought of it that way."

"I was devoted to our father-in-law," Eliza continued. "And I couldn't help admiring his single-tracked and ruthless ambition. But you must admit, Jessie, that it was a bit much for him to assume that by producing five sons, he could establish the Clarks as operators of coal in perpetuity."

"Well, at the same time, he did a lot more than produce the sons. He trained them. At least he trained Dexter and Fred."

"But something went wrong. You can't play God, as he tried to with his family."

"True, and sadly borne out by the present generation of six grandsons. Danny was the only one with the brains and the interest to carry on."

"Why didn't we foresee all this years ago, Jessie? At least why didn't Dexter and Fred foresee it?"

"For Dexter, the thought of life without the mines or away from Clarkston would have been impossible. They made up to him for not having any children and—" Jessie stopped abruptly.

"I guess that's true," Eliza filled in. "I guess he was so totally involved in the daily demands on him that he didn't think of the future. But Fred's never been like that. He's taken the mines not as a vocation but as a terrible responsibility laid upon him by his father and his brother."

"And you'll have to persuade him that he's carried that responsibility long enough and should shift it now to concern for the living. After all, selling the mines should take care of all the Clark women and children for years, maybe generations, to come."

"God knows, Jessie, I wish Fred would sell. He'll destroy himself and me in the process if he hangs on. But he's gotten stubborn in his despair. I can't even mention it to him anymore. Or even to Anna. The last time I did, her eyes all filled up with tears. Said it would break Freck's heart."

"That's nonsense and you know it, Eliza. Forgive me, but Freck's a spoiled boy playing at being lord and master of the mines. He loves to run trains—that's all."

"I know, but unfortunately Freck as the head of Clark Brothers is Fred's dream."

The miners returned to work on October 23, 1902, with the understanding that the commission would hand down a judgment on the dispute later on. Unexpectedly, ten days after the strike ended, Fred came home early. Eliza, looking up in astonishment from the piano, sensed that something momentous had happened. Fred seemed both relieved and agonized.

"I've done it, Hodie," he said, throwing down his derby. "Signed the preliminary papers turning over all of Clark Brothers interest in the mines. All I've kept are the family houses and a few parcels of land where there's no coal."

"Oh, thank God!"

Fred looked serious. "I guess we're lucky. Lehigh will have a pretty tough time of it, if you ask me. It will be six months or so before the commission makes up its mind. And then they're more than likely to rule for a raise in wages. Trouble is, Hodie, the public's fed up and for the first time they're siding with labor. I suppose Jessie will give us a lot of trouble and I don't even want to think about Freck's reaction. As for me, I can't help wondering what it's all been for."

"Freck will be all right, Fred. As I've tried to tell you so often, Freck wasn't cut out to run the mines. He really only loves running the trains and he'll get over it. It's your dream for him that's died, Fred."

She saw a shadow pass over his face and wished she hadn't said it. She reached up, took his hand, led him over to the sofa, and sat down beside him. "As for Jessie," she went on, "you won't have any trouble with her. Ever since the strike began, she felt you ought to sell out. She said she'd talked to you about not selling her house and you'd agreed. She also said she would miss us because she was sure we'd move to Philadelphia, but that she'd stay here and go right on doing what she's always done."

"You know, Hodie, Jessie has never been quite as sure of herself since the Black Creek Hall fire."

"Because that's when it first dawned on her that Dexter might be having an affair with Gertrude?"

"That's right. When he and Danny and I came home late that night, he was terribly shaken. I suspect being caught by Danny and me brought the whole business to an end—but not before he'd roused Jessie's suspicions."

"It never could have lasted anyway," Eliza said, grateful that Fred's gloom had momentarily been lifted, "and she was lucky to have found that nice John Sterling to marry. I had a letter from her the other day, by the way, saying they'd bought a house on Murray Hill and they'd now have plenty of room for us any time we'd come to visit them."

"You'd like that, wouldn't you, Hodie?"

"I'd adore it and you know it. It's almost too good to believe, Fred—Philadelphia and New York—and no more Clarkston. In fact I don't believe it yet."

He moved away from her a little on the sofa and turned to face her squarely. "Well, it's done, Hodie, and I guess I had to. Lehigh seems happy about it. In fact they're even optimistic about the future. I'm not—I think there's going to be hell to pay. Or maybe I'm just too old and can't face it all over again. Anyway, I'm going to put the family ghosts out of my mind for good. Perhaps now we can see enough of all our grandchildren to enjoy them and we can catch up with old friends in an easier life, Hodie. God knows you deserve it."

She turned her head so that he would not see her tears.

Jessie had finished lunch and gone upstairs to her room to read some poetry and take her afternoon nap. That morning she had said good-bye to them and felt unaccountably tired. She heard the sound of clattering hooves and went to the window. It was Fred's express wagon laden down with luggage, on its way to the station. John, the gardener, was driving. Next came the closed carriage. Janos was in front, Eliza and Fred inside, in the back. Jessie raised her hand in a gesture of farewell, although she knew they couldn't see her. The carriage continued on its way, the *clip-clop* of the hooves diminishing. It rounded the corner and was gone.

Jessie looked down at the volume of poetry she had just picked up. She opened the book and her eye fell on the lines:

> *Men are we, and must grieve when even the shade*
> *Of that which once was great, is passed away . . .*

How many years ago had she learned those lines? A silent parade passed in front of her eyes. Dexter . . . Schlenker . . . Danny . . . the men marching . . . Katie . . . And, eventually, the time will come when the colliery whistle will blow no more. Slowly, Jessie closed her book and put it on the table. Two P.M. She would rest until three, then she must get up and explain the workings of the Sunday school to the new clergyman. Tomorrow would be time enough to discuss the fall planting with Tony; that would give her a chance to practice her Italian, learned so many years ago at school in Florence.

She would get accustomed to the empty house next door, she thought. I'll fill this house with my sister's grandchildren from Philadelphia next summer. . . . They can work a few hours in the morning, Tom and Elizabeth at their drawing and Nancy at her violin. Oliver's still young enough to ride the locis like Freck. . . . The girls can help in the sewing class, and all of them will be useful in the Sunday school. . . . Jessie glowed at the prospect of improving so many young lives, all in one vacation . . . but they must have some healthy diversion, too. The boys can play tennis and the girls can ride Ruby and Daisy. . . . I'm glad I had those mountain bridle paths cleared. Let Eliza live luxuriously in Philadelphia and bring up her grandchildren in idle pleasures, and let them all forget about Clarkston. . . . If any of them remembers, it will be Freck. . . .

After forty years all the Clarks have abdicated and left me to look after the place and the people. . . .

She smiled with satisfaction. There's plenty to keep me busy, she thought.